P9-DYA-691

The Puppet Turners of Narrow Interior

Stephanie Barbé Hammer

Detroit, Michigan, USA
Windsor, Ontario, Canada

Copyright © 2015 by Stephanie Barbé Hammer

All rights reserved.

No part of this book may be used or reproduced in any manner
without written permission except in the case of brief
quotations embodied in critical articles and reviews.
Please direct all inquiries to the publisher.

Published in the United States and Canada by
Urban Farmhouse Press
www.urbanfarmhousepress.com

First Edition

ISBN: 978-0-9937690-3-0

Cover and interior woodblock prints by Ann Brantingham
Book cover and layout design by Cheryl Knobel
Translation of Victor Hugo's *Les Misérables* quotation by
Stephanie Barbé Hammer

For Larry Behrendt

Table of Contents

From the Geister College Archive
(unsorted: local Confidence Valley songs)

Children's Round

clap clap clap hands!
Danker dollies dance and chant!
clap for England clap for France
clap for all the German lands
that brought the Dankers to our sands
but most of all clap for Japan
whence came our mother Christine-san
who taught the puppets how to chant
clap clap clap hands. . . .
(repeat)

1. Henry then:
Parzival is dumb

This is what I remember.

I am almost nine. It is summer. I am playing outside at my grandmother's house. Near the sound, which is like the ocean, but the water isn't wavy so you can swim in it and not worry about drowning.

I balance on the middle rung of Oma's split-rail fence. I am a cowboy getting ready to have a shootout with Mr. Death.

I can't see him yet. But he's coming.

He took my father, and he's gunning for my grandma. She is old, although she looks and acts young.

"I'm giving you till sunset to get out of town," I say. I take out a Kleenex and wipe the pretend sweat from the pretend desert off my forehead.

If someone else were here to play with me, they could be the other characters in the story: the saloon keeper, a dancer girl who is pretty but who can fight like a man, and the trusty friend who is a sharpshooter but who drinks too much whiskey.

"I'm the law in these parts," I shout at some seagulls. I fix the pretend sheriff's badge I pinned to my shirt—the one that my big brother Patrick brought me from the airport. Then I take my toy guns out of their plastic holster. The guns are orange to prevent confusion with "real guns," my mother says. She is busy running the Holbein hotel business, and she doesn't talk to me much.

But I have my grandmother, and I got my guns.

I practice shooting them. Then I put them back in their holsters.

Mr. Death slides into my line of vision.

I squeeze my legs against the rail of the fence.

Mr. Death faces me, his bone-hands hanging over his pistols. He's got a skull face, of course, and he wears a shiny black shirt with those Western snaps, and he has black jeans—just a little dusty—and black boots. He has human eyes, though: blue. He wears a black hat.

I wish I didn't have to see him. But artists see things. That's what my grandmother says, and Oma was a dancer, and she plays three different instruments and can speak a bunch of languages, so she knows what she is talking about. She says I'm an artist because I have a great imagination, and she says that's what artists do; they pretend things and then bring the pretend things into the world. But the price you pay is being sensitive. And being sensitive is a pain.

My legs are shaking, so I have to sit down on the fence.

I suspect that Mr. Death has something to do with the fishy goings on in Grandma's hacienda. Strange noises at night. Folks coming and going at all hours. I don't see 'em, but I hear their voices and their footsteps when I'm trying to get some shuteye in my bunk.

Mr. Death wiggles his fingers over his holsters. He's trying to spook me. Make *me* leave town.

But I aint't no coward. I'm going to act natural-like and do my chores.

"I gotta rustle up some grub for Oma," I tell him. "*You stay away from her, you hear?*"

I get off the fence.

Mr. Death tips his hat to me. I tip mine back. We are enemies, but we are polite.

I walk back to the house. I don't turn around. If I do, Mr. Death will know I'm scared, and he will follow me right inside.

I take off my guns and my badge. Put them in one of the empty flower pots sitting by the front door. No point in upsetting the women-folk.

I go into the kitchen. Now I pretend to be a rich kid in a fancy country house in the East . . . even though the house is really a ranch, and I'm just a plain speakin' fella.

Bonnie the housekeeper smiles a big smile. She is blonde and nice. I'll bet she has a passel of admirers.

She opens the box that has the coffeecake inside. The teakettle rumbles like a buffalo or a bull.

"It's nice that you are making breakfast for the Duchess, just like your Opa Friedrich used to do."

"Yes ma'am," I say, as I open up the frozen orange juice can that is standing on the counter. "I mean—yes!"

You have to be careful about showing who you are to grownups. They get skittish sometimes.

My mom, for example. She doesn't like it that I "play pretend."

But Bonnie doesn't notice. I plop the tube of orange juice gunk into a pitcher. She fills the cans of water from the sink, and I pour them in. Then I stir with a long metal spoon. It clanks against the glass. This must be like the noise that horses make when you feed them stuff to eat in a bucket.

I fold a paper napkin and place a knife and teaspoon on the black breakfast tray. Bonnie spoons instant coffee into the aqua plastic coffee cup.

Now Bonnie pulls the big bread knife out of the wood block that holds the knives.

"Can you handle this, young man?" she says.

I figure that if I can keep Mr. Death corralled out there near the fence, I can cut a gosh-darned cake.

"Yep," I say, and I think Bonnie has figured out that today I am Henry the cowboy, and not Henry the knight, or Henry the detective, or Henry who is Peter Pan, or Henry-san the samurai, because she says, "There you go, partner."

I take the bread knife by the handle, I aim the knifepoint down and I saw away at that coffeecake varmint. Then Bonnie puts the tray into my hands, and I walk slowly down the hall so the coffee won't slosh over onto the saucer.

Oma is sitting up in bed with two pillows behind her. A poodle and a Pekingese lie on either side. The water from the sound murmurs from the open sliding glass doors.

I take a gander through the doors.

No sign of Mr. Death.

Oma smiles.

"Breakfast in bed!" she says, clapping her hands.

I put the tray down and hug Oma, and then I sit next to her, squashing the Pekingese a little. But he's used to it.

My grandmother is really little, and she has hazel eyes that are kind of slanted. Her father was Russian, and she has what she calls Mongol eyes.

"The Mongols conquered all of Russian Asia," she told me once. "But then—Asia conquered them. They eventually teamed up with the Tibetan Buddhists. Which means that we all, even the most savage, lean towards the light."

Oma cuts her coffee cake in half.

Every day we share the cake, and she tells me stories.

Yesterday, she started a story about a guy named Parzival.

"Where were we?" she asks.

I say, "Parzival was hidden away by his mom."

"The mother did this," she says, "because Parzival's father died in a horrible war."

"Like my dad, although not the war part," I say.

Oma nods.

"So Parzival is brought up on a farm, and he doesn't know that he's the son of a valorous knight."

She lifts her coffee cup and winks at me.

"But one day Parzival is working in the fields, and what do you think he sees?"

I am chomping on my piece of coffee cake.

"A bad guy?"

"No," says Oma.

"His mother?"

Oma laughs. "No! He's a grownup, so his mother isn't checking up on him all the time."

I think being a grownup will be great.

Oma pauses. "He sees a knight in shining armor—"

"On a horse?" I lean forward. We are getting to the hero part of the story!

"Right! So Parzival says, 'I want to be like that man.' He gets an old workhorse from the farmer, and he runs away from the farm with a rusted sword and some old leather padding that he thinks will look like armor."

I make a face. Why does Parzi-what's-his-name have to have an ugly horse? And why doesn't he just go to the market or fair and buy a good sword?

Also, you can't just run away from home in the daytime! You have to sneak out at night with a bandana on a stick, and you have to climb out a window and go down a ladder or a tree. Or fly out. And the stars guide you.

I stand up.

"Oma, I like King Arthur better, and Gawain. This guy Parzi-what sounds kind of dumb."

Oma laughs. "We'll do Sir Gawain tomorrow," she says.

"Or the Grimm Brothers!" I say. "Those stories have some blood and guts to them."

"Or perhaps," she says, "I'll tell you the further adventures of Tripitaka, Pigsy, and the Monkey King."

"Can Monkey beat up some more robbers?" I ask.

"Perhaps," she says. "Or perhaps that magic cap the gods put on him will keep him under control."

"I like it when Monkey King goes crazy." The Pekingese crawls back to his place next to Oma. We sit for a moment, smiling at each other.

Then I remember about Mr. Death.

"I'd like to be excused," I say.

I run out the front door and put on my guns.

2. Quirk now:
Listen to your octopus

"**You** need to come home, Allison," the parents told Quirk when they finally figured out about Geister College going bankrupt. "We are not putting any more money into your account at Narrow Interior Bank."

Quirk swung one leg over the window frame, lit up, and blew smoke out onto Main Street where those idiot high school kids were skateboarding, not realizing that long boarding was where it was at now, if you cared about such things, which she—Quirk—most emphatically did not. Her octopus tattoo hissed in solidarity: the big tattoo she had placed on her chest and neck against the desires of just about everyone, including Mazie, whom she supposed she loved (although Mazie did every girl on Front Street, every girl on campus, and every girl as far as Riverfield, from what she could tell [and almost a boy—but that was a mistake]).

"No," said Mazie. "Octo is too big."

"No such thing," Quirk had said. There's no such fucking thing as too big, and she had the tattoo needled onto her, lying on the leather barber's chair on Lyric Street near the Anglican church; and Mazie went to some party and had sex with some girls there, including one who wouldn't let go of her and was becoming a big pain in the ass.

A boy with green hair on a skateboard looked up at the window and said, "Look, there's that Goth bitch again."

Goddamn it!

"I'm not a fucking Goth," she yelled at them.

She lived on Gothic Street is all. What the hell! She threw the cigarette, still burning, at the kid below. She thought *spark*, and the high school kids shrieked as the cig went off like a little firecracker before hitting the pavement. She put on her black Doc Martens that she'd gotten with some of the money for winter tuition and walked down the stairs.

Ali was on the front porch talking to someone. He had his Bollweevil Café and Literary Pizzeria delivery shirt on, and he was looking Palestinian-handsome.

"Hey," he said. She said nothing, but her tattoo waved a tentacle.

"Why don't you sssspeak with him?" said the octopus.

"Shut up," said Quirk. "I'm queer, remember?"

"SSStill," hissed the octopus, "he'ssss ssssso beautiful."

Well, it was true; he was.

Quirk walked around the corner. The board kids were gone. The yuppie mothers with the strollers were out. The ancient hippy-war-veterans were sitting on the steps outside the ice-cream parlor, smoking. She'd talk to them.

"Yo," said one.

"Yo," she said.

Must go to the ATM. How much money left? How many days before the inevitable reckoning with the parents who had thought she was studying? They didn't see the report cards; they weren't allowed to anymore, but they had finally figured it out.

She walked to the ATM outside the fancy store with the too-expensive rubber boots and the clothes in sizes so miniscule they couldn't fit anyone real, or certainly not anyone like her.

They could fit Mazie, who wore a size zero on a fat day.

Quirk input her code, NOTAGOTH, despite her black hair and black jeans and black boots and black eyeliner. No, she wasn't a Goth. She was—

Your balance is $200.

Enough for a few days, two maybe, but the rent on the apartment was due tomorrow, so really only one day. Mrs. Cavanaugh was strict about the rent, and Quirk didn't have much stuff, so all that could be given away or put in suitcases. The Sankai Juku poster and the bass guitar and the computer—those would come with her—so, enough for the bus ride back home to the city. She wasn't a runaway; she wasn't that stupid, and she wasn't going to live in a doorway the way Christie's cousin did in Portland. They were all nuts out West. No. She'd go home, and the parents would fuss over her failure, pretending it wasn't one, but not pretending very well.

But it *wasn't* her failure; it was the school's—its ruin on many levels, the primary one being fiscal. But the truth was she was flunking out before the school failed. Or barely passing, or whatever you call it.

She withdrew one hundred dollars.

Quirk counted the cash, stuck it in her pocket.

"Hey Allison," said the Botticelli boy with the perfect complexion and the flowing blonde cherub hair, who took French with her last year, and who sold her drugs when she had some money. He always hung out by the cash machine.

"Fuck off," she said. She refused to name him although she knew him—had known him (too) well. "Get losssstttttt," echoed Octo.

"Nice to see you, too," he said, leaning against the building as she strode away.

She took out the cash as she walked. So to be honest, that left today and maybe tomorrow. To say goodbye, achieve closure, or whatever it was one did to attain something real and meaningful.

Quirk walked by restaurants and bars and a hair salon. She needed a haircut. She walked up the street, and the college came into view. There was a fence around it, and on the fence a sign said FORECLOSURE. Next to the sign was another that said FUTURE SITE OF A HOLBEIN LUXURY HOTEL! A bunch of guys in hard hats were digging a hole with bright yellow shovels behind the sign.

How can a fucking school go bankrupt? It was a private college. The students—many of them—had lots of money. It was weird. But it happened. Was happening all over.

Quirk lit another cigarette.

"SSSSomething ssssubverssssssive may be in order," said her octopus tattoo.

There were some old people and little kids filing into the Anglican church on the corner of Main Street and Lyric. She liked looking at people. They were soothingly ridiculous.

Ever since the college closed she did that: watched people be stupid. It was part of her observation work that was going to be part of some magnum opus she hadn't created yet.

An even older-than-old guy got out of a white van that said NARROW INTERIOR AMBULETTE.

"This is a goddamn travesty," he shouted at the people in the front seat. He had a voice like gravel and a car wreck, mixed with an anger cigar.

Hands lifted out the van window in gestures of despair and supplication.

"Now, Mr. Olsen," said the voice. Then blah blah and something about someone having the day off so he had to come here to the church.

Why do people always talk to old people like they're kindergartners? Quirk would want to fucking kill herself if anyone talked like that to her.

That's how the parents sounded on the phone.

"You know, sweetie," said the mother, "you will need to come home and make some decisions."

FUCK ALL DECISIONS.

"Goddamn it," said the old man, presumably Mr. Olsen.

A church volunteer in a dress and sensible pumps stood by the van as the Mr. Olsen geezer grabbed a bunch of metal and unfolded it into one of those walker things, and then lumbered up the church steps and through the red door on two or six legs if you included the walker, which Quirk did.

The volunteer caught sight of Quirk.

"Excuse me!" she said in a bossy sort of vocality. Quirk turned away, but the lady volunteer ran after her. She was faster than she looked.

"You! Come help us. We are short of young, agile people."

The lady looked her up and down and frowned. "You're not one of those Goth kids are you?" she said.

Quirk was about to answer with something withering, but the volunteer lady just took her arm.

"Of course you're not. You're a lovely young lady from the college, aren't you?" she said, not waiting for an answer. "Come along, we're going to do a senior citizens + pre-schoolers art project."

Quirk smelled some horrible sneezifying perfume. Lily of the valley? Tuberose? Freesia? Damn, it was awful.

"Ridiculous enough for you, Octo?" said Quirk. She was confident that the volunteer lady couldn't hear tats speak.

"Oh yessss," said the tattoo. Tentacles waved and tickled under her chin.

The volunteer smell lady took Quirk into the church and into the recreation hall or whatever that weird room is in a church that isn't the sanctuary, or whatever they call the God place, but is the other place where they make the coffee and serve the really dry cake.

There were like twenty people sitting at a long table, with bins of stuff and jars and baskets.

"All righty," said someone in that terrible in-charge voice. "We are going to make our own hand puppets." She/it paused. "And then put on a *show!*"

Jesus. It was old people and little kids sitting at tables with tube socks in front of them.

"GOD HELP US!" said the old man whose walker stood behind him folded up and defeated against the yellow wall.

Quirk got directed to a second side-table, where someone told her to open up bags of buttons, get out the sparkles, uncork the glue, and pass it all out.

The kids looked afraid. God, art projects were stupid.

"You show them," said the lady volunteer. "Model what to do."

Quirk sat down on a folding chair. Horribly uncomfortable.

"I don't like these," said a girl with braids and a mouthful of gaps. The others looked mournfully at the white socks.

"Goddamn it," said Quirk. She untied one Doc Marten (the shoes are arch-supportive, but I'm not a fucking Goth!), and forced it off her foot.

"Your toes smell yucky," said the girl.

"Shut the hell up," said Quirk. "Do you want a different color sock or don't you?"

"Do," said the girl.

Quirk took off one of her own socks. Black. She took scissors and ripped it open.

There were rumbles of old voices and squeaks of young voices…sounding shrill and empty, and they made her sad and mad at the same time. The old ladies with their dyed hair and baby powder voices. The little kids with their pony t-shirts and teddy bear pants.

She stuck empty spools of thread through the holes of the sock for eyes. She shredded up red yarn and stuck it with glue to the head. One kid said, "I have a loose tooth," and before the kid could say squat, Quirk reached over, yanked out the tooth, and stuck it on the head of the sock, like a horn, with Elmer's Glue.

"Ooh," said two kids. "A monster. Let's make another one."

Quirk took the other Doc Marten off, threw that black sock on the table, and started putting the tube socks on her feet. She re-laced the boots.

"That's a pretty goddamned unusual puppet," shouted the Mr. Olsen man looking down the row of little kids at her monster-sock who was circulating with great success to the sounds of grrrr and rooarrr.

"Well," said Quirk—really, she hated old people—"it's better than an angel or a doggie."

The man looked at the white tube sock that had been placed in front of him. "I could use some help down on this end, young lady," he shouted.

From a distance, the volunteer smell lady gesticulated towards the old man.

Quirk walked down the line. But when she got there, he grabbed her wrist. Hard. Fast. He grabbed so fast she gasped. He had long fingers, and his hands were not old really, but masculine and a bit hairy.

"Get me the hell out of here," he said to Quirk. "They are going to make us sing songs, and I can't stand it."

A boy with freckles like tiny pinpricks looked across the table at the old man. The little boy opened his mouth.

The old man glared, and the boy shut his mouth and looked down.

"What'll you give me?" Quirk said.

"Cold hard cash." With his other hand, the old man drew a bunch of green in a gold clip out of his trouser pocket.

"Fifty dollars." She was leaning over him. He smelled of bay rum and lime and death.

"Deal," he said. "Assist me on my way to the men's room, and then we'll slide out the side exit."

He sure knew his way around the church.

Two kids started fighting over some purple glitter.

"OK, sir, let's take you to the john," she said. The old man grunted as he stood up and leaned on her shoulder.

They limped out into the hall.

"Left," he said. "Hurry."

The side door creaked open. The sky slid out, blue and fresh and springalmostsummer.

"The money," said Quirk.

"First," said the man, "I need you to take me to a bar where I can get a libation to recover from the outrage of this experience."

"That'll cost you extra," she said.

He leaned on her more heavily as they proceeded downhill away from the church. She'd forgotten the fucking walker!

"Actually," he said, "I can walk fine with a person. It's just my balance."

Actually, he didn't walk fine. But yes, they managed.

She rushed him past the Bollweevil Café. She didn't look through to see if Ali was there.

"Yo," said the veterans sitting on the steps. "Looks like you made another getaway, man."

"Goddamn draft dodgers," muttered the old man. But what he said to them was, "Indeed!"

Polite. Fucking polite. That was kind of funny, even though the old guy was almost definitely a right-winger. The clothes were a giveaway. He was wearing a pinstripe suit with a narrow (but indie narrow) tie. And he had a pinky ring with an insignia. She kept seeing the ring on her shoulder when she turned her head.

"Here," he said. "Here."

There they were in front of the Maple Leaf Bar.

She'd never gone in here. The Maple Leaf had dark oak paneling and was old and looked smoky.

"I don't have my ID," she said. My fake ID, she meant.

"Not a problem," said the old man. "I know the bartender."

"I'm in a hurry," she said.

He laughed big, and she could see the gold fillings all up and down his back teeth.

"You've got all kinds of time."

"Listen, sir," Quirk said. She was beginning to feel tired with the weight of him. Also, she had so much shit to do, and this was her last day before having to go home, and she didn't want to waste it with this old guy. "I have to pack and I have to get out of my place and I have to go back to the—my parent's house."

"Then you have to have a farewell drink," he said. "You have to say goodbye to a place with a cocktail; otherwise, you'll become an alcoholic. You'll keep on trying to have that drink you should have had in the first place."

That's some logic.

3. Henry then:
Stakeout one

I am still almost nine, and it's still summer at Oma's house by the sound. I am exercising with Jack LaLanne in the kitchen after breakfast. Bonnie does it too, and we are both getting stronger. My dad used to do the Canadian Air Force exercises, and I used to watch him do them in his bathing trunks out in the country on the patio.

"Nothing to it, son," said my dad. "Being fit is important. It keeps you healthy your whole life long."

His life wasn't very long, though. But that's because he fell off a mountain in Switzerland, and not because he wasn't strong.

"Let's do some extra jumping jacks today, Henry," Mr. LaLanne says to me from his black and white studio.

"OK, Mr. Lalanne," I shout back, and I start doing the jumping jacks.

While I'm jack-jumping I think about how I'm still a cowboy inside, but that I also need to be that Sherlock Holmes guy who lives in London, which is kind of like the city where I live. He solves mysteries. I like the cowboy clothes better, but Sherlock is smarter than a cowboy.

"Good job everyone," says Mr. Lalanne. "See you tomorrow!"

So after the Jack LaLanne show, I go look through my dad's old clothes in the bedroom next to mine and get a trench coat of his. I put it on when I'm in my room with the bunk beds and I walk around the room with a pencil in my mouth (like Sherlock's pipe) and I say things like, "Watson, what are the details?" Watson is Sherlock's sidekick.

Sherlock is good at figuring out the facts based on clues. Here's what I have so far for what's happening at Oma's:

• Noises start at midnight every night for the past two weeks

- Sounds of cars, front door opening
- Footsteps going down and then up the stairs to the basement
- Weird singing-screaming
- Popping sounds
- Cabinets of drawers or something being opened and shut
- Cars driving away

I take off my trench coat and hide it under the bed. Then I go back into the kitchen to watch the movie that Bonnie has on while she waxes the floor. In the old movie I am watching after the Jack LaLanne show, Sherlock says, "The game is afoot!" Which I think means, you have to catch the . . . suspects . . . while they're doing what you think they are probably doing or what you don't know they are doing but want to find out about.

So I plan what Sherlock calls a "vigil." I think it's fancy for a stakeout. And since the "game" happens in the basement, I'm going to hide there and just wait for those varmints, I mean rascals, I mean suspects.

That night I tell my Oma goodnight, and I pretend to go to bed, and since I'm such a "good boy" she doesn't check on me, and Bonnie goes home after supper, so I just wait and sneak down the stairs to the basement in my slippers and pj's (with the trench coat over them).

Oma's basement is actually a fancy room because it's where Opa used to see clients for the clothes he made for ladies. So it's not like a real basement with a ping pong table and a dartboard and a big TV and maybe a bar like Uncle Peter has and that my cousin Sean gets to hang out in all the time, because his life is cool and fun and he lives in the suburbs and not in an apartment in the city.

Oma's basement has got fancy red wood paneling on the hall walls and in the main room. The room has sliding doors that go out to the water, but that view is blocked by heavy black curtains. There is a giant Buddha statue sitting and looking right at two mirrors facing each other, so there are millions and millions of big Buddha reflections staring at each other. Except now there is a red wooden screen that stands in front of one of the mirrors.

My dad always said that the Buddha statue sort of scared him.

"Nonsense," said my Oma one time when he was doing his exercises in his bathing suit outside. "The Buddha is *good*!"

My father shook his head. "Uncanny," he said once. "Uncanny."

I don't know what or who the Buddha is. I guess he is an important person. Which is why he gets a "the" in front of him—like "the president."

I bring a flashlight and a magnifying glass (Sherlock always has them). I bring a pillow from my bed and a blanket too, because Sherlock is always drinking tea and looking comfortable in his pajamas and sitting on a sofa. The screen is dark red and filled with people doing stuff (I don't know what). I looked at it once, but the Buddha statue stared at me and made me kind of scared. Once behind the screen, I can see myself in the mirror when the flashlight is on, so I know I'm there, and that space changes into kind of like a secret place for me, and I like secret places.

The problem is I am so tired from Mr. LaLanne saying, "more Henry, give me ten more Henry," (which he does, although Bonnie doesn't seem to notice) that I fall asleep and sleep until I hear the car sounds fading into the distance.

I wake up, and it is very dark, and I can hear the cars driving, and then quiet.

I get up, and, wishing Watson were here, I shine my flashlight around.

That's when I see the little dead people.

They are lying in their small coffins. They are the size of little kids, babies almost. But they have grownup faces, almost like those people in *The Wizard of Oz* movie.

I try to make myself feel brave. But all those faces.

And the worst part is that some of them don't have all their parts. One is missing a leg, and another is missing his head.

When I see the headless dead little person, I drop the flashlight and run up the stairs. I jump in bed and pull the covers over my head. Then I realize I am completely defenseless, so I get out quick, pull out my sword from the circus and an orange gun and the cowboy hat from under the bed, climb up to the top bunk where Patrick used to sleep when he came here, and I put on my cowboy hat, because if I die I want to die with some dignity.

I wait for the killer, but he (or she) doesn't come.

It begins to be almost morning, and I fall asleep again.

That morning, I sleep late and miss breakfast. Oma looks at me a bit funny when I come out of my bedroom into the living room, where she's sitting reading a book in French.

"It's the exercising with Mr. LaLanne," I tell her. "I need more rest."

What I don't say is this: "Oma you are in danger!"

I go outside and sit on my fence with my guns. I review the facts of the case so far.

Oma is not the murderer, because she is good.

Bonnie isn't the murderer either, because she is good also.

But Oma may be next on the murderer's list because although she is bigger than the little dead people, she is still pretty small, and she is awfully old, so I had better do my job.

Mr. Death is nowhere to be seen, which is not surprising given the ruckus that's been going on in these parts (pretend-talking like a cowboy is *much* easier than talking like Sherlock).

Then I realize.

Mr. Death might be hiding out downstairs with his victims!

I get the big flashlight from the garage and take a deep breath, and I go downstairs.

But first I pee, so I don't wet my pants in fear, or "fright," as Sherlock would say.

The bodies in their coffins are gone.

I feel glad not to have to look at them. But now I'm wondering what has *happened* to them?

I go upstairs to do my exercises in the kitchen.

"Welcome back, Henry," says Mr. LaLanne. "Let's do some push-ups!" And then he says, "I believe in you."

Which is lucky. Because I believe him back.

I have to.

4. Quirk now:
Listen to your octopus, continued

She walked the old man into the bar. He stopped leaning on her at that point and stood still like an ancient acrobat getting ready to walk a tightrope. He led the way, walking carefully. The old guy was tall, super tall, like six-and-a-half feet, and he held himself old-school erect.

It was true that the bartender knew him; he waved as they came in, silently placed the little napkins down in front of them and poured two glasses of scotch on the rocks.

They talked. They drank. The bartender did not card her. He kept filling up the glasses.

The old guy told his stories.

His name was Mr. Olsen, and he was a retired something or other. His wife had died. His kids moved far away. He lived in a house with a caregiver, but it was the caregiver's day off. He did something with local politics. He talked about being a C student at some weird school somewhere in some western state that no one heard of.

The scotch made her begin to drift off. Failure. The poster and the guitar. The parents. She didn't want to go home.

Mr. Olsen reached into his breast pocket and pulled something out. "That was some puppet you made," he said. He placed the black and red and kid's-tooth sock on the bar.

"You palmed it!" she said. "I can't believe it!"

"Who me?" he said. "Never."

He placed a hand on her hand. It should have felt creepy, but it didn't.

"You've got character," he said. "I like that in a person. You have a mysterious air as well. Like Ava Gardner."

Before she could retort that she, Quirk, looked nothing, I mean nothing, like a movie star, he leaned over with his drink.

"Now, Ava, how can I help you?"

Quirk sat back and settled onto the barstool. Now why hadn't anyone ever asked her *that* before?

"SSSSearch me," said the octopus. "But it ssssure issss sssweet."

An old black telephone rang on the bar. The bartender lifted the heavy receiver. He said, "I ain't seen him," into the phone, hung up, and looked at Quirk and the old man.

"They're on to you, Mr. Olsen," he said. "I predict they'll be here in about five minutes."

"Jesus Christ," said Mr. Olsen. "It's that goddamned church ringleader." He turned to Quirk. "Ava, that female is so damned unattractive; that's why she feels she has to run everything." He drained his glass. "Little picture thinking. Little people living little lives of detail and death."

He stood up, slowly clicking the unwilling vertebrae into place. Pulled his cuffs below his jacket. "Do you have a car?" he inquired.

"No," said Quirk, "but I live right around here. You can hide out till they go away."

Octo slithered on her neck. "Missssssss Quirk, you can asssssssissst him to essscape."

Yes! And then—she didn't know. What. Her heart started beating quickly. Mr. Olsen put some of the green bills down on the bar. "Thanks, Phil," he said. "I appreciate it."

The bartender nodded. "Go out the back," he said. "They always come barreling through the front door, remember?"

The old man lay a heavy hand on Quirk's shoulder and limped towards the door.

"It's not far," she kept telling him, *it's not far*. They staggered through the alley behind the bar. Step. Limp, step, limp. Rest, balance, step. One hundred, four hundred, seven-hundred-plus steps like that. Walking, leaning, walking. And then veer right.

Her apartment was there.

Mr. Olsen was breathing heavily. They got in the front door.

They looked up.

"SSSSSShit," said Octo. "We forgot about the sssssstairs."

How could she have forgotten three flights?

"No problem," said Mr. Olsen in the gravel cigar voice. "I'm in damned good shape for my age."

But he collapsed halfway up the first flight.

"Just a moment," he said.

She thought he was going to die right there, and she took her cell phone out to press 9-1-1.

A heart attack, she thought. *What a fucking weird expression.*

Mr. Olsen sat for a moment gasping. She waited for him to grab his arm. Isn't that what happens? Your arm hurts before your heart attacks you.

"Don't call the goddamn paramedics," he said finally. "It's just the hips and the knees. Not the heart. It's the bones, young lady. The bones die first. The rest takes longer. Generally."

She stood with him on the stairs. Voices outside. The front door opening.

Quirk could smell the dead flowers even before the volunteer lady came around the edge of the old wooden door. She stood, backlit like a mad scientist, next to some looming-big monster guy.

The old man looked up at the specters. "Ah, Calvino," he said, "you've found me out again, have you?"

The tall guy in a white coat—a nurse?—said, "Sir, we saw your pink shirt as you crossed the gap in the alley visible from the street."

"Damn," said Mr. Olsen. He looked at Quirk. "I should have worn neutrals, Ava!"

Octo was silent. Stunned.

Quirk's chest tightened. A heart attack.

A heart attack is when something bad happens, and the badness breaks your heart, swallows it up, and then laughs at you. A heart attack is when you're pumped because you're watching some magnificent SF adventure on cable, and then the writers totally pussy out on the ending, and the girl who ought to be the hero but never is goes splat, and you start yelling at the screen, *NO DON'T KILL HER.* But they do. They kill her every fucking time.

Quirk put herself in front of the old man still sitting on the steps. "You can't have him," she said to the volunteer lady and this scary-ass Frankensteinian Clavino or Clamato or whatever his name was.

"Mr. Olsen," said the volunteer lady. She walked up a step and tried to bend around Quirk. The smell of dead flowers flowed around Quirk, like being in a mortuary where they ordered too many carnations and it's all hot and all decay and the fragrance makes you want to puke your lungs out.

"Mr. Olsen, you can't stay here on the steps! You have to go home and take your meds and have your physical therapy."

"That's right," said Clavino/Clamato. He towered over Quirk even standing on the step below her, and he leaned an incredibly long leg past her on the stairs (Who was he? A reincarnation of Abe Lincoln as a nightmare nurse-man?).

"There's no running away from your age, Mr. Olsen," he said.

Quirk looked at the old man. He slowly closed his eyes.

"I feel tired," he said. "I don't feel well at all."

Mr. Olsen began to deflate, slowly collapsing into himself like a giant blow-up punching bag—one of those shaped like a clown or a hated president that you get at a novelty store—having sprung a leak. He folded from the neck and then from the waist in that sad sudden way that tells you your lousy birthday party is over, and if you're going to punch anyone it's going to have to be that cousin the parents made you invite or your fucking irritating, defenseless classmate who no one likes but has like a deformed face and so you pretend to be nice to them. Or that defeated college president who said basically the equivalent of *oops sorry* at the final convocation, right after Quirk's French professor had yelled in class about Victor Hugo and resistance in literature. But nobody here ever resisted in real life. The world was filled with so many already vanquished people that you just wanted to beat them into defiance or at least get them TO FUCKING WAKE UP.

The now almost completely flattened Mr. Olsen held out his hands: one toward Clavino/Clamato and one toward Quirk. Mr. Olsen moved to place his palm in her hand in a pathetic sort of high-five, but Clavino/Clamato pushed Quirk's hand aside and lifted Mr. Olsen as though the old man were a wooden marionette, all light splints and joints.

Volunteer Lady stepped down. A sigh of satisfaction spit out of her, like rain splattering on a dirty street. She straightened her dress.

"We'll see you next week, Mr. Olsen," she said. "We are going to get into groups to write our play!" She opened the creaking door and held it open.

"I don't have your walker," said Clavino/Clamato to Mr. Olsen, "so I'll just carry you out to the car." With this, the old man shrank even more and withered like a backwards baby in the arms of his caregiver.

Quirk shivered.

"Thissss issss like ssssome horror movie," opined the octopus.

The monster-nurse walked towards the door.

"Sorry, miss," he said to Quirk. "That's just how it is with old people."

The volunteer lady wasn't so kind. "Don't even *think* of helping out at the church again," she hissed, glared at the octopus tattoo, and slammed the door behind her.

Quirk sat on the stairs.

Once upon a time there was a girl named Quirk. And nothing ever happened to her. Nothing interesting, or good, or alive. Just schools closing down, and parents refusing funds, and monsters stealing nice old guys. So she stretched her legs down the stairs, because nothing shittier could unhappen today.

Her Doc Martens bumped into something on the lower step.

Lars Lenard Olsen
Narrow Interior Historic Buildings
Preservation Committee

The money clip filled with green lay there, and so did a small ivory card:

She picked up the card and the money.

The door opened again, and Quirk pulled her arm back, ready to fight this time.

But it was only Ali the beautiful pizza delivery boy coming in with two pizza boxes.

"Hi," said Quirk. She could hear her voice bouncing in her chest against Octo, who was tremblingly silent, once again.

"Hi," he said back.

5. Henry then:
Stakeout two

When I go back out to Oma's fence, Mr. Gilbert and his mother are pulling up the driveway in their truck.

Mr. Gilbert is German. He built Oma and Opa's house, and his mother is old and comes with him to work to make sure he is doing a good job. They always ride in a big truck with a bunch of tools and ropes and boxes and stuff in the back.

Mr. Gilbert is a contractor and a handyman; he can build or fix anything as long as it isn't too complicated or needs a cement mixer.

He comes out every week to check on the property and see if Oma needs anything.

I walk around the outside with Mr. Gilbert and his mother. I'm the one who notices that the blue flowers that Mr. Gilbert has planted around every fence post look sick. Some are black with little bugs crawling on them. The ones that aren't black are brown, and they're hanging over their stems like they need to puke.

Mr. Gilbert's mother notices too. She hobbles to the flowers and starts waving her cane at them.

"*Die Blumen sind kaput Ulli!*" she shouts.

I think Mrs. Gilbert understands English, but she won't speak it.

Mr. Gilbert takes a pocketknife out of his pocket, opens up the big blade, and cuts away at a dark spongy part of the fence-post.

"Something is rotting the wood," Mr. Gilbert agrees.

Then I see how some of the fence posts are standing kind of crooked. I come closer, and I notice how dark they look at the place where they come out of the earth.

"There are holes," says Mr. Gilbert. "Where the wood is gone."

Aha, Watson, I think to myself, *Mr. Death must have shrunk himself, slipped through the cracks, and murdered those little people.*

I feel my body getting hot. If Oma's fence goes down, there'll be no corralling Mr. Death at all anymore.

I run back into the house. "Oma," I say. I almost cry but remember that cowboys and Sherlock Holmes do *not* "blubber." So I gulp and say, "I think the fence is breaking."

Mr. Gilbert follows me in. "The wood of the fence posts is rotting," he says to Oma. "The posts will have to be replaced."

I think of the dead people in their coffins.

I go guard the fence while Mr. Gilbert drives to the lumberyard.

When Mr. Gilbert comes back with a bunch of wood posts, he and I get to work. His mother stays in the truck with the door open, listening to classical music on the radio. I can hear violins floating on the wind.

He has me hold one wooden cross-plank while he pulls up the bad post and then replaces it with a fresh one.

He puts them in the ground and smashes them into place with a thing that looks like a hammer.

I remember that, in the Monkey King story, Monkey has something called a "cudgel" that he beats up bad guys with.

"Now," Mr. Gilbert says to me, "you try setting the post into the ground. There's nothing like feeling a post sink into the earth. You've marked your boundary, showing where you end and someone else begins."

He picks up the next fence post.

"In the old days, the fence was used as a marker more than a gate. Fences showed a farmer where your planting and plowing started, but these fences weren't really ever meant to keep people out. Because in those times, if the land didn't belong to someone very rich, it belonged to everyone."

In the truck Mr. Gilbert's mother sighs. "*Ja,*" she says, and her voice is sad. "*Das wollten die Bauern im Bauernkrieg. Sie wollten das Land mitteilen.*"

"She's talking about a revolution long ago by the farmers in Germany," Mr. Gilbert says. "But now is now. Let's work."

He grins at me. He has a funny wide face and crooked front teeth.

"You shove the post in, and then you tamp it down with the mallet."

Mr. Death slides into view. He's smiling and shaking his head at me. He knows I can't do it.

Mr. Gilbert's mother hobbles out of the truck. "*Heinrich*," she says, and I think she's going to tell me to go into the house and stop playing with these grownup tools, but instead she adds, "*schliess los!*"

"What?" I say.

Mr. Gilbert nods at his mother.

"Come on, Henry, hold the wood."

I grab the post with both hands. Mr. Gilbert places his hands above mine. One, two, three, push down. We push. Hard. Mr. Gilbert gives me the mallet. Then he stands behind me and puts his arms around my arms, so we can hit this thing together.

"Raise your arms up and swing them down."

The mallet makes a hollow sound, and the earth sighs, swallowing the post.

"*Wunderbar!*" shouts Mr. Gilbert's mother, clapping her hands and almost dropping her cane.

We go down the fence-line. Him and me. Pounding the posts.

Each time, the earth accepts the wood.

Mr. Gilbert's mother walks after us, encouraging and admiring.

Mr. Death follows us too. When we finish fixing the fence, he takes off his hat, bows deeply to Mr. Gilbert's mother, jumps high in the air, and disappears.

"*Wir brauchen nur die Glocken, den Treuen zu warnen,*" says Mrs. Gilbert.

"What's she saying?" I ask Mr. Gilbert.

"Bells," says Mr. Gilbert. "In the old country where our people are from, they hung bells on the fences to warn the faithful that . . ." he hesitates, "the adversaries were coming."

"I wish I had a bell," I say.

That night my mother telephones.

"Are you all right, Henry?" She is calling from our apartment, and she's on her speakerphone so I can hear at least two other phones ringing, a printer printing, and people next to her talking about a new hotel in California. "Are you staying safe?" she says. I can hear her fingering her necklace. The one with the metal hand on it.

That's what she always asks me. Not, "What did you do today?" or, "Are you having fun?"

Before I can answer, someone calls her away, and my brother Patrick gets on the phone. Patrick is sixteen years older than me and is an architect.

"Hey, Henry," says Patrick, "how's that crazy Buddha in the basement?"

"He says hi," I say. "He says you should pay attention to your brother."

"Ha-ha," says Patrick.

"He also says there are some mighty strange goings-on in the basement at night, but not to worry; him and me are going to take care of those little people!"

"What?"

I hear my mother calling him in the background.

"We have to get back to work," says Patrick. My mother shouts, "I love you, Henry," as more phones ring. I say good-bye and hang up.

This time, I go to bed early and set an alarm for 11:30 p.m. I get up and go downstairs with my blanket and flashlight, an orange gun, and a magnifying glass. I'm wearing my dad's trench coat. Before I put it on, I smell it. Bay rum aftershave. Dad still smells brave.

I sit behind the screen and wait.

The noises come.

The cars. The footsteps. I look through the gap where the hinges of the screen panels do not quite come together. I see Oma coming down the stairs with a lamp. I see other shapes of people coming down. One, two, three, four, five. The shadows mix up at the bottom of the stairs.

The lamp goes out. There are flickering lights and whispers. Then the scraping/slamming of things opening and closing.

And now something goes clonk, and a there's a shrieky sort of guitar noise. And a creepy high voice sings/screams:

> *Once upon a tiiiiiimmmmmmmme*
> *There was a woman who dresssssed like mannnnn.*
> *She came over the Eastern Sea down the coast of Chileeee*
> *All the way to Italyeeeee*
> *But first there was a storm . . .*

My feet get cold, and my face gets cold, and my throat kind of closes up, and my stomach hurts. I slide my slippers along the floor and look through a different gap in a different hinge, and I see . . .

The little people. They are being carried around by big people in black. Wearing black clothes and black hoods. They have no faces.

Mr. Death has sent his—what do you call them?—"minions."

Something happens. Someone in me who isn't me says quietly, "We got to take 'em on, partner, so as to rescue Grandma."

Another someone says, "Watson, we must act."

So me and the men inside me take a deep breath.

I jump out from behind the screen with my orange pistol and my trench coat, and I yell, "Hold it right there!!!!! What have you done with my grandmother?"

One of the black hooded ones gives the little person to the other black hooded one. The bad guy takes his hood off.

It's Oma.

6. Quirk now:
Listen to your octopus, continued

Ali made his deliveries, then sat on the stairs with her. He was friendly, in a foreign sort of way. He took classes at the state university in Chankopee. But the US was expensive, he said, and he had noticed that all public college attendees acquired jobs.

"Why pizza?" she asked him that first time.

"Why not?" he replied. "It's very American."

On subsequent trips on subsequent days, they talked on the stairs, and then on the landing, and then in her place. About her rescue plan.

Quirk showed Ali Mr. Olsen's card.

"It's a calling card," he said. "Very English. Very high toned."

"But we need his fucking address or telephone number!" said Quirk.

Ali allowed that such information was crucial.

They looked for Mr. Olsen on the Internet and in the local phonebooks at the college library that was still open, even though the college wasn't. Ali and Quirk flipped through the directories while a scary Big Bear Russian man in suspenders yelled at two women librarians who ignored him mostly and talked behind their hands about a ghost on the second floor that the handyman saw when he came to fix the water fountain.

Nope, Mr. O. wasn't listed.

Phil the bartender didn't know where he lived either.

The old man was off the grid. This is what happens when you get old. Either everyone knows where to find you. Or no one does.

"Don't you think you'd better just go back to the church?" Ali said, lighting up, inhaling, then exhaling beautifully. He smoked too. Expensive imported cigarettes he got at the tobacco shop. She tried one. Strong. It had bright pink thread holding it together.

"And let him know you are—how do you say it—on the job?" They stood by the window. "So he doesn't have a heart attack if, after you succeed in locating him, you then just appear at his doorstep?" Ali spoke great, fancy English.

"Oh, right," she said, smoking ungorgeously. "But they'll recognize me."

"You must disguise yourself." Ali stubbed out the pink-threaded cigarette and placed it neatly on the windowsill. Long tapering fingers. Deep nail beds.

"How?" She stubbed and tossed hers out the window. Refused to change habits. Remained herself. Grounded in the whateverness that was her.

"The opposite," he said. "Disguises should always be the contrary of what you really are."

He left, and they didn't meet for a few days. She sat and thought and smoked and smoked. The kids with the skateboards came back and yelled at her, but she was too busy to yell back. She was using Mr. Olsen's money. But just for groceries and this month's rent. She didn't want to waste it. She kept records and had a ball of receipts. She was going to pay him back. She was.

It was beginning to be real summer.

Days getting longer.

The parents called. "When," they said. "When?"

She said, "Soon," and hung up.

One getting-to-be-warm afternoon, she walked down the back streets with a messenger bag, for stashing puppets and any other emergency items. The pretty streets where the very tall Mennonite women lived. The streets where the Mennonite women lived had little white picket fences running down the property line, with tiny tinkling bells hanging from the posts. Molly Street was her favorite. A grey cat lying on the sidewalk, wanting to be petted. One Mennonite woman stood hanging her clothes to dry on a line. Quirk watched her as she quickly pegged the clothes, tied her bonnet, got on a bicycle, and headed in the opposite direction.

What must it be like to be a woman like that? Horrible? Wonderful?

The summer wind blew. On the line, a dress and a cap. Stockings. A big woman. A fat woman.

Octo said, "SSSSStealllllll."

A quick lurch at the white gate on the fence. No don't open, just hop over it. Then a second fence less than a foot inside of that first one. Weird. A bell tinkled somewhere nearby.

Walk quickly and just pray to some god, the god of stealing (Hermes?) that no one sees. Blanket yourself in invisibility. Clothes. Jean Valjean and his candlesticks. Wait! He didn't steal those, the French professor explained.

Messenger bag that you have this one time. Thank you, patron saint of thieves.

The next day:

Another meeting at the church for tots and seniors. Leave Ali at home. She changed in the alley behind the Bollweevil Café. Hid the bag behind a dumpster. Took the back way through parking lots to the church.

"Well," said a perky someone, seated at a card table right inside the church, "we don't get many, um, from your community stopping by to help."

"Say . . . " It was horrible Volunteer Lady walking by, "you look familiar."

Quirk waited for her to say, "You *stole* that dress from off the clothesline, and the cap!"

Quirk looked down and then looked up quickly. The shoes . . . the Doc Martens were all she had.

"Oh my goodness," said Quirk, putting one Doc Marten behind the other, "I just moved here with the Mennonite community, but we are trying to learn more of the other good Christians in our land."

"What's your name?" said VL, looking at her sharply.

"Larynx," said Quirk, "as in Larynx of the Lord."

"Mrs. Brewster!" called two rabbity-looking young women.

Volunteer Lady turned towards them and launched into command mode. Do this, do that.

The gingham, or whatever it was, covered Quirk's chest. Octo scuttled uneasily beneath the homespun.

"OK," said the girl at the desk. "You might as well go in and just start helping out."

Quirk now Larynx walked into the recreation room. At first, people gawked but then looked quickly away. The Mennonites at last trying to blend in! So let them. Let them at last become true Americans. It's about time. Yes.

The children said, "That's a funny hat!" And the older people shushed them.

Mr. Olsen sat down the line at one of two long tables. He wore a blue blazer with a yellow shirt. Tired. The pockets under his eyes the size of little garbage bags. But the military bearing. Undefeated.

VL, a.k.a. Mrs. Brewster, clapped her hands. "It's time for the show, everyone! Are we ready?"

Unwilling pretend enthusiasm. Oh yes oh yes we are.

The air smelled of Elmer's Glue.

A little boy stood up with a paper top hat.

Why always a boy? Quirk a.k.a. Larynx the pretend Mennonite wondered. *Why still always them?*

"Welcome, everyone. And now, on with the show! Our theme today is America the beautiful and *strong*."

A cardboard refrigerator box was brought out. A trio of children hid behind it. Wheelchairs were wheeled behind it. The old ones on crutches ducked as best they could behind the flaps.

"God bless America," sang two wavering elderly voices while six green sock puppets appeared above the rim of the box. They marched and shot at six navy blue sock puppets with orange pipe cleaners.

"Oh no! Curse the infidel," shouted the blue socks, and four tiny American flags pilfered from someone's martini glasses were raised and waved. The green socks marched proudly among the tiny flags as the pink and red baby socks clustered adoringly around them. Someone was playing a drum.

"YOU ARE NOW FREE!" shouted a child's voice: the master of ceremonies.

"Yay," murmured three kids' voices softly. "And now let us pray."

"Jesus H. Christ, get me out of here," said Mr. Olsen.

"SHHH," said Bitches Brewster. "And now for the next skit!!"

Quirk started arranging pipe cleaners into their long skinny boxes and squeezing splayed plastic-handled scissors back together. She moved down the line, smoothing paper tablecloths, enacting the doing of cleanly Mennonite things.

Mr. Olsen looked down at the table, drawing an invisible figure absently with one hand.

Quirk bent next to him, pulled a sticky sponge from across the table, and started wiping.

"Mr. Olsen?"

He looked at her. "What?" he said, "I'm watching, aren't I? I'm behaving, aren't I?"

"It's me," she said. "It's me."

He looked at her blankly.

He's forgotten me, she thought.

They did that—the really old people. Her grandmother did not know Quirk at the end and looked at her blankly with those empty eyes of the dying. It was the saddest thing she'd ever seen, to have someone she loved so much look at her and not know her or know anything.

"Who the hell are you?" he said.

"Allison," she said. "But you said I looked like Ava Gardner, so you called me Ava."

"What?"

"AVA," she semi-shouted.

Mrs. Bitches Brewster lifted her nose and smelled the air. She was a bloodhound for rebellion.

"What are you doing over there, Larynx?" she said in a stage whisper. "The next act is about to begin."

"Your address," said Quirk to him as she set the sponge down with a splat. "Your address so I can—"

"QUIET," said VL/BB.

Mr. Olsen's brow was so wrinkled you could really plant stuff in it. The furrows were deep; they were dark and weird looking. He wrinkled them even more as he squinted.

She had to walk away and help a child who had to get his pants buttoned back up after a successful trip to the boys' room.

"I like your hat," the boy said. "I think it's like the olden days."

Five sock puppets began doing a hip-hop version of the Pledge of Allegiance.

"I pledge I pledge I p-p-p-pledge."

Quirk /Allison/Ava/Larynx put the boy to rights and took the triumphant green sock puppets and put them in the box. No, she explained to the children from the last skit. No playing with your puppets after you have performed. It is now time to listen quietly and with respect to the other players. Everyone is a star. Everyone is.

A new skit was beginning.

"This is a story my grandma told me about a girl named Molly," said a clear girl voice. "And she came to our town from England a long time ago."

Mr. Olsen was murmuring to himself at the table. He had apparently refused to act the part of a puppet.

The other children looked up. A girl from long ago in our town?

A white sock in a black dress made of paper, with long brown yarn hair glued on its head, got onto a paper bowl with a stick stuck in the middle. On the stick a long piece of toilet paper. Two socks in dresses and one sock in paper pants stuck on the front waved goodbye with stubby non-arms.

"I set sail for the new world, friends," said the girl-sock named Molly.

There was a pause as a soft older voice told her what to say.

"To found a new . . . religion in Christ. To sing and dance the . . . inner light. With the Mary's that are for . . . bidden here."

"Beware the Puritans of the colony," said one of the other girl-socks, speaking in an old lady voice. "For ye are radical, even more radical than them they call the Quakers."

"I do not fear," declared Molly the sock as she and the bowl-boat drifted to the left.

"And now," said the four people behind the refrigerator box, "a song."

"AVA!" said Mr. Olsen out loud. "Ava! Of course!"

The children and old folks behind the box started singing:

Dankers burn your dunking lights,
Dive from the lakeside late at night.
What actions take behind your fences?
Christian prayer or puppet dances?

It was an old tune that everyone in the room recognized. It also had different words didn't it? No matter. The children and the old folks caught the melody and began to hum along.

Dankers Dankers what's that song?
We hear in the meetinghouse all night long?

"THAT'S ENOUGH," shouted Bitches Brewster. "This skit is running over. You need to give the others a chance."

An elderly lady in the audience raised her hand. "But this is very interesting, Mrs. Brewster, and I didn't know—"

What foreign tongue speaks the holy word?
Who plucks such chords on harps unheard?

"No," shouted Bitches Brewster. "No." She ran in front of the singing puppets. "STOP!!!!!!!!!!!!!!"

She shouted so loud that three girls near the front began to cry, and the children and old people behind the box started arguing. Then the box fell over.

"The stage," someone cried. "The stage is ruined!"

Quirk whispered to a kid next to her, "Let's play telephone. Give me your address; pass it on."

The whispering and giggling went all the way down the line and around the long table.

The volunteers pulled the kids and seniors away from the box stage, sat them down, and started distributing cookies and juice.

The elderly lady sitting on the other side of Quirk turned to her.

"You have a pretty dress," she said and chortled. "Here, this napkin got passed down too."

126 *Geisterseher Street* was written on the napkin in crayon. Quirk shoved the napkin in her dress pocket. The dress had deep pockets. For secrets.

Juice and cookies circulated, but everyone was rattled now. Kids tried to drink, but the little cups sprang leaks, and the bottoms of some of them fell out. The round vanilla cookies rolled off the plastic plates and onto laps, into wheelchair crevices, and then rolled on the floor. Seniors had to pee. Kids had to pee. Some people—old and young—began to cry once more.

Elderly people said, "I'm tired, I'm upset, all this fuss!"

Children said, "I miss my mommy!"

The boy who had the pants-button problem said to no one in particular, "What's a danker?"

Mr. Olsen sat quietly amidst the hubbub.

Quirk/Larynx/Allison/Ava put two cookies in each pocket. She grabbed the Molly puppet too. She didn't know why.

She walked out into the hallway.

Bitches Brewster came running after her.

"Larynx," she said, "where are you going? There's clean up still to do!"

I do not fear.

"I must away," said Quirk. "The Lord calls me."

"Wait," said Bitches Brewster. She stared at Quirk. Spotted the Doc Martens. "You're—"

A long blue-back suction-cupped ribbon flew out of Quirk's chest as small buttons burst from her dress and spattered on the floor.

Octo's tentacle pressed over the Volunteer Lady's open mouth.

"SSHHHHSHSHSHSHSHSHSHSH," said Octo. "JUSSSS'T be SSSSSSSILENT."

The Volunteer Lady's eyes crossed, and she stood motionless in the hallway, her mouth pressed tightly closed, as the Mennonite girl in the heavy black boots retracted a serpentine something, turned, pulled the church door open, and ran out.

7. Henry then:
Almost

"*Got sei Dank!*" says someone else. "We don't have to be so quiet now!"

I hug Oma.

"My Henry," she says. The lights come up, and the bunch of people in the red paneled room take their hoods off.

Bonnie is there, and Mr. Gilbert, and Mr. Gilbert's mother, plus the lady who runs the garden store downtown, and a man with a little round thing on his head, and two ladies who have eyes like Oma, and a woman with a scarf over her head.

"What are you doing?" I ask.

"Heinrich," says Mrs. Gilbert, "we are celebrating the inner light."

I know this is important because she says it in English.

I hold onto Oma. I keep squeezing her.

"Is this like a show?" I ask. Squeeze. Squeeze.

The two ladies with Oma's eyes begin to shake their heads. "*Iye*," they say, "not show."

The woman with the scarf on her head answers. "In a way," she says. "But we are *not* a spectacle."

"It's a hands-on, participation kind of thing," says the man with the round thing on his head.

The cowboy in me is happy the womenfolk are safe. But Sherlock Holmes pokes me. He wants some answers.

"Why is this a secret?" I ask.

"Because it always is," says Oma. "The *spiel* has always been performed in secret and shared only with those who demand to know." Then she turns to the group.

"Shall we continue, everyone?" To me she says, "Henry, would you like to see the whole story?"

"But . . . the little people," I say.

"Show him!" says the woman with the scarf.

Someone brings over a little body. I close my eyes. I shudder.

"*Nein, Heinrich,*" says Mr. Gilbert's mother. "This is a puppet."

I open my eyes. The little body has all its parts: arms, legs, and head. The lady with the scarf knocks on its chest. "See?" she says. "Wood."

I breathe a sigh of relief. The small person is really a giant puppet. I look more closely. She looks like a lady with black hair and a beautiful face.

"And look," says Bonnie, "here is a man who is sometimes the Lord."

"But not always!" chuckles the man with the round flat hat. They show me a man with long hair dressed in an orange robe. As the figure moves, though, the robe changes color; it becomes white.

"And here is Kanzeon!" The Oma-eyes ladies bring her forward.

"She is the best of all. She is bigger than the others."

Mr. Gilbert puts his hands on my shoulders.

"We will perform the story," he explains, "then we go into the sea."

I let go of Oma.

"You swim after?"

"Oh yes," says someone, "dank then dunk—that's the rule."

Sherlock pokes me again.

"Who taught you?" I ask.

"My mother taught me this play," says Oma.

"And my mother," says the woman in the scarf, "but I learned the French version."

"Ours too, although we learned it in Japanese," say the two women with Oma's eyes.

"I have learned it in German from my father," says Mr. Gilbert's mother.

Mr. Gilbert says, "The *spiel*—what we remember of it—has been passed down for many years in different places."

Bonnie has been quiet this whole time, but she speaks now. "I learned about it like you, Henry. I worked late at the house one night, and I came back to the house because I forgot my cell phone, and I saw these goings-on!"

The group laughs.

"And I thought it was pretty weird, but now I just think it's fun, and playing with the puppets makes me feel good."

"Let's open the curtains and the sliding doors, then," says Oma. "It's always so stuffy in here."

"Do you think it's safe?" says the man with the round hat.

"Sure, now Henry knows. What's to fear?" says the woman with the scarf. "Don't be so nervous Yaakov!"

She turns to me and shakes my hand. "I am Shereen," she says.

They start the play again. I get to help hold the Kanzeon puppet, which is really big. She is also very beautiful, with a red robe made of shiny cloth and a high hairstyle.

"You yank on this stick," says Mr. Gilbert. "That makes the legs move. But not yet. Kanzeon comes later, so just hang on."

"Ok, everyone," says my grandmother. "Let's resume!"

Once upon a tiiiiiimmmmmmmme

the high voice sings, and now I can see it's one of the ladies who speak Japanese. The other is playing a guitar-type thing, but it is square.

> *There was a terrible stormmmmmm.*
> *They had to make landfall in France.*
> *Oh* Dieu *what a chance.*
> Mein Gott *what a chance.*
> aa kamisama! kore ga daisuki!
> namusanbou namusanbou.
> Oui, Ja, hai, *YES!*

As the narrator-lady talks-sings-screams on the stairs, Oma and Bonnie make the lady puppet ride pretend waves made of ribbons that the woman who runs the garden store and the man with the round hat are making flow up and down, kind of like a jump rope. I stand and wait with Kanzeon while Mr. Gilbert and the lady with the scarf bring a thing that's supposed to be a boat. Oma and Bonnie put the lady in it and have her almost falling off into the water.

The guitar gets louder.

> *But will she live to spread the word?*
> *NO no no says the wind,*
> *No no no says the sea,*
> *Yes yes says the heart!*

My own heart thumps. I am afraid.

No, I am not. This is the best play! It's like the secret pretending that I do! I didn't know grownups did secret pretending.

Now everyone chants together:

> *I am stronger than all of you!*
> *With Kanzeon, the lord, the martyrs, and the inner light,*
> *I shall bring the poppets to all shores and tides!*
> *From Muenster, to Berne, and to Montpellier, from there*
> *to London, to the New World, and now to here,*
> *I am the messenger who manipulates the clear*
> *Word of—*

That's when Patrick and my mother and the chauffeur and my mom's bodyguard show up outside the sliding doors. Opening them was a mistake.

"Stop this!" shouts Patrick.

"Mother-in-Law," says my mother, "I thought I told you *never to do this in front of my sons.*"

"It's what we do, Tilda," says my grandmother. "It's who we are."

"I warned you that this cult crap has got to end," says my mother. "Henry," she adds, "come with me."

"But the summer isn't over, Mom," I say.

"It is now," is her answer.

Oma crumples like a leaf into the arms of Mr. Gilbert.

"Oh no," she says faintly.

The group starts quietly taking off their hoods and packing up the puppets.

"It was *you!*" I say to Patrick. "You told Mom what I said about the secrets."

Patrick presses his lips together in a way that makes me want to punch him. "I have to keep you safe."

I look around at the silent people screwing the heads and arms off the little bodies and putting them in their cases.

For a brief moment, Mr. Death presses his face against the sliding glass door. Two bony fingers make a double thumbs-up. Then he shimmers through the glass and into the room, cowboy hat cocked at a jaunty angle. He nods at me and points his skeleton finger at Oma.

I can't prove this, but I swear that all the puppeteers turn their eyes towards him.

"The adversary," the man with the round hat says. "The adversary is among us."

"How *dare* you speak to me in that way," says my mother. She grips her necklace, making her hand into a fist.

The me who isn't me says, "Silence, Watson. Now is the time for us to retreat and formulate a new plan." Even the cowboy says, "Yup, partner, we done got beat. All's we can do is go back to the hideout, lick our wounds, and figger out the next step."

So I hide. Inside.

It feels like drowning, when you hide like that. So I close my eyes. Imagine water.

"I'm sorry, Mom. I'm sorry, Patrick," I say with my eyes closed. I can feel rather than see Oma, trembling in Mr. Gilbert's arms while Mr. Gilbert's mother murmurs, "*Schande, Schande.*"

"Patrick," I say, "may I please go get my toys?" I say it in a pathetic way that is really fake—the way kids on TV talk, or in a movie.

But Patrick buys it.

"Ok," he says.

I open my eyes. My mother nods curtly and goes out to the car.

I take off the trench coat and start folding it up to show I'm serious about packing up and leaving.

"Hey," asks Patrick, "isn't that Dad's?"

"No," I say. "It's just some junk I found down here."

I walk past Shereen. She stuffs something in my arms.

I go upstairs, and I put the trench coat full of something in my big suitcase.

I put one of my orange guns and my sword and my cowboy hat and the magnifying glass inside.

I don't know where the other gun is. Or my badge. But since Patrick gave it to me, it's spoiled, and I don't want it now.

I get in the car.

When I get home, Oma has something called a stroke. She lies in bed all the time. Staring at the ceiling. I hope that in her mind the *spiel* is going on, and that she is playing all the parts, and that afterwards she can swim in the sea.

I hope that—although in my heart I know it's not true.

8. Quirk now:
Listen to your octopus, conclusion

After the puppet show, Ali and Quirk waited a couple of days. Mr. Olsen pulled an escape stunt about once a month, Phil the bartender told the two of them later—after they'd formulated a kind of plan.

"So, he has completed his monthly performance of resistance," observed Ali. "The powers will rest easy, their attention slackened."

They sat together in her apartment. On the futon that served as a sofa. Ali sat straight up as though at a formal dinner: almond eyes in the middle of an oval smooth face.

"Say," she said, "are you Palestinian or Syrian or what?"

He smiled slightly. "I think it would be better not to share my origins or national identity."

On the wall the chalk-faced, all-male Sankai Juku dancers nodded their androgynous approval from their poster. Octo writhed periodically with spasmodic pleasure, and Quirk kept putting her hand over her chest to prevent the tentacles from shooting out and grasping the boy who sat on the lumpy seat.

"You still need a vehicle," he said. "A truck or a van or something so you can get him out of there."

"We'll borrow Dr. Caligari's van," she said. "I did some research for her once. Just tape over the letters that say 'Institute of Sexual Healing.'"

Ali raised an eyebrow. "And then where will you take him?"

She hadn't figured that part out. "A house?" she said.

There was a nice house that was being worked on. Not in the town center, but not too far away either. The Vietnam vets had talked about it, and she had seen it a couple of times on her walks. A fence around it, one side covered with roses. Furniture already inside, but no one lived there yet, the vets said. It was being prepared for the hotel man. The hotel man was coming, they said, to put something inside that great big hole next to the college. But not for a month or so. Because the hotel man was very important, and important people are busy. Quirk knew the house had electricity because she could hear jackhammers and electrical equipment going inside.

Ali was dubious. And wondered about Olsen's medical condition.

"I'll fucking figure that out," she said.

"All right," he said, "I'm with you. I'll drive the van, and we'll take him to the house, and then you and he can confer as to what to do." He stood up. His pizza shift about to begin, or else he had to go home—to a place she'd never seen. She looked at him, wondering. Why did he never talk about his family or say where he was from? The parents would worry he was some sort of radical. But that was stupid. Ali mosdef had a secret, but it wasn't a secret like *that*.

And anyway, she didn't talk about her family either.

"The old gentleman certainly keeps on trying, doesn't he?" said Ali. "There's something poignant about his determination."

They set the plan for Friday night. The house workers would have finished early; they'd have the weekend. The wild card was the nurse-man.

"The tall guy who takes care of him?" said Phil, when they asked about Clavino/Clamato. "No, he never comes in here, but I do see him pass by the windows on Friday nights. Then he crosses the street and goes to the bookstore."

Quirk decided that it's a good thing that small town people have such boring lives that they watch everybody doing everything all the fucking time.

"I'll drive the van," said Ali, "but I won't come in. If there's trouble, I'm leaving. I'm on a student visa, after all. I would prefer not to get arrested." He lifted his hands up, "My family ... would ... be ... embarrassed."

"It's fine," she said. She was amazed, frankly, he was willing to do this much.

"He likessssss you," said the octopus.

"Possibly," said Quirk.

Friday night came. They drove to Geisterseher Street. They had flashlights for signaling and a kitchen knife. Just in case.

They parked a few doors down in front of a house/office that the chiropractor and the psychiatrist shared.

Quirk walked up the path to the front door. She looked through the windows of his house. It was faded, elegant, and sad. Green leather club chairs. A fire in a fireplace. Chinese lamps like her grandmother had. A lone dark cherry colored glass thing stood on a table. There was a picture of Cézanne's apples on the wall. She remembered that from art history.

She was going to climb in through a side window, but Mr. Olsen was there in his suit, drinking a cocktail. And she remembered, *Don't scare him*.

So she rang the doorbell.

He walked—caneless, walkerless—slowly, so slowly, to the door. He paused. Picked up a baseball bat on the way. He was ready to fight if he had to!

Cool.

He opened the door slowly.

"Ava!" he said. "Do come in!"

He remembered!

She stepped in. The walls were blue, and they were crying big tears of embroidery.

"I have your money clip," she said. "But I'm really here to—"

And then she realized how incredibly stupid this whole thing was. This man had a nice house, and he didn't need saving.

"You look pale," said Mr. Olsen. "Come here, and I'll fix you a whiskey. I can still do that much."

I don't want to save him, she realized.

I want—

Why was this always so hard to think about? She shook her head at herself. *What's wrong with me? Everyone wants things.*

She stood and looked out the window, got out her flashlight while Mr. Olsen's back was turned. As he was carefully pouring from a decanter at a real old-fashioned type bar, she gave the 'I got in OK' clear signal. She thought she saw Ali straining to look through the window of the borrowed van.

She started to sink into one of the expensive green leather chairs. "I want," she said, and then, realizing he was formal and cared about such things, stood up again. "May I sit down?"

He nodded.

"I want to stay in Narrow Interior," she said. "I don't want to go home."

"What about college?" he said. "A young person has to have a college degree in today's economy."

"I tried," she said. "This college went bankrupt."

"Yes," he said. He drank a big gulp of whiskey, still standing at the bar. "Goddamned board of trustees." He poured again, limped, sat down, and his ruined knees clicked something sad and funny under pinstriped pants.

"Now we've got two companies who own different parcels, and we don't know what to do with the goddamn library! The commission is debating—"

He stopped. "But that's all boring crap for a young person," he said. "So tell me, what about your parents? And what are your job skills?"

They were talking like this (she had some fucking skills! Parents were a fucking pain! [But he knew this already: goddamn pushy family]), when Clavino/Clamato walked in.

Fuck.

"I forgot something," he said, "and—" He stopped and looked at Quirk.

"You!" he said. "Again!"

"I want a job," said Quirk, "and—"

She looked around. Chinese statues and the collected works of Sherlock Holmes. Ashtrays made by children and a big table held up by a wooden Indian elephant. The house was a strange mélange of styles, clearly crap he'd been left with.

"I want to live here. I'll barter my work for rent and food, and I'll figure out college."

Clavino/Clamato looked at her, his eyebrows raised high on his huge Frankenstein forehead.

"Assssssk the quesssssstion," said her octopus.

"So…what do you say?" said Quirk.

The nurse man looked at Mr. Olsen. He went to the telephone.

"Pleazzzzzzeeee!!!!!!!!!!!!!" Shouted Octo. "Have mercccccccccccy upon ussssss!"

"What's that hissing sound?" said Mr. Olsen.

Mr. Calvino put the phone down and stroked his right forearm thoughtfully.

"Do you really think you are capable," the tall nurse said to Quirk, "of keeping Mr. Olsen from running all over town?"

Mr. Olsen looked inscrutable.

"I'll run with him on your days off and when you have to pick up his meds," said Quirk. "And you can keep track of him more easily, because he'll be with me at . . . the library, studying . . . and stuff like that!"

They looked at Mr. Olsen. No one seemed to want to mention the Maple Leaf Bar.

"You are the boss after all, sir," said Calvino.

"Right," grumbled Mr. Olsen. "It's about time you remembered that, Mr. Calvino!" He nodded to himself. "Let's try and give it a whirl. Why the hell not?"

Quirk looked out the window.

"I have a friend outside," she said. "May I bring him in?"

"Of course," said Mr. Olsen. "I enjoy young people."

"Wait," she said. "He's an Arab."

Mr. Calvino piped up, "A most misunderstood ethnic group, like the Italians!" He rolled up his sleeves.

"Let me make us something to eat."

On Calvino's forearm was a big-ass tattoo. A monkey with a crown on its head, winking and waving.

"Thankssss for your asssisstance, majessssty," said Quirk's octopus. The monkey bowed, his head stretching Calvino's arm skin slightly.

Quirk went and opened the door. She felt her own arm moving in an unexpected gesture.

When she went to see Sankai Juku with her grandmother before the Alzheimer's got bad, the dancers' bodies seemed to fly out towards the audience without so much as moving. Only their arms stirred, waving across and back, while their usually immobile faces expressed longing under their white makeup for the people who watched them in the dark. So, Allison/Quirk/Ava moved her arm across her body, pulling her hand palm up and out. It was an awkward maneuver, yet it seemed to exert its own peculiar power. For, after a moment's hesitation, Ali got out of the van and walked slowly and with an understandable degree of caution towards the open door.

She put her hands back in her pockets: self-conscious again and shy. It was then that she felt the sock puppets. She pulled them out. The monster and the puppet with yarn hair. The one called Molly. She put them both on her hands and wrapped them tight around Ali's tall, thin frame.

9. Henry now:
Me, grown up

So, I become secret. I study unspecialness and silence. While most people in America work to develop ersatz talents, individualistic quirks, and even the occasional eccentricity, I let mediocrity shine like a beacon of nothingness. A black hole of personality.

You've seen me. Or thought you have. I'm the pudgy rich kid that everyone likes in the private International Baccalaureate high school and at the under-rated, high-priced East Coast university. I bring the good booze to the kegger. I routinely give some inebriated individual a ride home in my used Italian car. Because I never take a girl or boy home for sex. I play basketball with a group of guys. Badly. People say I'm nice, but they mostly look through me. That's ok. Often, I don't see them either. Because I'm hiding. With my eyes closed.

I graduate unremarkably from college and return without incident to the penthouse in the big city, where my mother lives.

It is the beginning of summer. I meet my friend Patti for lunch around the corner from our luxury high-rise. Patti has been my neighbor as long as I can remember. We met as bored children waving to each other on the Fourth of July from our respective penthouse gardens while our families sipped professionally bartended drinks at the catered parties on the roof.

"I'm going out," I announce to my mother, who sits on a Louis XVI divan covered in faxes and two computers with her personal assistant of the moment leaning over her.

"Be careful," she says.

My mother is currently consolidating the Holbein hotel empire. Holbein Hotels boast palatial establishments everywhere, even in the most dangerous, terrorist-ridden countries. Patrick designs the hotels, and my mom and he hire lawyers and money-managers and smart, ambitious people to run them. Lately, they've gotten into retrofitting older buildings. Which means they make them super grandiose with a fancy lobby and overpriced restaurant. They demolish what was special about them and put in a gift shop.

"Business going well today, Mom?"

"Mmm," is the answer. Patrick and my mother do their best to keep me out of Holbein affairs. But I listen in on the conversations. Glance through the paperwork lying on the desk. There's been a lot of paperwork and phone calls lately. I can tell my mom is nervous because she's playing with her necklace a lot. The necklace with the hand-pendant that is always pointing down and not up.

Today Patti and I meet at the Hamburg, a tiny eatery on the corner of our block.

"Henry!" Patti is a big hugger, and since she is fat her hugs are particularly physical. Comforting.

"I can't believe we are both done with college," she says as we plunk ourselves down on the old-fashioned leather stools at the counter, which comprise the entire restaurant.

On the other side of me, Mr. Death takes a seat.

He is wearing an LL Bean hiking outfit complete with backpack. His skull face looks at me from underneath a green hat that says *I <3 the out of doors!*

I nod. If I don't greet him, he tends to jump in and out of my vision repeatedly until I acknowledge him.

"Why can't I meet a handsome man who wants me?" says Patti as she waves to George, the owner/short order cook, and he gets to work on the "usual": a double bacon cheeseburger with fries and a chocolate milkshake.

I shake my head, wag my finger and make a drinking sign.

George places the "other" usual, an iced coffee, in front of me and looks at me.

"Back on the diet, Henry?" he says.

I shrug. Both of these questions, George's and Patti's, are questions without an answer. Or without an answer that anyone wants to hear.

George fries up the burgers and the bacon, shakes the fries loose from their basket, puts them on the plate, and lays the whole thing down in front of Patti.

"I mean what do I have, rabies or something?" Patti picks up a piece of bacon and twirls it.

"And you—" she points the bacon like a floppy spear, "what do you want?"

"I'm hungry for something," I say. I sip and sip. "I just don't know what for."

"That's bullcrap." Patti takes two enormous bites of burger and smashes four fries into her mouth.

"Your problem is that your brain just powers down because you are so afraid, and then you don't want anything at all consciously, because you can't even think about it."

Patti has just been accepted to a graduate clinical psychology program and is practicing on everyone, including her dog.

Her father bought the university a building. Like me, she's not a great tester. But she *is* pretty smart.

"What the fuck are you talking about?" We talk in this crude way to each other because it makes us feel confident. It's like a coach talking trash to an athlete. Or so I have read. Anyway, when I talk to Patti, I feel something I don't feel very often.

Hopeful.

"It's all in the theory of Endicott," she says. The hamburger is half gone. The milkshake is two-third's gone, and the fries are three-quarter's gone. "You were so traumatized as a child that—"

I am tired of hearing about trauma. I'm sure it exists; we see the battalions of shell-shocked soldiers and those tons of hollow-eyed refugees on the news. But can you speak meaningfully about something that has been relegated to a sound-byte and a photo-op?

But no one wants to hear about that either.

I almost say that I would like an attractive *anyone* to fall in love with me. Or at least have sex with me. Or at least flirt with me.

"Patti, I—"

"You really should consider therapy."

I put my empty glass down. Hard. "Stop trying to fix me!"

She smiles. Leans back. Burps quietly.

"That was *good*, Henry!" she says. "I think you're having a breakthrough."

Why is it that any time a quiet person yells it's either because they've lost control or because they're experiencing catharsis?

Why can't a person yelling just *be* a person yelling?

I roll my eyes and look over at Mr. Death, who is doubled over in silent laughter. His jaws open up under his non-existent lips.

The check comes.

"I got this," she says. And then she asks the inevitable question. "Do I look fat, Henry?"

I can tell Patti she's fat and that we live in a society that frowns on fat people even as it serves up the fast food and the supersized bottles of cholesterol. I can tell her that we are both rich losers who will never have a real relationship with anyone because our wealth and extreme cultural privilege (although Patti's is somewhat mitigated by the fact that she's Jewish) will make it so everyone is going to think of us in terms of the great stuff they can buy.

"I think you look fine," I say.

She smiles at me.

"I have a graduation present for you," she says. I notice a shopping bag from the Walking Company next to her. "I know you walk for exercise. These shoes support your arches and your feet will never get tired."

"Thanks," I say.

Then I order a milkshake, and a hamburger too, because these are my favorite foods.

"That's the ticket," she says.

My response is to slurp as hard as I can through the milkshake straw.

"While you're eating, I'll read your tarot cards," says Patti.

Mr. Death gets up and goes around next to Patti as she whips out her cards.

"Please don't," I say as I chomp on my burger.

"Three-card spread," she says.

"I thought you were an atheist," I say. The burger is perfect. Pink in the middle, charred on the outside and a little crunchy.

"I am," she says. "You don't have to believe in a Mr. God to believe in spirituality."

I sigh and drink my shake. Patti went to college on the West Coast, where all manner of peculiar idea combinations seem to hold sway.

"Besides," she says, "The Tarot is very Jewish. It emerges from Kaballah. Look."

She shuffles and has me tap the deck. I look at her and do it. I love Patti, and tarot gives her a feeling of control in a world of chaos.

She lays out the cards.

The Tower

The Five of Pentacles

Death

"Jesus," I say. "Thanks a lot."

"No," says Patti as she takes a bite of my hamburger. "The Tower is the past trauma I was talking about; the Pentacles is the present; and the future is—"

I look over at Mr. Death. He is bending over his own card in a bemused fashion. He pushes back the LL Bean cap and scratches what I guess used to be his forehead with a finger.

"Yeah, I know what *that* future means."

Patti now swipes my milkshake and takes a big gulp. "Look carefully— it's a really good, exciting card."

I move my eyes and notice that on his back, Death is carrying a tiny baby.

Which reminds me.

"I got to go," I say. I hug Patti, take my bag of shoes, and go back home to do some practicing.

10. Sean now:

You have to serve somebody

So, my Aunt Mathilde phones me at like 2:00 p.m. and says—get this—"Sean Gavin, I need your help."

I sit up on the foldout bed in my mom's basement in our house in Rhododendron, the old whaling town just rotten with history.

"What up, Auntie?" I say, lighting a Marlboro. Then I use the same match to fire up a little New Pure Land Materialist Buddhist™ incense. And start ohming to myself too, just to get the karmic juices flowing.

Mathilde is my mom's sister and she married into this family of hotel kajillionaires, the Holbeins. She is a widow and she has two sons: Patrick the jerk, and Henry, who is my friend. Patrick helps her run the hotel empire. Henry is—well, there's one person in every family who gets set up to be the "problem." Henry is the "problem" in the Holbein family. I'm the "problem" in mine.

He's rich, though. And I'm not.

But I'm getting off the point.

"Make your plot points clear in the opening and *stick to them*," my mature but hot screenwriting teacher Sherry always used to say. As I listen to Aunt Mathilde tell me—her favorite male relative (other than her dead husband that is)—her problem, I can also hear Sherry yelling, "SHOW DON'T TELL FOR GOD'S SAKE, SEAN!" (That was before we started dating, which happened after we ran into each other that one time in the unisex bathroom at Super Fit Fitness.)

Oh yeah. Sherry says flashbacks are problematic too.

"We have purchased this hotel site, dear boy," my aunt tells me on the phone. "But there are problems."

Interesting. Holbein Hotels usually runs smooth as silk, thanks to Cousin Patrick. And that Mathilde would call me about the hotel is even weirder, unless this problem somehow involves Henry. Which is what I suspect.

But the fact is I'm pretty short of cash right now and there's a Karmann Ghia I have my eye on. If I can help my aunt, she might throw a couple of Benjamins my way, and that would be good. I love cars, and I can fix them and alter them so they can run on sunflower oil, which is a lot more ecological than that fucking French fry car they came up with at that fancy schmancy hippy college that Ken Burns went to.

"The Civil War documentary series is very skillful," Sherry said in our class at RCC Extension. "But doesn't that recurring violin music start to wear on you?"

"It makes me want to fucking kill somebody, metaphorically speaking," I said, raising my hand.

That was when we connected.

Oops. Another flashback.

So I say, "Sure, Aunt. How can I help you achieve serenity in this world filled with *māyā*?"

"Come into the city," she says. "We'll have high tea at the Hotel Plantagenet and discuss this properly." She hangs up without waiting for an answer. Aunt Mathilde's a busy woman.

You'd think a macho hunk like me wouldn't go for high tea, but I love my food, and any occasion to eat for free is an occasion not to be missed. So I swing my feet over the foldout, throw on a clean saffron robe, buckle up my vegan sandals, quickly blend myself up a banana smoothie with my Zen-Green energy powder in it, drink it down, chase it with some semi-sweet chocolate chips, light up another Marlboro, and head for the commuter train on my bike.

It attracts babes. What can I say? And keeps my legs in shape. Also, I don't happen to own a working car right now.

Now, I got to be honest: I don't like the train. It stinks to high heaven from all those pissed off early morning commuters, and when I go—which is generally in the middle of the day—there's always some old lady asking me if I'm a Muslim and/or a member of the Hare Krishna. And telling me to go get a job like a regular person.

Then I have to explain about my monastic order, what New Pure Land Materialist Buddhism is, and how we are really cool, nice people, who are visionary entrepreneur types who don't live in monasteries because they are freaking uncomfortable, and so we like op in the real world in such a way as to more easily transform cultures like the film industry, and we are also great lovers (I generally save that part for a much younger woman).

See, that's the other problem with the train at this time of day; there are rarely babes on board. You get the old ladies I just referred to travelling into the city to see the matinees or visit their grandkids or go to the dentist. But you have to be nice to them too. That's like part of how we Buddhists roll.

So, true to NPLMB form, I smile at the elderly females sitting across from me with their pearls and purses, all psyched to see the latest restaging of *Les Misérables*. I chat with them about the stuff I learned about Victor Hugo in my French Writers In Exile extension class. I mention the fact that Hugo wrote the book on some freaking island (no wonder that book is long! See the film, if you can, instead: awesome with Liam Neeson). Not the musical. Idiotic.

Then I look out the smudged window and think about the electric guitar I want to get, and how sweet that Fiat Spider will roll once the part that I've ordered from Georg arrives. Parts are hard to find because the car is so old, and well, anyway.

I get into the city and take the subway to that fancy Holbein hotel that overlooks the park, and is all turn-of-the-century.

But then guess what happens?

I see Patrick the Ivy League Rhodes Scholar Wharton School, Phi Beta fucking Kappa jerky older brother sitting in the fancy lobby with the chandeliers and not Aunt Mathilde! She's in an important meeting apparently about a property in the former East Germany.

Bummer. Seeing Patrick threatens (but does not of course manage) to bust my super duper Zen buzz. He's so uptight and so disgustingly successful that he doesn't know which university tie to wear. I've never seen a more joyless person.

He's an architect by trade, but an asshole by vocation.

But, man, you want to talk money? He's a Poindexter when it comes to figures, and I guess that's why his mom relies on him so much for business stuff. He can do big calculations in his head. Used to do it over Thanksgiving all the time to make me and Henry feel dumb.

Hey wait! If this was a movie, wouldn't we need some kind of establishing shot of the restaurant?

Here it is:

Camera goes through doors (always a cool effect) and pans opulent lobby area in courtyard in hotel. Huge, over-sized palms in pots.

Voice over: Patrick being here means this hotel problem is serious.

Umm—where was I? My Introduction to Narrative Sculpture teacher at RCC Extension, Miss Lola Kasnikov, said I had a way with stories, but I needed to get to the point of making an actual art project, which I never did, so I got an Incomplete.

"Sean—" my mom said to me last night over her faux-tini (this is a fake martini with a bunch of olives and club soda), "why are there only Incompletes on your college transcripts?"

"Mom," I said, sipping on my Spaten Optimator, "what does completion even *mean* in this universe of multiple incarnations?"

Shit. Two flashbacks in a row isn't good narration either, Sherry always said.

"It confuses the viewer," she told me. "Sean, just unfold the fucking tale already."

Goddamn it. I think that makes three fb's.

Focus, Sean.

The hotel lobby. High tea.

So I say to Patrick, "HEY, BRO!" Because I know that kind of talk pisses him off, and I have to confess (although this is not very enlightened) that nothing delights me more than PISSING PATRICK OFF.

He looks pained but determined.

I slide my ass along the pink banquette of the fancy tea joint in the lobby of the hotel and stick my sandals out, so you can see my bare and not totally clean feet. The maître d' glares at me but he realizes I'm with Mr. Patrick HOLBEIN. So the guy clenches his teeth, waits for me to settle in on the banquette, bows stiffly, gives me a fancy heavy-paper menu, and retreats.

I lean back. "So how can I help the family THIS time?" I ask.

Patrick is wearing some fancy Brooks Brothers get up. He always dresses like he's a Wall Street broker from the early sixties.

He—I'm not kidding—snaps his fingers at a waiter.

We order.

Patrick gets tea. I get all the tea sandwiches they got, crumpets, two mini éclairs, three mini napoleons, and six mini fruit tarts, and a bottle of white wine to keep my tea company.

Patrick wastes no time with small talk. He launches into biz and tells me about this new hotel site.

While I attack the sandwiches on their three-tiered tray (kind of like what Mr. Spock plays chess on in *Start Trek*, *TOS*, and in *Star Trek II*), Patrick tells me that Holbein Hotels bought this property in this place in the country. The town is really old, and Patrick and his mom figure they'll get in on the ground floor of some historic Williamsburg type restoration with hired help running around in historically accurate costumes and demonstrating making soap and other junk that they had to do in the day.

I finish the sandwiches and eat the crumpets.

The éclairs are sliding down, all chocolate cream and flakey pastry, when Patrick explains that there's some super old building standing on the property for the hotel. But the town won't let Holbein hotels fix it or change it, so they'll have to build around it. But they don't exactly seem to know what it's for. No one wants to talk about it either. Which is weird.

I belch: polite in most eastern circles.

Patrick stops talking and looks at me.

I'm about to say, "Dude, I don't understand why you wanted this piece of land in the first place." But then I remember it's not for me to think such un-entrepreneurial thoughts. I try to be Zen and in the moment and like, *can I get some French fries, even though they aren't on the high tea menu? And do you make banana splits?*

The waiter runs and gets me some fries; they arrive in a big silver charger. Another waiter brings the banana split.

"Sean!" says Patrick. "I need an answer! Will you go to Narrow Interior or not?"

"Say," I say, my mouth semi-full of quite deliciously salty fries, "isn't that the name of Bashō's book?"

"Who?"

"Bashō, the Japanese poet who named himself Banana and was this cool haiku type dude."

Patrick is manifestly uninterested in Bashō, which is too bad, because Bashō actually was pretty successful at merging a Buddhist aesthetic with what one might call a commercially viable artistic profile. A.k.a "brand." That's what my RCC Extension teacher Miss Yakitori said when I took that class on Japanese poetry.

She was gorgeous. Married. Two kids. There was that time I almost—

"The deal is you go to Narrow Interior," Patrick says, "and keep an eye on Henry."

Bingo. So this *is* about Henry.

If this was a movie, there'd be a close up of me and my white wine glass, thinking.

My cousin Henry is—well I guess you'd call him weird, but I like him. His mom and bro think he's dumb. But he isn't that. He's just kind of unrealized. A person who hasn't yet happened.

He went to private school and has been sort of overprotected, because his father died when he was a little kid. When he wasn't at school, he was out at his grandmother's country house near the ocean. He's never really seen life.

He reads a lot and watches television, and he used to play with Legos and Play Mobil.

If this was a movie, we'd now have a flashback of little kid hands moving Lego people and building cool pretend structures. There'd be a voice-over saying that Legos are deeply cool. You can build whole worlds with them. And Play Mobil is even better. Henry had a castle and a bunch of knights and an awesome dragon.

That reminds me; my mom gave away my Legos and my Play Mobil pirate ship just the other day. She's been giving a lot of stuff away lately.

Patrick is drumming his fingers on the table, waiting for me to respond.

"What's up with Henry these days?" I say. I spear the last huge heap of French fries on my fork and jam them in my mouth, along with some mayo, like they do in Belgium. That's what I learned in my Food Cultures of the Low Countries class.

Patrick's eyes get large with pissed-offness.

"I hear he just graduated from college," I say encouragingly as I chew.

Patrick rolls his eyes. "If you can call Sorry State University a college," he says. "It's a third-rate institution."

Of course I'm (personally) still taking courses at someplace even less, uh, PRESTIGIOUS. I'm more of like a part-time student.

But I rise above the intended insult.

I beam at Patrick. I have nice round cheeks, and I look kind and intelligent when I beam. Sherry said so.

"Great!" I say. "So what's Henry up to now?"

Patrick mutters something.

"What?" I put down my ice-cream spoon and grab my ear. I pull on my first three earrings for dramatic effect and let the little jade elephant that hangs from the third earring tinkle in a merry sort of way.

"PUPPETS," yells Patrick.

The rest of the high-class tea drinkers in the hotel lobby look anxiously at one another. There is a pause in the polite hum in the pink room at the fancy joint that my older cousin owns.

"He's obsessed with puppets! Goes to puppet shows all the time, and Mother caught him—"

Wow, I think as I finish up the banana split, *this is really getting interesting.*

"—playing with one of them in his bedroom."

If this was a movie, we'd now have like an anime fantasy sequence of Henry as a life-size puppet with two really gorgeous girls from like Slovenia, who were here on a lapsed student visa, like those topless hotties in *Hostel* before the movie gets all gross and boring, OR it would be a live-action scene in fast motion kind of like that one in *A Clockwork Orange*. My screenwriting teacher Sherry (did I mention that she was really incredibly hot?) said that was a great example of—

"Sean, ARE YOU LISTENING TO ME?" shouts Patrick.

I put my hands behind my head. I did it. I got Patrick to yell! TWICE! And it's only like twenty minutes into the meeting.

But Patrick immediately recovers; he's fast. He smoothes his hair back on his head and straightens his tie.

He leans over. "Look," he says, "we want to send him away until he finds himself."

Good on you, Henry, I think. *Escape from your fucking brother is your only hope.* If this was a movie there would be a shot of me encouraging Henry like Steve McQueen (in a cool torn shirt) encourages Dustin Hoffmann, who's nerdy and kind of scared in *Papillon*.

But now I focus all my karmic energies because it's time to run my scam.

"Oh gosh, Pat," I say, shaking my head, "not again with this babysitting of your brother!"

I pretend I don't like Henry and spending time with him is a chore. I've been doing this for years. It's great because I always get paid.

The script generally goes like this:

Mom/Aunt Mathilde/Uncle Hans/Patrick: Go sit with your cousin, he's the only other kid here on (**name of holiday**

here).
Me: Aw gee, Mom/Uncle Hans/Aunt Mathilde/Cousin Patrick, do I have to?
Mom/Aunt Mathilde/Uncle Hans/Patrick: Please, Sean!
Shhh, here's a dollar/ten dollars/twenty dollars.

I'm thinking about the cars and the guitars and the screenwriting software they say you just plug your movie ideas into.

"I don't know," I shake my head at Cousin Patrick. "I have a very full schedule. How soon do you need me up there?'

"Right away," is the answer.

Hmm. When Patrick says right away, you have to ask yourself how much money you want to play for because the deal is going to go off the table pretty fast. I learned this the hard way when I was twelve, and I hesitated to go with Henry to his eighth birthday to Disney World back in the day. Patrick was already on the job bribing people to be nice to his brother, so I said I had to go home and think about it.

By the time I called him back, Henry was gone on a private jet with some kid from his school, and I spent spring vacation shoveling snow in the driveway with my pissed off, not yet divorced from my mom, very drunk dad.

"All right," I say.

"I want you to get up there this afternoon, spend the night, and take a look at the property."

"How much?" I say.

Patrick smirks. It's not an attractive quality.

"Five hundred to go up there THIS AFTERNOON and spend the night. Plus all expenses." He leans back. "Then we'll negotiate."

I say OK, walk out of the hotel and into the Holbein limo. Jimmy's driving, like always. They got a suitcase already packed for me. Because that's how the Holbeins roll.

11. Henry:
Not again

After my lunch with Patti, I go home, ride up the elevator, and walk into the apartment. I shut my bedroom door and put on black pants and a black hoodie, and I put a black Halloween half-mask over my face.

The official histories state that the art form of Bunraku began at the same time as Kabuki, a theatrical form started by a woman. But there is an older Japanese name: *kugutsu-mawashi* ("puppet turners"), and some think that the puppet turners have been around for much longer and that they too may have originated with women.

I limber up my arms and shoulders. I clench and unclench my fists and wiggle my fingers.

In traditional bunraku, the turner's face is covered and he does not speak. But I like it because you get to stand in front of the audience with your puppet. So you're there, but you're visibly invisible. A perceived absence.

Now I reach into the back of my bedroom closet and pull down the old plaid suitcase that is jammed back there, crammed between my father's copy of *Howl* and some old videotapes of a TV show called *Dobie Gillis*.

I open the case and take out the puppet that Shereen—the woman with the scarf—gave me and that I smuggled out of Oma's basement.

But the puppet is not the beautiful lady.

It's a furry-headed monster who is supposed to be the Monkey King.

I pick him up and slip my arm up the back of him and into his head.

What happens next is Son Gokū's fault (his name is originally Chinese—Sun Wukong—but he prefers the Japanese version).

But perhaps what happens is my fault too, because Monkey seems to absorb whatever he is close to, which in this case is the Beat poets and 1950's television.

When I bow to him as I slip my hands into his body, he opens his eyes wide and says, "What's jumping, daddy-o?"

Then he jumps off my arm and starts clambering up the curtains.

"Get back here," I say. "I need to talk to you." The truth is I want him to remember his origins and tell me what he was doing in my Oma's play.

Today I try a different tack.

"Your majesty," I say, putting my arms across my chest, "why do you think you were made into a bunraku puppet at all, being as you are not generally a figure in that theatrical tradition?"

"Beats me, man," says Monkey as he swings from curtain rod to curtain rod. "I don't know why I'm not big with those know-it-all, long-hair theater squares. The real people dig me, and by real I mean those video-game hipsters and those color TV watchers. I'm pretty famous with the comic book kids too. Isn't that cool enough for you?"

Monkey does a somersault off the top of the valence and lands on my bed. He proceeds to do something that looks a little like the can-can. He ends the can-can with a split. Then he lifts his human-looking arms and scratches his uncharacteristically furry puppet head.

"Man, this hang-out is strictly dullsville! Where are the cocktails?"

He leaps off the bed, does two back flips, and propels himself into my arms. I spot him, his head and back encase my hand and forearm, and as we make contact, he rolls his large eyes and wags his finger at me.

"And *where are the chicks*?" he inquires. Then he laughs raucously.

When he gets too loud and too restless, I take the wooden sticks that I bought at the Japanese Cultural Center, and I bang on them, and that action makes him go unconscious—if a puppet can ever be said to be conscious in the first place.

But this time, I don't have the sticks out.

My mother knocks on the door. "Who are you talking to, Henry?" she says. She knocks again.

"Nobody," I say, but Monkey keeps on laughing.

"Hey, daddy-o, who's that chick pounding on the door? Is *she* the reason you aren't out making the scene someplace orbital?"

My mother walks in.

"Radioactive!" says Monkey.

My mother looks at me with my hoodie, mask and the giant monkey puppet on my arm.

Monkey's head bobs up and down appreciatively at my mother standing just inside the doorway. "You got a classy chassis, dolly!" says Monkey. He emits a poppet simian version of a whistle. "What if you're a little old for me? I can tell you're fast. You kill me, to tell the truth. So what do you say, you and me hop into a machine and play a little back seat bingo?"

My mother doesn't get quiet very often, but she gets quiet now.

"Oh. My. God." she whispers and runs. I can hear her feet pounding down the long hall to the other side of the apartment.

"Wait, don't split!" Monkey jumps off of my arm and starts heading for the door, shouting things like "I dig you!" and "I'm real gone!"

I grab the wooden rods out of the suitcase. Monkey is about to turn the corner and go out of earshot. I stick the rods under my arm, grab his tail, and pull him back into the room. Then I jump in front of the bedroom door and strike the sticks together. CLACK.

Monkey collapses on the very nice Persian rug.

I exhale. Pull the mask up on my head.

12. Sean:
You have to serve somebody, continued

If this was a movie, we'd cut to an establishing shot of a picturesque and quaint American town.

Jimmy sets me up at the creaky-staired historic inn right smack in Narrow Interior's downtown. It's a charming old joint where the famous authors of the Nineteenth Century stayed; Hawthorne stayed at the Narrow Interior Inn, and Whitman stayed there, and Melville stayed there, and hell, President Washington would have stayed there if he'd been alive in the Nineteenth century (was he?), and it's all nice and crisp and pleasant, with samplers on the wall and fluffy pillows on the bed.

But it's way too small for a convention or for anybody to have a sizeable wedding, and I see where Aunt Mathilde is coming from. This town could use a modern hotel. With catering, Wi-Fi equipped meeting rooms, fitness center, and all the amenities.

I score a late breakfast, have a smoke on the front porch, phone the contractor and tell him I'm stopping by the hotel site, and walk around town.

In the film adaptation of this situation, there'd be some hokey "our town" type music and a montage as I attempt to kill some time before my meeting. You'd see me in a set of medium long shots, perambulating the streets of one of those burgs that's going through the ups and downs of yuppiedom: a lot of empty buildings, manufacturing places, breweries and tanneries, old five-and-dimes, and elegant old banks that are all deserted. Up on top of the hill, you'd see some old college that looks like it's completely empty, just sitting there. And sprinkled in among all of that is an Urban Outfitters and a GAP and a CVS (product placement). Then there'd be some posters on a guitar shop indicating that rock and roll indie people have moved up here to have kids and are doing concerts for free.

Right then there'd be the cameo of the singer Cassandra and her baby briefly, coming out of the local hair salon. Her husband, who's like the bass player, grabs her and sticks her and the child in an SUV.

An androgynous guy with long blonde hair like an angel and a super smooth complexion floats over to them all ethereal.

"Need anything today, Cassandra?" he says in a surprisingly deep voice.

"Not today, Carter," Cassandra's husband says to him.

Cool, I think. Here's the college town's pretty-boy drug dealer.

This would be a good set-up for a bio-pic starrring Cassandra and a buddhist bystander who happened to become the love of her life.

Now where the hell are the girls?

I wander around some more. I stick my head inside a semi-decent looking bar called the Maple Leaf. There's just an old man sitting there with a blobby Goth girl, and he's talking to the bartender with that loud hard-of-hearing voice.

I walk out. I go up the street to the ice-cream parlor.

Sweet! There are these two, young but not as young as me, moms with strollers. I walk up to the counter and pass them and check them out.

Both blonde and cute in that chipmunky way I like.

But there's one thing that's a little weird about them: they move in an odd way. They've got great bodies, but they are kind of stiff; the babies are a bit weird too, if only because they are making these totally regular cries like those baby-dolls you turn upside down that say "Mama." The women bend over at the same time to hush the regularly crying babies and straighten up stiffly at exactly the same time. Almost like invisible strings are working them. When they approach the counter, their heads bob a bit, and if this was a movie, you'd think of Daryl Hannah pretending to be a doll in *Blade Runner* (she was HOT! and then there was that stripper movie she was in: damn).

But who am I to judge how people move? I mean, maybe they're dancers or Pilates instructors or something.

Or maybe they need to relax. And Sean Gavin Francisco knows how to relax a girl.

I lose any lingering doubts when they look my way. They fasten very dark blue eyes on me, and I can tell that they are hungry for something other than ice cream and gossip.

I beam at them! I get a cone and lick it, pressing the ice cream down into the cone, so you don't get a bite of cone without a bite of sweet coldness.

The moms watch this procedure with interest. They ask about my get-up.

I tell them (of course) about New Pure Land Materialist Buddhism and that I'm a pacifist, a spiritually and sexually enlightened smoker who likes to fix cars.

"Buddhism AND Cars?" they say. "Wow!"

"Where are your husbands?" I ask. They are both wearing rings.

Lick, press, lick, and press.

"They work in the city and leave us with the children." They speak at the same time and nod tightly in unison, like bobble-heads on springs.

We start talking about the movie *Unfaithful* and how it's really a very compelling portrait of a woman with needs, and one puts her hand on my shoulder, and the other puts her hand in my lap, and they say they want to know all about my religion, and do I have to take vows, and what are they.

"Richard Gere," they say. "Wow!"

They are a little duet of cute sexiness.

We go back to the historic hostelry, and I help the moms and kids into the limo, and we all drive to one of their houses. If this was a movie the style would change, and we'd be in *cinéma vérité* mode, with that shaky artsy hand-held camera and a lot of suggestive shots of necks and ears.

While the babies lie in their crib for their naps, I convince those girls that the three way that they did in college was really not the right time and place to try it.

We are kissing and fondling, and I am both the director and the actor, and I'm forgetting Henry, RCC Extension, and the fact that I still live at home. The moms have full breasts from the milkiness, and these women are totally thin and stacked and beautiful, and they want to fuck a lot, and I want to fuck them too, as it's been a while since I've had sex with anyone.

We lie down in a big four-poster bed in this very nice old house. I have unrolled myself from my robe, and they are topless and getting bottomless, and they are all giggling and saying "wow" in weird tandem, but it's ok because we are about to get into some seriously sacred sexual shit.

This is when the script goes all to hell.

I have closed my eyes for a moment to achieve oneness with the universe. When I open my eyes, there she is.

The mini-domme standing at the foot of the bed.

She's a tiny blonde who is like four foot eleven and wearing an enormous black hat, and she's got a tight latex black dress on, and she's speaking very sharply to those moms, which wakes the babies, and they start crying in the other room.

"Go no further!" she instructs them. The moms blink their eyes, shake their heads, roll out of bed, and start to put their clothes on. They are fumbling with their bras and their panties, all out of lock step. They look a bit stunned. But they are moving like normal people now.

"Did we do ok?" asks the taller one. "Did we fulfill the requirement?"

The lady nods and points imperiously at the taller one's still unbuttoned shirt.

"Uh," I say. I pull the covers over me and try to sit up. "I'm beginning to feel a little self-conscious here."

The little lady stands on the corner of the bedstead and extends both hands towards me. She looks like a nutty magician or a hypnotist in a bad Ed Wood movie.

"Will you serve the light?" she says. The moms are almost dressed now, and they turn their heads expectantly as they slip into their jeans. In the distance the babies are crying: jagged, irregular, sad.

This really pisses me off. I was all about to get lucky with these chicks, who could really have used a sensual experience because look at how much more relaxed and human seeming they are after just a little foreplay.

So I blurt out, "Fuck NO!" I leap to my feet on top of the bed. I don't know what comes over me, but I start jumping up and down.

"No, No, No," I yell. "I want those girls!"

The crazy cougar lady does a back flip off the bed like an acrobat and sticks her landing perfectly—both feet landing firmly on the floor.

She's spry: I'll say that much for her.

"STOP THAT JUMPING!" she says.

I don't know why, but . . . I do stop.

The moms are pretty much dressed now.

One of them (the taller one) says, "What did you say your name was?" Then she looks at her friend. The shorter one shakes her head a little, as though she were dizzy. "Have we actually met?"

It's funny; her voice sounds completely different. Much more resonant. Much more her own.

The cougar domme takes each mother by the arm.

"You will find no rest until you serve someone other than yourself," she says to me. "You shall find no peace and no pleasure until you—"

"That's the stupidest fucking thing I've ever heard," I shout. I pick up the sheets and hurl them at the lady who's taking my women.

"Don't you dare leave!" I holler.

All three of them look at me. Unimpressed.

"Until that time," they all speak together, "you shall remain as you are: a man who is less than a man; an animal propelled by outsized desires that cannot serve you, but that you serve, unknowing."

With that, the little lady pulls those two mothers out the door.

I seethe in rage, jump off the bed, and run to the window.

A white van with the words CALIGARI INSTITUTE FOR HYPNO-THERAPY AND SEXUAL HEALING is parked outside behind the limo. The babies get packed back inside the van, along with the moms. The little lady gets in the driver's seat.

And they're gone.

I am left alone in this giant house. The front door isn't even locked.

I put my robe back on and strap up my sandals.

I lumber outside and climb in the limo.

"Jimmy," I say to the driver, "let's go home."

"Wait, sir," says Jimmy. "Your appointment with the contractor! Remember? You called him, and you wanted to go look at the hotel site."

"No," I say. "I want out of here. My chi is completely blocked or messed up or something."

And it's true. I feel. Strange.

"Mr. Sean," says Jimmy, "if you don't mind my saying so, I think you got to keep your appointments and do what you say you're going to do, you know what I'm saying?"

Will you serve the light? What the fuck does THAT mean?

I sigh. Jimmy's right. I promised Aunt Mathilde I'd help.

"Shit," I say. "Let's go see this goddamned building."

13. Henry:
Not again, conclusion

I wait ten minutes. Then I put on my dad's trench coat and slowly edge down the hall.

My mother is on the speakerphone in her bedroom. I listen outside.

"Update me on the Narrow Interior Project," she says.

"Mom," says Patrick's voice on speaker, "we have purchased the parcel I told you about, and I drew up plans for the retrofit of the meetinghouse/shack thing that is currently there."

"This is so we can take advantage of the tax breaks?" says my mother.

"Precisely," says Patrick. "State law provides incentives to building projects that refurbish historically significant sites, so long as the project preserves the historic character of the building." He pauses.

"The state is excited about the idea of having more towns that look like historic Williamsburg as a way to bring in tourists."

"What history is in Narrow Interior?" My mother's voice is sharp.

"Well, there isn't any that we know of," says Patrick. "But your original thinking—to provide a way station in the area between wineries and Revolutionary battlegrounds with a bevy of shops and fine restaurants—looks good to go."

There is a silence as my mom strikes a match. "Fine," she says.

"But," says Patrick, "we've hit a small snag—"

My mother inhales hard. Exhales. I smell the cigarette smoke.

"What's the problem now?" she says.

Her voice sounds tired and sad, and for a hotel magnate worth millions of dollars, she sounds like a tired housekeeper who would just like to put her feet up.

"It's not a big deal," says my brother. "Narrow Interior's Historic Buildings Preservation Commission has reviewed the plans and rejected them. So we're suing them."

"Jesus," says my mother, "not another lawsuit."

"Mom, it's fine," says Patrick. "Felice, Hughes, and Whatchem will win the lawsuit, but it wouldn't hurt to have somebody go up there, and, in the words of our Jewish friends, 'make nice' with the commission and go through the motions of trying to reach a friendly settlement."

"Well," says my mother, "I don't have time for that and neither do you." She pauses elaborately. "I think we should send—"

She switches off the speakerphone. She is talking very softly.

"I must—" she says. "He's all I have left." Then she adds, "What's going on with the IRS investigation?" There is another long silence as she listens.

I hear the click of the phone going off.

Silence.

I press my ear to the door.

My mother cries.

I stand outside the door. My mother weeps the whole time I stand there. She sounds like a young woman with a soft high voice. The sobs rise and rise. Then they fall. She becomes silent. On the other side of the door, I too am devoid of words.

When I walk down the hall, I see Mr. Death in a business suit on the landing to the stairs. He is jotting something down on a memo pad with an elegant Cross pen.

He hands me the piece of paper.

It's blank. But still, I put it in my pocket. I go back to my room and pack my trench coat and my sticks and the Monkey King.

And wait.

14. Sean:
You have to serve somebody, continued

As Jimmy drives me back downtown, I try to forget about the incident and just be chill and eat some of the banana chips I always bring with me for snacks. As I chomp on them, I figure the little cougar lady standing over me didn't freak me out too bad.

Then we get to the hotel site.

And there is this THING in front of us.

It was like a shack only bigger. Black, burnt looking wood and yellow crap all over the windows.

A blond guy with a ponytail and a tool belt comes on over and shakes my hand.

"Those yellow strings are the mold," he says. "John Russell. I'm the contractor."

"What *is* this place?" I say to John.

"Well, according to the commission on historic preservation, it was once a Danker meetinghouse."

"A whatta house?"

"Danker," says John. "No one knows very much about them. The place is kind of a local curiosity, and it's nice that your—what is she?—your aunt and your cousin want to build to incorporate the historic structure. It's too bad about the lawsuit, but I'm sure you folks will sort that out."

"What lawsuit?" I say. Patrick didn't mention that part.

"It's a typical small town ruckus," says John. "But I put my money on your family. They'll win their lawsuit and be able to update the building, get rid of the mold, and put in a gift shop, and do the historic Williamsburg kind of development that will put this town on the map."

He points at the empty space. "But for the time being, we can't build."

I look at this shack covered in yellow mold.

"Sean!" someone cries.

"What's that sound?" I say.

"Those are the Narrow Interior Lake swans," says John. "They have a strange mating call."

"No," I say. "I think a *person* is calling me."

I excuse myself for a minute, walk down the path to try to hear a bit better and also to get in touch with my feelings and be like Bashō, whom I admire, and who knew how to get paid and be an artist. I'm also hoping one of the hot moms has gotten away from that nutty little lady in the hat.

"Sean!"

No, it's not either of the moms. It's a voice I've never heard before. A beautiful voice.

I walk down by the lake and I get to a big, twisted up tree. It's a pine tree, but it's not like any pine tree I've ever seen; it's got big needles, and its trunk is all gnarled, and somehow that tree scares me. I mean nothing scares me, but that tree does. It starts creaking and groaning, and I realize that the voice is coming from the tree.

"Let my truth be known," says the tree voice, which is a woman's voice, and suddenly something comes over me and I feel so sad, like I've never felt before in my life. I look down at my feet, and I think for the first time how ugly they are. The toes are hairy and really kind of long.

Suddenly there is a woman standing in front of me holding something. It's a bundle of cloth and it looks like a baby.

She holds it out to me.

"The dolly," she says. "Sean, make my truth known." I'm about to take the baby from the woman because she is beautiful and looks like, all the women, somehow.

But then she starts to burn. Flames burst out of her mouth, and her face catches fire, and she crinkles up like burning paper.

The smell of burning skin and hair: it's so bad I want to puke, but I can't, and anyway the burning thing that was a person grasps my hand with her horrible hot paper bag skin.

I love women, but this is no woman, this is . . . I . . . don't know what.

I look into the burning eyes of the paper bag woman. I can't look away, although I want to. The burning fingers hold my wrist tightly as the scorched paper face comes closer and closer. My face hurts. My hair begins to singe and snap. Sparks on my scalp.

"Let go of me!" I try to shout, but my voice comes out in an animal whimper, and her hand is like a claw that digs into me, and with the other blackened crumpled arm she shows me what's in the bundle of rags—

And I don't know what the fuck it is.

It isn't dead, and it isn't alive.

You know like in *Eraserhead* where the girl says, "I'm NOT EVEN SURE IT IS A BABY"?

It is like that.

Only worse.

All I can see is the thing's piercing black eyes as it squawks at me in some high-pitched monster language.

"You must take him," says the ghost/burning paper bag woman. "He is the original."

She holds out the bundle of the baby thing that isn't a baby, and I'm finally able to tear my arm out of her/its grip, and I fucking run for my life.

I'm not much into cardio, but I can tell you that I run all the way back from the lake, past the burnt black meetinghouse, and past John Russell, who's standing by the limo with Jimmy. I pound the pavement till one of my sandals falls off, but I keep running because I'm so fucking scared that I'm shrieking, and I just keep running down the hill past the old college and the banks and stores till I get to the Maple Leaf Bar.

I burst through the door and throw myself down on a barstool. Only then do I turn around to see if she is following me.

I look at my left wrist. A bracelet of burn marks all around it.

It's quiet in there. The Goth girl has left, but the old guy is still sitting. The bartender polishing the glasses.

"See something you shouldn't?" says the old man.

I just sit there. Breathing, sweating. Like a motherfucker.

You know, some people look at me and say there's a fat white guy in a sari! But no, don't be fooled. I'm deep, and with my New Pure Land Materialist Buddhist deeposity, I can see that this Narrow Interior joint is into some heavy Karmic bad mojo shit.

The old man looks at me from beneath shaggy old man eyebrows.

"Don't worry about it, young man," he says. "The inner light will emerge." He thumps me on the back with a surprisingly strong hand.

"And even if it doesn't, at least you escaped. This time."

I look at him. I can't tell whether he's kidding or not. The bartender is silent. Still polishing the glasses.

15. Henry:
I depart

A couple of days pass. I run into my cousin Sean on the street. He hugs me for no apparent reason.

From her spot on the divan, my mother tells me she needs me to undertake an urgent piece of family hotel business.

"Thanks for believing in me!" I say. I kiss her cheek.

She winces. She does not like to be touched.

I am already packed, so I just walk out of the apartment building. Jimmy is waiting outside with the limo. He hands me a cream-colored envelope.

I don't have to look at the handwriting; I know it's from Patrick.

"Jimmy," I say, "I think I'm going to take the train."

"Oh, Mr. Henry, the train is so dirty, and—" he pauses. His forehead wrinkles in five deep accordion creases.

As he talks I think, *already he looks so old*.

"Your mother wouldn't want you—"

It bothers me that I don't know jack about Jimmy. About his family or girlfriend or boyfriend or kids. Whether Jimmy is a son of parents who are alive. If he is someone's big brother or little brother. I always ask how his family is, and he just says, "fine."

I interrupt the litany about the unsanitary and undesirable nature of the train.

"Jimmy," I say, and I place my hand, my soft hand that has done no hard labor, on the already stooping shoulder of the man who is my age maybe and who is—let's face it—my servant.

"I appreciate very much how much you care about me and my family."

I'm just filled with fucking *noblesse oblige* today.

Jimmy nods and smiles at this. His teeth are not as white as they should be; one tooth looks grey, which means it needs to have a root canal and be capped, and I wonder if we even cover dental.

I should speak to Mom about that. Or Patrick.

No, probably just talk to whoever it is who does payroll for our family.

Who the hell *is* that?

I remember a play I saw with Oma. A king goes crazy and runs around in a storm, and at one point he says, "I have taken too little care of this!" and I always think that's what my dad would say if he ever came back and looked at us.

Jimmy's lips roll back down over his tainted teeth. "No problem at all, Mr. Henry. Shall I take you to the train station?"

I would prefer to take the bus, but I don't want Jimmy worrying that he's going to lose his job, so I just say, "Yes. Please."

The train station is a big restored museum of a place lurking underneath a skyscraper in midtown where two different avenues meet. You can't see the grandeur of it right away, but when you turn the corner off of Luther Avenue you see the giant Greek god statues and the huge windows, and the effect floors you because the place looks more like an opera house than a transportation hub. It is a monument to trains, where engines great and small congregate to take all of us across town or across the country.

I like old buildings.

"Narrow Interior," I say to the man behind the Gilded Age ticket window.

The man squints at me through thick glasses. "The train don't go there," he says.

"How far *does* the train go?" I say.

He studies a yellowed paper brochure. "This line is not in the system," he says. "It's not used much." He squints some more and finally says, "Confidence."

"Thanks for your encouragement," I say.

"No, wise ass," says the man. "You get off at the Confidence Valley train station and take the bus. The depot is around the corner."

"Ok," I say.

This train is a battered silver and blue. The conductor—a pretty girl with a braid—points me to my seat.

The air is cold; it's always cold in America when you're inside, no matter what time of year it is or where you are. And the air is always stale, because no one ever dares crack a goddamn window.

I hear some flat voices across the aisle.

"They seen better days, these trains have." The woman who is talking takes a picture of the man sitting in the seat next to her.

Behind me someone is speaking Russian, or perhaps it's Bulgarian, because at one point the someone—a woman—says *Da da, Bulgarien.*

The seat is lumpy.

An enormous family—two women in wheelchairs; three men; two more walking women; and a beautiful girl, who wears glasses and who has a backpack and is tall and shy-looking—say they're looking for the dining car.

"We are all together," one man explains to the conductor.

The women in the wheelchairs nod, and the young girl looks behind, sees me, and smiles an enormous, bashful smile.

I sit in my lumpy seat with my one backpack (Jimmy's going to UPS the rest of my stuff) and suddenly, I feel something.

I feel furious because these people are so clearly together, so clearly a family: the eyes and the noses and the ears and the tilts of the head and the positioning of the shoulders and the flapping of their hands revealing their connection.

I think this emotion is jealousy.

I shiver in the air-conditioning and wonder what would it be like to have so many people? So many people to call *yours*?

I put my sweater on and settle back in my seat as they troop off—the wheel chair women staying behind and calling out an order for fried chicken if they have it, and a hamburger with bacon if they don't. And pizza, not pepperoni but cheese, if they don't have the hamburger. And if they don't have pizza, well then you'll just have to figure it out.

The train starts moving. My stomach rumbles.

"That's too many people," says the woman with the camera. "You got that big a family, and it just gets crazy-complicated. No one wants to eat at the same time. No one wants to eat the same thing."

"Well," says the husband as she clicks and clicks, "there has got to be conversation, and there has got to be compromises."

"Screw that," says the woman. "What you want personally gets lost in the shuffle of those conversations."

I scoff (quietly) at that remark. What I want always gets lost in the shuffle in my tiny family. I don't even get asked. And as a result, I don't even know.

"Maybe," says the man. "Still—"

I don't feel lonely very often, but right now I do, thinking about how perhaps who I truly am—whatever that is—could emerge with a big family. I could find myself in the chaos of others.

"You say something, Mister?" says the woman who has not stopped taking pictures out the window of the train station tunnel and of her husband sitting in his seat.

"No," I say.

"You're talking to yourself," she admonishes. "People are going to think you're not right in the head."

I could find my voice in the gaps between the voices of so many people speaking.

I nod to myself as the woman across the way says to her husband, "I don't know why it is we always got to sit near the crazy ones." She takes another picture.

"Ooh, look," she says. "I love being able to see in people's backyards. The train is perfect for that."

16. Sean:
You have to serve somebody, conclusion

Jimmy finds me at the bar and drives me back to my mom's. The whole four hours in silence.

I come home and go down to my room in the basement. I ought to call Patrick, but I can't fucking face it, and my mom is out, and so is my sister, and the rooms feel small and horrible and burnt, and the air smells moldy, and every pile of blankets looks like there might be a weird squawking monster baby in it, so I go down my list of friends to call.

I have a lot of friends, but, it's funny, I feel lonely a lot of the time.

So I call Henry, because I'm thinking of him, but he doesn't pick up, probably because he doesn't like to talk on the phone.

"Telephones are gross," he said to me when we were kids. "They make me really sad. I hear the voice of the person, but I can't see or touch them. Talking on the phone is like speaking with a ghost."

I shudder. I don't want to hear them OR see them.

The fact is sometimes I just call Henry because I like to get his take on things. His point of view is always kind of wacky and interesting somehow.

But since he rarely picks up, I end up leaving a message and I just talk for a while.

Since I can't really talk about the ... thing ... I saw, I tell Henry's voicemail how I really think we all got to get on the gold standard, and how we all ought to eat organic, because regular food is killing us, like my friend Marcos says, who raises his own cattle now, and, as I keep on trying to tell my mother, the juice in cartons is just DEAD juice, from dead little oranges growing in a dead forest or a dead grove somewhere in Florida.

People think I'm crazy, but my Zen master Ken gets it, and you know what? Sometimes I think Henry gets it too.

I finish talking about the juices and remind Henry to buy a juicer: the Jack LaLanne one (because I know Henry's into Jack LaLanne, and it's true, he's amazing and lived a really long time and had a great looking wife), and then I make myself a banana smoothie and go out and wash the cars. And then I go to the Buddhist temple even though it's kind of late by now and hang out with Frank, who is the janitor, and we smoke some dope, and then I go home.

But first I stop off at the grocery store and buy a couple more bananas.

I sit in my room and eat them, and I decide I don't need to get involved with this Holbein real estate thing. That place is going to become historic Williamsburg like I'm the reincarnation of George Hamilton, although . . . the latter could be true if that guy weren't still alive.

I turn on the TV and go through the channels. I'm watching *Breathless*, because it's Sherry's favorite movie.

And in the middle of it, my mom comes home from AA, stands right in front of the screen, and says, "Sean, I need to talk with you."

Marvin comes into the room too. Marvin is my mom's boyfriend, and he is also in AA, and he's nice enough in a meek way, and he is standing off to the side looking thoughtful.

"I'm moving into the city with Marvin," my mom says.

She pauses and looks at me over her glasses. I hate it when she does that; because she thinks it makes her look pretty, and it just makes her look old. She's also got on that stupid hand necklace that I keep telling her makes her neck look wrinkled.

"*And*," she says, "we are going to sell this house and take a very SMALL apartment."

"What are you saying, Mom?" I ask. "Are you are throwing your son out of the house he grew up in?????"

Mom bursts into tears, still standing in front of Jean-Paul Belmondo and that really cute girl with the short hair.

Marvin says, "Sean, you're on the other side of twenty five. You need to do something with your life other than fix cars and meditate and whatever it is you do during the day while we are working."

Fuck, I think to myself, this part is *also* right out of *A Clockwork Orange* when they throw the poor hero out. (OK, he's a horrible guy, but please!)

"What about Sis?" I say, looking mournful.

"Oh Christ, do I need a real drink," says Mom.

"She's getting *married*," says Marvin.

I stand up. I'm enraged, hurt, humiliated. "So why am I the last to know?" I say.

"Because you never ask," says Marvin. He takes Mom by the hand and leads her out of the room.

"He's just a confused little boy, like Curious George," I hear my mom say to him. "Don't be angry with him."

"Hmph," says Marvin. "He's a goddamn mess is what he is."

I'm standing alone with Jean-Paul Belmondo and he's about to get shot for no good reason.

I've never understood this movie. It's beautiful to look at, but damn, it's depressing. All those Godard films are. It must be because he's Swiss. They're so Calvinist.

Christianity: man, it's a grim religion.

I pull out the fold out couch in the basement and go to bed and lie there thinking about Joseph Campbell's *The Hero with a Thousand Faces*.

You ever read that book? It would make a great movie. Talk about back-story! It's ALL back-story.

"Oh please, Sean," said Sherry my screenwriting teacher. "That's just nuts." She laughed. "That's the ape-shit craziest thing I've ever heard."

I think she loved me a little bit right then.

Here's a flashback and a montage. But watch out: it's sad.

I got her to go out with me for almost a year. She was amazing. Difficult, nervous. Smart, sexy. Did I say amazing? Yes.

"Sean, you have no depth," she said, when she dumped me six months ago. "You're like a cartoon character. I don't believe in you. I don't care what happens to your narrative trajectory." She stood up from the table where we were eating a pretty nice Italian dinner.

"The audience has to care, Sean, otherwise we walk out of the movie and go watch Adam Sandler."

"Adam Sandler?" I said. "You have GOT to be kidding."

"Unfortunately, no," she said.

Unfortunately no.

As I start to fall asleep, the original *Planet of the Apes* comes on. I dream about Adam Sandler playing the part of Charlton Heston. He's screaming while two monkey-men and a monkey-woman nod at him patiently and kindly.

"Being an enlightened monkey is better than being an out-of-control human," the elder simian sage says.

"Damn you all to HELL," screams Charlton/Adam.

I get up the next morning and figure I might as well go into the city and have some beers and see if I can stay with Susan's fiancé. He's a CPA and has got a nice place. There's also a friend of a friend that I want to talk to who has a great concept he's developed with another guy about making tires you can't puncture. I also know a guy who says he knows a guy who can design fragrance-free moisturizer that mosquitoes can't bite through. See, I keep on saying to everybody, I'm really a visionary.

So anyway.

I go into town.

The film I'm in now feels like grainy *Midnight Cowboy* outtakes, and I'm that slimy Dustin Hoffman character. Only Buddhist, and burly like John Goodman in *The Big Lebowski*.

I kick some candy-wrappers with my sandal and sit on the cracked plastic seats. I don't talk to anyone on the train. This newest batch of old ladies is going to see the latest restaging of *Rent* and they are all singing "La Vie Bohème" on the train.

"Are you going to see *Rent*?" One of them says to me. "It's such a tragic story."

"No thanks," I say.

"You should see it!" says one old lady. "It's sad but deeply uplifting. It's about," she waves her purse in the air, "*alternative* creative lifestyles, and not this petty late capitalist world we see before us."

"Whatever," I say.

I get off the train and go on the subway. The guy with the tire concept lives uptown.

You know, it's funny. This city is really just a small town. It holds millions, but I swear you can't swing a dead cat without hitting someone you know.

So what do you think happens? I am on the subway, and I get off, and there's Henry!

Henry is standing in front of some apartment building talking with that neighbor girl he likes. I don't mean wants to get with. I mean he likes her. She's rattling on about some psychologist she's studying, and I see his face, and he looks so SERIOUS. He looks like that all the time. It makes me really fucking sad somehow to never see him happy.

He sees me and I say, "YO CUZ." He looks at me with that serious expression.

"Hi, Sean," he says. "I'm seeing Patti off to her house in the country."

Patti is getting in the car with her mom.

I clap him on the back. "Dude what *about* that fucked hotel project up north?"

He looks at me, and I'm so excited to see him and talk to him about Narrow Interior that I start (just a little bit) jumping up and down.

"What in the world are you talking about?" he says.

That's when I realize: Henry doesn't know SHIT about that weird place Narrow Interior. It's a set-up. His own family is like *conspiring* against him and sending him up there to *deal* with the mold and the crazy lady with the hat and the weird moms and the ghost and the monster baby and who the hell knows what else.

I start to open my mouth and then my inner Buddha, who is never wrong, says *let him escape the tigers so he can become a butterfly.*

"Gosh," I say, "it's good to see you, man."

I force myself to stop jumping up and down. I smile really wide and give a little shriek of happiness.

Henry smiles a little smile back. "You too," he says. "I guess I'll see you at Thanksgiving or something."

"You never know, man," I say. "You might see me earlier."

And then I hug him.

One of the great things about Buddhism is you know that you really can love another guy and not be gay. Unlike . . . well, you know . . . the Christ thing.

He hugs me back, and then, fuck—

I just start crying.

I think about my mom and that asshole Marvin, and I think about Sherry. I think about the voice in the tree and the bundle of whatever it was. I think about my father, and I think about how I'm really alone and that I really AM kind of driven by desires I don't understand, and I just feel—

"Sean," says Henry softly, "you're going to be ok."

"You bet I am," I say, sobbing, resisting the urge to make both of us jump up and down. "And so are you! I'm going to see to that!"

Here's a final flashback. It's important.

I realized I really liked my cousin Henry when we blew up the basement when I was ten and he was six, using the chemistry set I got for Christmas. We started a fire and ran out onto the lawn, and my mom was screaming, and the fire trucks came.

But here's what Henry did. Immediately after the event, he started acting as though the event hadn't happened. Whenever the subject came up, he didn't say, "No, it didn't happen like that," or "my story is different," or worse, "Sean started it," (which was the truth).

He just said, "Why, Mother, that never happened!" Then he turned to his genius older brother.

"No, Patrick," said Henry, "that did not happen."

And he kept on doing this.

At first my mom said, "Are you kidding? Look at the singe marks on the wallpaper downstairs." But Henry was so adamant and kept it up for such a long time that, you know what? Now no one even REMEMBERS the explosion and the fire. Except for me.

And at times even I'm not sure.

Remembering that story, how Henry is somehow a master of invisibilization, and how cool that is, I do something really goofy.

I stop hugging Henry, and I kneel on the pavement in front of that fancy apartment building, and I say, "Cousin, let me serve you."

I say this because I realize that my dream is telling me something true. So, if I have to be a character actor, or an animal actor, rather than a leading man, or an assistant director in the *Henry* movie that seems to be in preproduction, then that's what I'll do.

After all, playing the goddamned monkey is *still* better than being Adam Sandler.

"Let me help you," I say again.

Henry stands before me smiling slightly like one of the Play Mobil knights with their kind painted faces, and in the distance the traffic roars like a dragon, like a monster, like a distant enemy that must be faced.

He puts his hand on my shoulder.

"Get up, Sir Sean Gavin," he says. "Arise, a knight."

Tears flow down my cheeks, and my saffron robe is getting dirty, but for the first time in a long time, I feel like I'm on the right track.

I stand up.

And the feeling doesn't go away. It stays with me.

It stays.

17. From the Geister College Archive:
(page torn from commonplace book. anonymous [circa early 17th C(?)])

Dankers! Dankers! dunking lights
Burn by the river late at night
What secret hides behind your fences?
What figures do those devil's dances?

Dankers! Dankers! what's that song
We hear by the meetinghouse all night long?
No Christian tongue ever spake such words
Nor e'er that foreign fiddle heard!

Dankers! Dankers! be ye damned
Though you hide your history as best you can
Confidence banishes you from this spot—
God have mercy on you for we have not!

18. Beatrice:
The Dean's List

The barricade Saint Antoine was a monstrosity; it was three stories high and seven hundred feet long. . . . It was a collaboration of pavement stones, rubble, wooden beams, iron bars, cloth, smashed-in window panes, chairs that had lost their cane seats, cabbage stalks, rags, tatters, and maledictions. It was big and it was little . . . It was the acropolis of those who have no shoes . . . Overturned carts fell haphazardly on the slope of it . . . An omnibus had been strong-armed with a kind of gaiety up to the top of the mess of stuff, as though the architects of this brutal edifice had wanted to add a touch of childish fun to the horror of it . . . The barricade Saint Antoine made a weapon out of everything; all that a civil war can throw at the head of a society came out of it; it wasn't an attack, it was an eruption . . . Over its summit the spirit of revolution spread its thundercloud, from where that voice of the people that resembles the voice of God rumbled. A peculiar majesty emanated from this over-sized basket of wreckage. It was a pile of garbage and it was also Sinai.

– Victor Hugo, *Les Misérables*

This bright June morning, I sit at the secretary's desk in the Geister College registrar's office and am just about to begin writing the eighteen-hundredth legal pad page of my scholarly monograph in progress, *Victor Hugo's Les Misérables: the Literature of Resistance*, when my handyman, subcontractor, and (I suppose) friend Mr. Adonai stops by to remind me that:

1. The city council has instructed the sheriff's office to evict me tomor-

row at 7:00 a.m. from the shuttered college registrar's office.

2. Marilyn over at the library told her assistant Serenade, and Serenade told him (Mr. Adonai) that those horrible hotel people, the Holbeins, have sent a dimwit family representative to oversee the retrofitting of Whispering Pines House into one of those typical postmodern giant glass hotel monstrosities.

3. A German man in a peculiar historically anachronistic costume (my words not his) is *still* hanging out near the Early American section of the (former) Pinckney Library, now Narrow Interior Library North, harassing anyone who appears on that floor.

"Please come back later. I am writing!" I say.

"You're gonna get evicted!" says Mr. Adonai as he dives into the reception area with two bags of groceries, a bouquet of flowers, and his chattering pet monkey. "And the hotel people are gonna build that big hotel. And the German man in the library really scares me! When I went up to fix the men's room toilet—you know the old one on the third floor—he followed me all over. He kept on hassling me in German, wanting to show me something in them books."

I hate being interrupted when I'm working on my manuscript. But this hysteria demands a reasoned response.

"First of all, Mr. A," I say as I push my mortarboard forward over my forehead, "the sheriff is a wispy weakling who takes orders only from his wife, so he's not going to do anything, and besides, the closure of the college is only temporary. I've been here since January, and now it's June."

Mr. Adonai lays the bouquet of flowers on the reception area counter. He always brings me and the women at the library flowers when he comes with my weekly supplies.

I don't want the wet stems to stain the weathered maple of the counter, and since I have to do all the cleaning of the building myself, I forsake Victor Hugo's discussion of the Revolution of 1848, leap up, take the flowers, and put them in a vase that once sat in the president's office upstairs.

I arrange the flowers and try to talk him out of this nonsense. "The college declaring bankruptcy is only a stop-gap measure until the board reconvenes and raises funds. It's only a matter of months before we reopen."

At this stage, Mr. Adonai's monkey climbs out of his shirt pocket and gets up on his shoulder. Mr. A inherited the creature from a deceased homeowner who bequeathed it out of gratitude, since Mr. Adonai had taken such good care of the house, and he—Mr. Adonai—didn't have the heart to give the animal away.

"As for Holbein Hotels, I'll believe *that* particular construction event when I see it."

The monkey squats on Mr. A's shoulder and defecates a runny, brown stool.

"As to the German, Mr. Adonai," I continue as I try to ignore the monkey, "are you sure he isn't some confused exchange student who didn't get the letter canceling summer school and who is now wandering around attempting to locate his first class?"

Mr. Adonai pulls a tissue from one of his many pockets with one hand and wipes his shoulder. The monkey stands up and starts chattering.

"You know, Professor," the little monkey says to me in a high-pitched simian squeal, "Mr. Adonai is the child of Holocaust survivors, and as such he may well tend to see Germans *everywhere*."

I close my eyes for a moment and shake my head. I positively hate it when the monkey addresses me directly, because it causes me to think that I might be getting—to use the words of my ex-husband Benjamin—"a bit loopy."

"Mrs. Beatrice," he—Mr. Adonai, and not the monkey—bursts out, "he ain't no student."

"Mr. Adonai," I say, "for the hundredth time, please don't address me as 'Mrs.'!"

I extend a sleeve of my academic gown. I point to it with the other hand.

"It's *Professor* Bell. Or more properly, *Dean* Bell."

"Sorry," Mr. Adonai says. He shrugs as the monkey clambers onto his other shoulder (where it defecates another small grayish yellow mound) and sets the bags of groceries on the counter. "He wants to show me something with them books."

At moments Mr. Adonai sounds like an Arkansas farm worker instead of an Israeli.

I sigh. "With *the* books, Mr. A," I say. I take four deep breaths like my ex-husband Benjamin showed me.

"I wish you could just calm down a bit, Beezie," he said right before I threw him out of the house. Which was right after he quit an excellent job as partner at the firm of Felice, Hughes, and Whatchem.

"Work is everything," I told him. "Without meaningful work, we are nothing."

"Beezie, that's bullshit," he said. He tried to put his arm around me, but I wouldn't let him.

To be frank, he didn't exactly protest when I told him to move out. In any event, I wasn't there when it happened. Because I was attending the Five-Year Plan for Excellence meeting or else participating in the Revision of the Breadth Requirement Workforce weekly convocation.

"Before you lose your temper, Professor Bell," says the monkey, "I would remind you that Mr. Adonai is no longer on the college payroll. Therefore, his stopping by with groceries and firewood and offering to do odd handyman jobs for free (which included patching the registrar roof this past February when the snow came in) is really more of a courtesy, a kindness, and an act of charity, wouldn't you say?"

"Fine," I snap at both monkey and man. "We shall investigate this German man incursion right now." I slip my running shoes on my feet and adjust my cap and gown.

"It's kinda funny that you always wear that graduation gear," says Mr. Adonai.

I stand up. I feel my face getting hot. Mr. Adonai can be very dense. All men are. Benjamin never understood how hard I worked for tenure and how difficult the running of a college is.

"Beezie," Benjamin said to me late one night when we were in bed, "why are you serving on ten committees? And why the hell do you allow students, faculty, and staff, not to mention the goddamned alumni association, to phone you at home at three in the morning?"

"They are calling from Singapore," I explained, my hand over the receiver. "The Birches want to discuss the new branch of the art museum."

"Jesus Christ," said Benjamin, pulling the covers over his head.

Back in the present, I consider Mr. Adonai and his monkey. As aggravating as he is, I'm an educator, so I am morally obliged to try to explain my reasoning.

"Mr. A, the wearing of traditional academic garb every day was once commonplace on college campuses, and they still do it at universities in Canada and Great Britain. Our regalia designate our degree areas should someone stop us on the street and have, say, a question about philosophy or anthropology. We *stand* for something, after all."

The monkey raises his tiny hand to ask a question, but Mr. Adonai interrupts.

"What about the university and the Third Reich?" Mr. Adonai says.

"On a TV show on the PBS they said the university professors took the oath of loyalty to Hitler right after the army did."

The monkey looks at me, shrugs its shoulders elaborately, and lifts its hands, inviting a response.

"Admittedly," I say, as I smooth my sleeves, "we haven't always been *consistently* brave."

I shoo Mr. Adonai and his blasted monkey out of the registrar's office, and then I egress, carefully locking the door. Mr. Adonai stands on the porch, leaning on the exterior of the venerable brick building. The monkey balances easily and plays with Mr. Adonai's ears.

"You don't gotta lock the door," he says.

"The student records!" I say. "Transcripts, self-statements, faculty recommendations and commendations! They must be kept confidential. We don't want chaos when we reopen do we?"

Mr. Adonai takes his monkey and puts it in the pocket of his oversized jacket. He picks up a second bouquet that is lying on the porch.

We walk across the lawn to (the erstwhile) Pinckney Library.

From inside the pocket, the monkey declaims in muffled but audible tones: "Look, Professor, at how green the lawn remains, thanks to the lack of students tromping off the paths. In disappearance there may be virtue, as the sages tell us. Behold how short the grass is! Mr. Adonai mows it. And weeds it too by the look of things. He is very virtuous, is he not?"

We walk up the stone steps of Pinckney.

I enter the library and inhale deeply.

Knowledge has a fragrance. Study has an aroma to it. And the different fields all have their scent. Books are the flowering plants springing up miraculously from the seeds of everyday words, and as I enter Pinckney Library, I turn the key to a veritable secret garden—a sprawling preserve of olefactory flora.

As I walk by the reading room with its elegant first editions, the smells waft up in gorgeous variegation. The irises of ancient Greece, the gardenia of the Chinese Boxer Rebellion, the forget-me-nots of French Romanticism. The harvested coffee beans brought to eighteenth century Paris. The roses of the French Impressionists. The fruits of France's former colonies: tobacco, orange, papaya. It's no wonder France is my favorite. It has so many smells, the knowledge of France does. The sharp dandelion scent of the Huguenots.

Marilyn, the circulation librarian, looks over her glasses at the main desk. Behind her, Serenade, her part-time assistant, is cataloguing books and keying their new call numbers into a laptop computer, which she keeps on taking outside to the patio, where the librarians not so secretly smoke.

"Hey, Dean Bell!" says Marilyn.

Mr. Adonai places bouquet number two on the desk.

"We got a German bothering the books," he announces.

Marilyn picks up the flowers. Breathes in the scent for a moment. Then she points towards the reading room.

"You mean that guy in the pink shirt who's researching puppets over by the encyclopedias?" Marilyn replies.

I turn around; there's a nondescript person with a pink shirt on and khaki pants sitting at one of the large tables.

What a dull looking young man, I think to myself.

"No," I say. "Mr. Adonai says this man is in costume, and he's in the stacks upstairs."

Marilyn looks at me cryptically. "Oh," she says. "That."

"Hey, Dean!" says Serenade, "there's a letter for you!" She goes over to a stack of mail and pulls it from the pile.

The college mail, or what's left of it, now comes to the library, and the "ladies"—Marilyn, Serenade—shred it or, in this case, pass it on.

I feel a jump in my heart. Perhaps it's a letter from Benjamin finalizing our divorce.

Then I look at the envelope. Heavy, old-fashioned creamy stationery. The Prankton University logo.

In Veritas Superlitas: In Truth Superiority.

I open it.

It's from Ginnie Hayworth, my former graduate school classmate.

Dear Bea –

I am writing you formally since I have been unable to reach you by email or phone. I hope that you will consider giving a paper at this year's Modern French Cultures Conference in Allentown this coming December. The subject of the panel is "Re-Imagining Hugo's Nineteenth Century." Your work on Victor Hugo would fit nicely, and it might be congenial to have an older scholar weigh in on such a canonical author, amidst all the dazzling junior people from Harvard and Yale.

Merde, I think.

Might I suggest that it is crucial for you to resuscitate your research credentials as well as your professional contacts in order that you might locate another academic position? I gather that Geister College has folded at last. These are hard times in the academy, although you may take comfort in the fact that our chancellor insists that better days are upon us as soon as some of these retirements come through, which should in turn trickle down to the lesser schools, where you may have a chance.

I stick the letter in the pocket of my robe.

"Good news?" Serenade asks, but before I can answer, Marilyn spots Mr. Adonai's simian passenger, his head poking out of the pocket.

"Yusuf," she calls him kindly but firmly by his first name, "you can't bring that thing in the library." She points at the large sign: NO PETS, NO BEVERAGES.

He wrinkles his forehead again. The folds of his skin crumple like book pages, bumping their words against each other.

"Just tell me where you saw him," I say.

"Third floor," he says. "Near the elevator. Near the uh . . . ladies' room."

"Got it," I say. "I know this library like the back of my hand."

I take the stairs. It's good to get a little exercise. I didn't run today and those Canadian Air Force exercises that I do upstairs in the president's office get a bit boring.

I try to run five miles or so a day.

Benjamin thought I was insane.

"Just because the Brits were long-distance runners, doesn't mean you have to be," he said. "Anyway," he added, folding his arms behind his head on the sofa, "wasn't one of your grandmothers German or something? Maybe that's where all that rigidity comes from!"

Benjamin was a walker, not a runner.

I jog, taking the stairs two at a time.

I reach the third floor and follow Mr. Adonai's directions exactly. The air feels cold, although it is summer, and although the air-conditioning— such as it is—is not being used much.

I pass the entrance to the ladies' room. The water fountain outside is dispensing a thin stream.

It hisses and, almost, speaks.

I shiver and smell an unexpected memory when I pass a section with the words "Faculty Publications" crossed out.

"There is no tenure when the school ceases to, for all intents and purposes, exist," said our president at our last formal faculty meeting.

"Nonsense," said Professor Spivak from Mathematics. "You can't fire us. We are here forever."

But he got another job in Chicago and was gone by Christmas.

The Faculty Publications shelf is empty now. Failure smells at once metallic and fungal: a combination of old steel furniture and dirty feet.

I hold my nose and move down the row of books.

Ugh. Early American religious history. *The Puritan Dilemma*: I read it years ago. *The Radical Reformation in America*: dull. *The Anabaptists: a forgotten ideal*. Never read it.

I have always preferred France.

I let go of my nose and suddenly smell pine. A beautiful, sharp, fresh smell.

A tall, thin man is standing in a no man's land between the volumes on the Puritans and the Quakers; he is taking books off the shelves and flipping through pages with long fingers. And *not* putting them in the reshelving area, which is going to completely disorganize the order.

I find his cavalier attitude infuriating. "Young man!" I say in my sternest college administration voice.

He removes a broad hat and bows over his breeched pants, stockings, and poorly fitting shoes.

"*Ich heisse Bernhard Hofmann aus Muenster*," he says as he lowers his head and raises it again sharply, holding his hat at his waist.

I understand a bit. My grandmother used to talk to me in German sometimes. My name is Bernhard Hofmann, and I come from Muenster.

"I don't care *where* you are from," I say, putting my hand on a shelf to steady myself. "You're making a mess of this research section, and I must ask you to leave these books where they are and request assistance downstairs for whatever it is you are seeking. The library is extremely understaffed due to the transition and—"

"*Ich muss mit Ihnen sprechen*," he says.

Sprechen = speak

"Well, whatever you have to say, Mr. Hofmann, you'll have to take it up with the library if this is a book matter, or with the board of trustees if this is a college matter."

I stop for a moment, as I am feeling short of breath.

"If this is a research matter pertaining to my area of expertise, you need to email me for a formal appointment."

He gazes down at me intently with quite attractive brown eyes.

"In any event, you cannot use the facilities here without a proper library card, so I will need to have you proceed downstairs directly to speak with circulation."

I realize I am repeating myself because I feel a bit flustered.

I . . . he reminds me of somebody.

The fluorescent lights bounce off Bernhard Hofmann in a way that makes him shimmer. I take off my glasses and rub out the worst of the smudges with my sleeve, my cloths for my glasses having long worn out.

As I clean, the Hofmann man mutters something.

"Midnight," he says.

I put my glasses back on.

The man is gone.

The smell of pine is gone too. The water fountain has stopped gurgling.

I walk back down to circulation.

"There *was* someone," I tell Marilyn, "but I sent him downstairs."

"I didn't see him come through here," says Marilyn. She turns to Serenade, who shrugs and shakes her head.

"But good. We don't want weird guys lurking in the stacks. It's just me here and Serenade and—." She almost says "Raskolnikov," but doesn't.

Raskolnikov is the head librarian, and he's a detestable, bear-like, tyrannical Russian.

Then she chuckles. "But I'd sure like to see you take on *you know who* like you did at that meeting about the *Les Misérables* undergraduate student conference.

I look at her.

That was last year before the budget crisis. Raskolnikov took his shoe off and banged it on the table during the last plenary session, when I suggested that his maintaining that Tolstoy influenced Hugo was an historical impossibility.

"That is unacceptable!" he shouted.

Marilyn grins at me. "Don't you remember how you grabbed him by his beard, yanked his face down, and shouted, 'If you mess with me again, you oversized apparatchik, I'll take your collection of Jack London stories and shove them up your ass!'?"

Something happens to me when someone threatens me. Benjamin said it was my Celtic blood. I'm Irish on my father's side.

"I just wish you wouldn't feel so threatened by everything all the time," he said when I came home after that incident.

"It wasn't a very academic reaction," I mutter.

"Are you kidding?" says Marilyn. "It was great! It was inspiring to see someone, a woman especially, and a woman in our, uh, age group, not afraid of some know-it-all."

A woman in our age group. Sixty something. A woman out of the running. Perhaps that's why I run so hard.

I walk out of the library and down the stairs.

Mr. Adonai is playing with his monkey outside. The monkey is throwing a golf ball, and Mr. Adonai is going and finding it. He lays it at the feet of the monkey, who then throws it somewhere else.

"Ha-ha!" says Mr. Adonai. "You see! I the pet and monkey the master!"

"We work with the slower bodhisattvas as best we can," chatters the monkey.

"The German man was there, but he's gone now," I tell him.

To his credit, Mr. Adonai does not say, "I told you so," although he does look a bit triumphant.

"Did you give him what he wanted?" he asks.

"Come along, Mr. Adonai," I say. "I have no time to speak with some weird, historical reenactment fan, renaissance fair aficionado from Germany."

I start walking back across the lawn to the registrar. "I'll pay you for the groceries and make you a cheese sandwich, and then I must go back to my writing."

He whistles, and the tiny monkey runs to him, does several flips, and catapults himself onto Mr. Adonai's shoulder.

But just as we are nearing the building, a dark green Corolla pulls up on Elm Street, turns into the driveway leading to the registrar's office, and stops. A man alights from the car.

He is wearing sunglasses and a cheap suit. "Hey there," he shouts, and waves.

We ignore him and walk more swiftly.

But the man runs up the driveway and accosts us before we can get to the door.

"Professor," says the man, "I am here on behalf of the Evictinators, and we are representing the Narrow Interior Sheriff's Office, who's received a complaint from the new owners of this property."

He holds out a huge sheaf of papers.

"Since your eviction is scheduled to take place tomorrow, I thought I'd come by with a copy of the guidelines for the procedures as well as a check-list of what you will need to provide for yourself in order to achieve a successful and stress-free eviction process."

He smiles brightly, takes out a pen, and hands it to me.

"There's the checklist right there at the top. You will need three movers, several rolls of plastic, in case of inclement weather, and, should you decide to leave before tomorrow, you must advise the sheriff's office in order not to incur a penalty charge of one hour's eviction time."

Mr. Adonai's monkey pipes up.

"Actually, young apprentice of the bureaucratic way, the dean is not a tenant. She is a squatter, and according to the state legal code there are two sorts of squattertude. Ergo the called-for procedure is not the one you cite involving the plastic, because the furniture belongs to the college that was."

"Wait a minute," I say to the man in the suit. "I know you!"

The young man in the cheap suit stops fiddling with his paperwork.

"You . . . you remember me?" he says.

"Yes," I say. "Alex Doreky from French Civilization: the French Revolution as trope in fiction, film, and art. You flunked that course!"

He takes a step back. "Well, gosh Professor uh—"

"Bell," I announce. "Dean Bell to be precise."

"Oh, right," he says, looking at a piece of paper. "Uh—"

He shifts from one foot to the other.

"Behold this poor young man's lack of enlightenment! He does not see what is right and wanders the paths of gross incorrectness," observes Mr. Adonai's monkey.

I take off my cap and remove my glasses. A long time ago, in France, someone tall and thin said I had nice eyes, even if they were not terribly large.

"Look, Alex," I say, not at all unkindly, "I am safeguarding student records at the registrar's, which is my job as Dean of Students. The college is going to re-open, if not in the fall, then in winter semester. It is not in the interest of the college or of the town to try to evict me, because of the immense confusion that will result if the office—"

"Lady," Alex interrupts, which is a very rude way of putting it, "you don't get it. The college is dead. It doesn't exist anymore. This whole campus, with the exception of the library and the lot on Elm Street, has been bought up by the I.S.A. Company, and you know very well that the land across the street—"

He regains his composure. Mr. Adonai's monkey dives back into the coat pocket.

"If you don't cooperate with the Evictinators, we will swear out a complaint and the sheriff and some police officers will come and take you out by force and—"

Alex Doreky pauses. Puts his sunglasses back on. "Embarrassing. You might get arrested. You'll have a tough time getting work if you're arrested."

He turns to go. "This is just a courtesy visit. I didn't even have to come here at all."

He swaggers to the car. This is just how he used to leave class, I remember. And when he didn't come in late, he left twenty minutes early.

At this moment Mr. Adonai's monkey leaps out of his pocket and stands in front of us and shakes his tiny fist at the intruder. "In a different incarnation, I'd beat you silly!" the monkey shouts.

Alex Doreky walks over to his car. "What the hell are you looking at?" he says to someone.

The car drives away.

The dull young man with the pink shirt from the library is standing on the street where the Evictinator car was parked. He waves at Mr. Adonai and me.

"Hello there, Professor," he says. And to Mr. Adonai, "Wow! I have a puppet that looks just like that monkey!" He pauses. "Although my puppet's much bigger!"

The monkey looks at the young man, puts its paws together, and bows formally, before back-flipping four times and leaping on to Mr. Adonai's shoulder.

"He's very smart!" says Mr. Adonai.

"But isn't he rather mischievous?" says the dull looking young man in the pink shirt.

"Yes!" I say.

"No!" says Mr. Adonai.

We stand awkwardly for a moment.

"I thank you very much for the use of the library," the dull-looking man says. "It's very kind of the college to allow members of the public to use the facilities."

"I can see you're not from around here," I say. "The college is uh, in moratorium, and the library is now part of the municipal library system."

"Really?" he says. "How impressive that a college can afford to just shut down operations and keep everyone on the payroll. Your school must have quite an endowment."

I wonder if he's being sarcastic, but he has such an open broad face, and such a young, naïve look that I think he's being honest.

Mr. Adonai cocks his eyebrow at me. I incline my head in a professorial, non-committal way.

The young man scratches his forehead and looks at a piece of paper. "Now, would you folks be good enough to tell me—am I walking in the right direction to get to 999 Elm Street?"

I nod and point down the driveway to the street. He thanks us and goes.

"Say," says Mr. Adonai, "that guy—he looks kind of German, doesn't he?"

"No, he doesn't," I reply. "Don't be so silly."

"Yes, he does," says Mr. Adonai stubbornly.

We go back inside the registrar's office, and I make the cheese sandwiches.

But Mr. Adonai doesn't sit down. He stands by the door while the monkey climbs out of his pocket and crawls onto the counter and actually takes bites out of a sandwich I've made.

"Shoo!" I say, slamming my baguette down on the counter.

"I guess," Mr. Adonai says as the monkey scampers back up his arm, "we better pack up your stuff tonight, and then tomorrow you can go stay with a family member."

I put my sandwich back on the plate.

"I have no family," I say.

There was really just Benjamin.

"I'll write when I get settled someplace," my almost ex-husband told me when he came back to oversee the movers take his furniture from the house we shared. "I'm thinking about a little place in the mountains. I can do some lawyering there, and you—you could finish your book. There'll be no internet, minimal heat, but it'll be ok. My cousin has a place I think he'll let me use. He's an old hippy. Very cool."

I never heard from him. But that's fine. We're almost divorced after all.

"But you must have *somebody*," says Mr. Adonai.

I purse my lips, take out the letter from Ginnie Hayworth.

P.S. I'll be away all summer at the Cape, but you can reach me by phone, email, or snail mail. Do take advantage of this opportunity, Bea. It's really in your interest. I'm so happy, *she added unnecessarily*, that I finally have the chance to do something for you.

"I have a colleague," I say unwillingly to Adonai. "She 'might' put me up at the Cape—might."

The monkey climbs on top of Mr. Adonai's head. Stands up.

"You see?" Says Mr. Adonai as the monkey stands and sways, "you can go there."

"How?" I say. "I don't have a car, and I am . . . low on funds."

"The fact is," says the monkey to Mr. Adonai in a low conversational tone, "the professor has lost her house and has been living off of her savings for these past months."

"You can take the bus!" says Mr. Adonai. "And then your friend will help you!"

I imagine myself like Victor Hugo's fugitive Jean Valjean appearing on Ginny's Cape doorstep.

Mr. Adonai leaps to his feet. The monkey rides his head like a surfboard.

"I'll go get the bus schedule downtown." He starts to go out and stops. "Hadn't you better call her?"

"Good idea," I say. "I'll go over to the library and use the landline." They cut our office phones months ago.

"Farewell, Professor!" calls the monkey, as we walk out the door. "I hope we shall meet again."

I don't go to the library to use the phone.

I walk the perimeter of the fence around the college, and I check the doors of our dorm buildings. Everything is in order. All awaiting the re-opening.

I keep on walking. I see and smell the green. Spring comes late here, but when it comes, it comes strong. The willows near the river are blooming green, and what used to be the botanical garden is still somehow thriving. Tulips and roses, gardenias and camellias.

After he quit his partner job, Benjamin became an avid gardener. "You remind me of a rose sometimes, Beezie. Despite the thorns—beautiful, delicate, and resilient beneath your protections."

That was five years and about twenty pounds ago when he said that. But he saw things in me. He gave me hope.

I walk through the botanical garden. There is a hole in the chain link fence at the back of it. I duck through.

Now I'm on the side of the street. There's a little lake here, and right next to it is Whispering Pines House, the oldest building in Narrow Interior. It too is fenced off with the ugly chain link and a huge red and purple sign saying, "Coming soon to make your town all it can be: A new Holbein Hotel combining luxury, modernity, and rural charm!"

In the middle of the lot is a gigantic hole. Next to it are earthmovers and shovels. A few construction workers are getting into cars, ostensibly leaving for the day.

I press my face against the fence. The building's blackened roof sags, and the small dusty windows have strings of yellow mold running down them. No one knows how to fix it, although no one can bear to tear it down either, because of its "historic" value.

"Wow," says someone. "What a mess!"

I turn and see the dull man in the pink shirt.

"Whispering Pines House," I say. "Tradition has it that it was owned by Mary Winston Geister, our college's founder, along with her brother, Jesse Wentworth S. Geister."

"Well, good luck with it," says the man in the pink shirt. "I'm heading off."

I spend the rest of the afternoon writing on my legal pad. I have gotten to the section of *Les Misérables* where Cosette falls in love, and Jean Valjean must give her up to one of Hugo's typically clueless young men. Valjean has given his whole life to her, and she must leave him, and the June Revolution is about to begin, and all is chaos. He will always remain an exile. He will always be alone.

I write:

And yet, Hugo does not disparage either the desire to love and give of oneself or the necessity of social resistance, even if it proves—in the short run—futile. The act of resistance for Hugo exerts a spiritual liberatory function on the individual and on the community, even when it fails.

And then the miracle happens. I lose track of myself and I just write.

The afternoon passes quickly. And then the evening. I keep writing, my blue pen flowing over the yellow pages of the legal pad.

Mr. Adonai doesn't come back, but it doesn't matter. I lose myself in the world of nineteenth century idealism and lost causes. Of stolen candlesticks belatedly given as a gift. Of a generosity without measure, despite/ because it cannot be returned. But the reader returns it. The reader loves Jean Valjean, and the boy Gavroche, and the desperate people in the novel who dare to dream of a better life.

The old-fashioned clock over the reception desk reads midnight.

I take a break, make myself another sandwich, and remember another midnight.

My last night in Montpellier. France. My last night of dancing on the beach in Palavas with a tall thin man with attractive brown eyes.

My Frenchman was the direct descendent of the Protestant reformer Jean Calvin, and his name was Calvin too. Calvin Calvin, to be exact.

Our last night was like all the others. We went to the beach in Palavas every Friday to meet others who danced with us. It was something very ancient, Calvin said: something from so long ago that no one could remember it. The whys and the wherefores. We danced in a group, and there were men and women, old and young. And sometimes we passed a doll around in a large circle. And then we went swimming with our clothes on. Always Fridays. And Japanese lanterns swung in the breeze.

We danced and swam till three in the morning, and then walked home in our wet clothes even in the coldest weather, a few peeling off as we got to our street. Montpellier was a small city then. It was miraculous, walking on those dark midnight streets. Fountains everywhere. The sea not too far away. The Rhône River passing by. The Lez cutting through the city. The way water dances.

That last night, Calvin Calvin kissed me and promised we'd meet in the States during my last year of college at the University of Ladylake to finish my degree in French. We would have a lovely long week in a large American city. Then I would study hard, graduate, return to France, and we would marry. And we would dance, and I would get a job and have children, and dance some more.

A telegram came to my campus mailbox the day before we were supposed to meet. There is another, better woman, the telegram said. Goodbye.

After that, I applied to graduate school. I would study France from a safer distance.

I met Benjamin through a colleague, and Benjamin, while not French in any way, was an ambitious smart person, and he was very kind.

But I never believed in him. I felt myself already an exile from the possibilities of love. I was already like Jean Valjean: a fugitive from the emotions.

I look back down at what I've written on p. 1848.

> *Dearest Molly, beloved in Christ*

This is not my writing!

And yet it is. As my eyes adjust, the letters slant the way mine slant. So it must be my writing. But the content. Is all wrong.

I look at the words that are and are not mine.

Here is what they say:

> *Der 23 Juni, 16—*
> *Dearest Molly, beloved in Christ –*
> *Today the clouds drift over the spires of Muenster, as they always do at this time of year. It is June now, and I cannot tell when you will receive my missive, but I write every day, I write to you, and I think of you. My Molly who sees the inner light, who sees the spirit, and who has dared to bring our ways to the new world to the wilderness of the Puritans and the seeming sense of the Quakers.*
> *In your last letter, which was when—6 months ago?— you tell of the meetinghouse, and you tell of the work being done there.*
> *I am so joyful to learn that the secret theater is being built in the cellar. Near the water. And that the fences are being erected. With the bells of protection, so when the Out-*

siders come, the friends can warn each other of it.

Molly darling, it pleases me to no end to think that our holiest rites are being brought out of Europe, dark Europe with its popes and kings, to this new land, which I hear is so green and so wild.

My father lies neither alive nor dead, and there is no hope for him other than to pray for his departure from this world of woe. And yet, I cannot altogether think this is a world of woe, for you are in it, my dear Molly, and our company of believers, whom you have fondly called the Dankers because of our gratefulness to Christ and his disciples who made magical shows to all those who would not believe. We continue their work, and while others may mock us and deplore us, we know the truth. The truth of the small bodies and what they contain. The ways in which inner light may manifest itself through the very thing that Cromwell and others foolishly condemned. But not all can see. Few can, as it would seem, and for those of us who can, we must enable others to see what is before them, to embrace each other, not in the spirit only, but also in the flesh. And how my skin longs for yours, dear Molly.

The candle's burning low, and I must conclude. I pray either for my father's recovery and blessing and the portion that is mine, or for his peaceful death and again, giving me means to procure passage, and then some, to bring others, and to come to you, with wealth and possibilities.

Ich bin wie immer Dein, meine geliebte
Bernhard

PS I have just received a letter from your father, telling that your brother Heinrich has been sent to study with the Protestant masters in Geneva. He has reclaimed there the family name Holbein, and hopes to bring the Danker faith to the townspeople there. Those who manage the hostels in the mountains, for there God is very present.

Bernhard Hofmann of Muenster?

I look around. Did someone break in here? Did they get past Adonai, and as some nasty mockery, some twisted sense of amusement, put this paper here? A forger or some outraged student or colleague imitating my handwriting?

I look through the rest of the pages. They are all as they should be.

Just this page is strange.

I feel dizzy. My head spins.

Who in the world are the Dankers? There is something about the date, but I can look that up later.

I turn my old laptop on, and then I curse.

My computer cannot go online from the registrar. The Wi-Fi was disabled long ago. I look across the lawn to the darkened library. I have the keys. I need to look these things up. I must look them up.

I take out Benjamin's rifle and a flashlight.

Benjamin was a crack shot, but he detested the NRA. "Take it," he said. "As protection."

I walk out and lock the door. I take my flashlight but don't turn it on. I creep across the lawn. I unlock the doors of the library and walk in. I look at the alarm panel next to the door.

The lights glow a dull orange. *Error*, it reads. *System not armed*.

The alarm system has not been turned on.

The man who calls himself Bernhard Hofmann is standing in the reading room with the encyclopedias.

"*Endlich!*" he says. "At last you are here."

"Who are you?" I say firmly. But my voice shakes.

"I am the man who wrote the letter."

He pauses. "In 16—"

But—

My brain feels like it's splitting in two, but somehow I know he is the man from the past, and he's here now.

He shrugs his shoulders. "I don't understand it myself, exactly. All I know is what I am supposed to do."

He presses on a brick in the fireplace. The wall opens and there are stairs. "Come," he says.

"Why should I trust you?" I say.

"Because," he says, "you know that what I say is true. What the man you loved in Montpellier showed you was a piece of this truth."

I know I should feel frightened, but I don't. Not exactly.

I think of the Phantom of the Opera luring that young woman to the cellar.

But I am not young, and I'm certainly not an opera singer. "But why?" I say to Bernhard Hofmann. "Why show *me*?"

"Because you are the woman who searches. Because you are the woman who wants to know. Because you are a student of history, and wise. Because your name is Sophia."

"My name is Beatrice," I say.

"But Sophia is your middle name."

And wouldn't you know it? He's right. I'm named after my grandmother. The German woman.

We go down stone steps carved into what should be the chimney. I turn on my flashlight.

But he snaps his fingers and holds light from a stick, like a wand.

"The inner light shines for us, but only for a time," he says. "We must hurry."

"There is the way to the meetinghouse." He points to stairs. "But this way leads to the lake."

"What meetinghouse?" I say, but I think I already know the answer. "It's Whispering Pines House, isn't it?"

"*Ja*," he says. "The ruined house whose truth has been lost."

And then suddenly we are walking up. He pulls down a trap door, and we emerge. Near the botanical garden at the lake.

"*Die Taufe*," he says. "This is our path to *die Taufe*."

I shake my head. "I don't understand you."

"I'm sorry," he says, and he tries to form different words. I can see his lips—beautiful lips, the lips of a young man—trying to make sounds.

"I can't," he says. "I cannot tell you. The power of forgetting is too strong against me."

"You came here to do what, exactly?" I say.

"We come here afterwards. After we have done our games with *die Puppen*."

"Dolls?" I say. "What about dolls?"

He's about to answer, but then something happens.

"Dean Bell!" calls a sharp, Eastern European voice.

Bernhard Hofmann begins to shimmer in the darkness. His wand sputters like a candle. He and it are about to go out. This time I know it's not my glasses.

"Don't go," I say. "Please."

"Heal us," he says. "*Heilen durch Spielen.*"

Gad, I think to myself, why couldn't he have been a French speaker?

"But protect our secret until it's time," he says.

He crouches on the ground near the water. I crouch down too.

"How do I heal you?" I am about to say when—

"Dean Bell, *what are you doing here*?"

I see the ursine outline of my least favorite person, and certainly my least favorite man in a day filled with unexpected, strange men.

He stands there baring his teeth, holding an evil-looking gun.

Raskolnikov.

"Someone has broken into the library!" he says. "Come immediately. We are not safe."

"I—" I say. But he interrupts. He always interrupts!

"Who's that?" He shouts, training his gun on something next to me.

I look down. There's someone lying there.

But it's not Bernhard.

It's the dull young man from the reading room. He's lying on the ground, soaking wet.

I crouch down next to him. "What's happened?" I ask.

"I . . . I don't know," he says.

"He's an intruder!" says Raskolnikov, aiming his gun. "He's a *spy*!"

"I think," murmurs the man, "my name is Henry Holbein of Holbein Hotels."

"*You* are the family's representative?" I say

"I was," he murmurs. "But now—I don't know."

I put my lips close to his ear. "Did you see a man?" I whisper.

"No," he whispers back. "I saw a woman. Three women."

I sit back on my heels and look at his face in the moonlight.

He looks different. Not dull anymore. "Well, Mr. Holbein," I say, helping him to his feet, "you've chosen a very poor time to visit the construction site."

"Yes," he says, "and how stupid of me to fall in the water. I must . . . I must be going now."

"You're just going to let him go?" says Raskolnikov.

"Yes," I say. "Mr. Holbein and I have already met at the registrar this afternoon. We are old friends."

The Holbein boy picks himself up and starts slowly shambling down

Elm Street. He is carrying something.

I turn back to Raskolnikov.

"And what are *you* doing here?" I say, brushing the dirt off my academic gown.

"I was alerted to an intrusion," he replies. "The city made us install a new alarm system, but I insisted that it go straight to my home because we do not yet have the funds to hire a professional security team."

He looks at me, sees my own gun and bows stiffly. Clicking his heels. Not at all like Bernhard of Muenster. "I shall proceed to the library now to investigate."

Suddenly I remember the fireplace stairs! "I'm coming too," I say.

"No, Dean, it is not safe!" says Raskolnikov.

I put Benjamin's rifle over my shoulder. "Either we go investigate together, or," I pause, "perhaps we should call the police."

"NO COPS!" shouts Raskolnikov, not mindful anymore of who may be lurking in the bushes to kill the head librarian. "They care nothing for books." He pauses and spits on the ground. "Or for the life of the mind."

"Agreed," I say. "But in that case I will come with you to check for incursions. I have my own rifle. I can use it."

He snarls with frustration.

"I'm coming with you," I say again. "For the last time."

"What do you mean?" he asks suspiciously.

"They come to evict me from the registrar's tomorrow," I say.

"Who?"

"The sheriff's office has hired the Evictinators."

Raskolnikov is, miraculously, silent. I begin to steer him away from the open trap door.

"Lead the way," I say. He does. Naturally.

I lean over, cough, and slam the trap door shut.

"What's that?" Raskolnikov growls back at me from a few yards away.

"Oh that," I say. "It's some old metal door from the botanical garden that got left down here."

We walk swiftly over the smooth lawns of the deserted campus.

The moon is out. It is beautiful here at night.

The library door is still unlocked. We walk in.

"You check the main halls. I'll go investigate the reading room."

He stands in the dark entryway.

"I'll turn on the lights," he says.

"*No*," I hiss, "for God's sake, you'll alert the intruder!"

Raskolnikov grunts. Leaves.

The room is more pungent than ever. Vetiver, lavender, tobacco, coffee.

I heave the hidden staircase wall against the bricks. It closes easily. How to open it will be a trick, but I can't worry about that now.

There's a computer on the table. I power it up and go online.

There is nothing about the Dankers.

"The web is treacherous," I say out loud. I will look at something older. I run my flashlight over the encyclopedias. *The World Book*, the *Britannica*, the encyclopedias of philosophy, religion. Nothing. Then I go to the lowest shelves, to the oldest collection items. The old books written at the turn of the century.

The Encyclopedia Stupendia, a Sir James George Frazer favorite. Well, if anyone will have something arcane and forgotten, the *ES* will.

I turn the pages and smell once again—fresh pine.

The Encyclopedia Stupendia

The Dankers – etymology unknown, but suspected to be connected to the word *dank* (dark and moist) and referring to the group's predilection for dark and often damp places of worship. Religious Protestant group flourishing in the 16th and 17th centuries in England, Germany, parts of France, and then through emigration in the upper reaches of Eastern North America. Founded by the Winston family, close friends of both George Fox and Lattimer, well known reformers who were crucial in the development of the Friends or Quaker movement. But Francis Winston (né Franz Holbein of Basel), and his wife Christine (origins unknown, although she is referred to in the archives as "foreign") soon came to blows with George Fox and other Reformers over a mysterious question, unexplained by evidence and remaining documents, many of which have been destroyed over some practice involving "dollies," "speels" and "leeb." Scholars debate as to whether this first word refers to the actual playthings of children, in particular little girls. There is some evidence for this, given the importance of women in the Danker movement, and an appreciation of the naive openness of the child or to the idea of movement. This meaning of the word "dolly" may also, according to certain scholars, look forward to the cinematic term, in which a dolly is a carrier on wheels, legs or both. In any event, the "dolly" controversy caused a split between the Quakers and the Dankers, and resulted in the latter's almost entire exclusion from all Protestant and Reformer discussion and subsequent history. A group of the Dankers, led by Francis Winston's daughter, Mary (or Molly) Winston, made for the Massachusetts Bay colony along with another set of renegade Quakers, Anne Hutchinson and others, only to be banished from same after interrupting church services and appearing naked in the street. Molly Winston, sometimes referred to as the Anne Hutchinson of the Dankers, may have moved farther west with her beloved friends, one whose last name was Hoffmann and who originated from Muenster (see "Kingdom of Muenster" entry). They are believed to have settled in Confidence Valley, where they set up a community that was subsequently wiped out. How exactly remains a mystery, although local historians argue that the ruins of the various meetinghouses need to be excavated and studied. A meetinghouse, believed to have been a Danker stronghold still stands in the downtown area of Narrow Interior.

Credos and Rituals: Unknown.

Texts and Scriptures: Fragmentary. See Geister College archives

I rub my eyes.

I feel tired. I sit on the sofa of the library reading room and all the smells I love are here. Lavender, and rosemary, and rose, and geranium, and gardenia. A touch of pine. I hold the encyclopedia and, despite myself, close my eyes.

When I awaken it is just getting to be light. There is an oversized coat thrown over me. It smells of bear.

"Dean!" says Raskolnikov. He leans over me. "I have searched and searched. I have found no one. The special collections are intact."

We walk together to the registrar's office.

"Do you know anything about an archive of papers related to the Dankers?"

"Who?" he says. Then he pauses. "I might have something . . . "

"Hey Bea!"

I look.

Marilyn, Serenade, and—at last—Mr. Adonai sitting on the porch of the registrar's office.

I sit on the stairs for a moment.

"Do you have the bus schedule?" I say to him.

Mr. Adonai starts to cry.

"For heavens' sake!" I say. "Now what?"

"Mrs. Beatrice," Mr. Adonai sobs. "I . . . figured out . . . I don't got . . . nobody either . . . I have no wife. My sons are grown up and they . . . they don't talk to me."

Sob sob.

I listen. This is the most Mr. Adonai has ever revealed about himself. "All I had was my monkey."

That's right! Where is that ridiculous critter? "Where is he?" I ask in a more charitable fashion.

"He . . . 's . . . dead," Mr. A sobs even harder.

"Jesus!" says Serenade. "What happened?"

"I go over to the post office to get my mail before I go to bus . . . and to . . . get your schedule, and my monkey . . . he scampers in front of bus and—"

I am silent. I hated that damned thing, but my God, it was just a poor little being.

Mr. Adonai takes out a bright blue bandana and blows his nose loudly.

"I figured it was a sign." He sniffles. "Leaving by bus ain't such a good idea."

"I'll just stay here with you, if you don't mind," he finishes. "I shall bear witness."

I don't know why, but my eyes start stinging, and I get a big lump in my throat. "I don't think there will be much to see," I say.

"We will keep you company at least," says Marilyn. She holds out a paper tray full of coffee cups. Serenade is holding a huge donut box.

"Don't be stupid!" shouts Raskolnikov. "The dean must not be taken!"

"Please, Mr. Raskolnikov," I say. "Let's be friends for this last—"

"Dean, this has become more than a college matter. I—must—impart—" Raskolnikov stutters. We all look at him, preparing for another explosion.

"The library," he says. "The library is going to be closed, too. They, the goons at the municipal library—we are all going to be let go."

"Oh my God!" says Serenade, leaping to her feet. "When were you going to tell us this?"

The Danker archives . . . I think. I need to locate them.

"Stop talking at once! " shouts Raskolnikov. "We must formulate a plan," he announces.

Then I remember something. "What's today's date?" I ask.

"June twenty third," says Serenade.

"I know something we can do," I say.

I explain my idea to everyone while we drink our coffee quickly, chomp expeditiously on our quite yummy donuts.

Then we get to work.

Marilyn and Mr. Adonai go off to the operations garage. They come back with a forklift.

While they are gone, I unlock all the classroom doors.

Serenade goes to the library. She returns with a small video camera and a laptop computer.

Raskolnikov and I together manage to pull the old college gates shut. We lock them with bicycle locks left in the Lost and Found Office.

Then Mr. Adonai, Raskolnikov, Marilyn, Serenade, and I start piling chairs and desks on top of each other all along the driveway in front of the registrar's office. In between them we wedge garbage cans, files, five-year plans, syllabi, and old blue examination books left behind in the faculty offices. In between those go the pamphlets for our summer school classes, the physics major, and our Education Abroad information booklets.

The work goes fast. We are able to lift and carry things easily. The furniture is light, and the pieces interlock neatly like the segments of a gigantic puzzle.

Raskolnikov and Mr. Adonai go upstairs, and between the two of them, they bring down the enormous steel conference table from the board of directors room: the one where they met and decided to kill our college. Then we, all of us together, hoist the big table to the top of the huge heaps of furniture that run from where the gate ends to where the chain link fence starts. The whole mass ends up being about twelve feet tall.

I push my mortarboard securely on my head, make sure my eyeglass earpieces are curled around my ears, and pull my gown up around my knees. Then I climb up the mountain of desks and chairs.

I stand on top of the conference table. Serenade films with one hand,

and with the other hands me the college flag that she has taken down from the flagpole. GEISTER, it says, and on it is a circle of twisted pine trees, surrounded by a fence and the waves of a lake and a shining sun.

The motto reads: SPREAD THE LIGHT.

Mr. Adonai keeps a lookout from the window of the president's office. "Here they come!" he shouts.

Marilyn climbs up beside me wearing a WE LOVE LIBRARIANS t-shirt. Raskolnikov waves Mr. Adonai downstairs and they both climb up on the front of the barricade.

The green Evictinator car pulls up. Parks on the street.

It's Alex again.

He gets out with his clipboard. He is reading something out loud to himself in a droning voice when a student chair falls from the top of the barricade. It lands in front of his feet.

Alex shrieks, looks up, sees me, sees Serenade filming, and smoothes his hair.

"Professor," shouts Alex. "This is so totally not a good idea."

He pulls out his cell phone. "Happily, I knew this was going to happen, and I have filled out the requisite paperwork and am now going to call the authorities. You have been hereby duly instructed to vacate the property, or you will be taken into custody along with your um . . . uh."

"Associates," I holler back at him. "Confederates."

"Allies and supporters," shout Marilyn and Serenade.

"Comrades," shouts Raskolnikov. "Damn it, man, there are so many words to choose from. Can't you even think of *one*?"

Alex can't. He stands by his car talking on his cell phone.

It is a beautiful sunny day here in Narrow Interior.

A police car arrives. Three men and one woman get out.

"Ok, lady," says one of the guy cops. "The joke's over. We're coming for you, and you are not going to like jail."

"You police are forcibly removing Narrow Interior's one remaining public intellectual," yells Raskolnikov.

"And we need the library!" I shout.

The second guy starts climbing over a file cabinet.

"You are committing violence against an institution of higher learning. You are murdering the mind of the people," shouts Marilyn.

That's a bit of an overstatement, I think.

"Hitler closed libraries and purged universities!" shouts Mr. Adonai.

Oh dear, I think, *not the Third Reich again.*

"Hey, Doug," Serenade shouts.

A cop looks up.

"You look like a complete asshole." Serenade turns to me and grins. "That's one of my idiot cousins."

But in the meantime, the cops have made it past the first tier of office stuff, and they are now climbing over the blue books and garbage cans.

"This will be done in time for lunch, Mandy," the third guy says to the lady cop who is pretty spry and who has already cleared a bunch of old printers.

And then something happens.

The first officer climbs over and falls backwards. He looks around. Tries again; something pushes him back.

The second man tries another route. He gets a little farther, and then falls backwards onto the hard driveway.

The woman tries a different approach. She crawls up the side, but suddenly she screams. "Something's got me!" And there she is stuck between a desk and a bookcase. "My foot is trapped," she says. "It hurts."

That leaves the third man. He tries and can't even get a foothold. He slides down a desk like it's a children's slide.

Alex slinks back to the car. "I'm calling for backup!" he says.

The local news van arrives.

"This is fabulous," says a reporter in a very short skirt, with her long dreads floating in the breeze.

She gets our names and then starts directing.

"Dean Bell, can you please wave that flag a little more? Richie, are you getting this?"

Another police car comes. Then another. There are now twelve policemen with dogs. A few parents with small children walk by.

"Mommy, what's that lady doing on all that stuff?" says one little girl. "You told us we couldn't play on the furniture, and look at HER!"

"Breaking story here in the sleepy town of Narrow Interior," says the reporter. "Stay with us as we watch the drama unfold between Dean Beatrice Bell of the bankrupt Geister College and her fearless co-workers, who are—of all things—librarians."

"And a handyman!" yells Mr. Adonai.

These latest police are big and burly and they start just moving the furniture. I begin to sway on top of the pile of stuff.

Policeman Doug calls to me, "Lady, you need to surrender and come quietly, before you get hurt."

Marilyn topples on her own separate stack of desks.

"You're not such hot stuff now, are you, Professor," jeers Alex.

As a university administrator, I can put up with a lot. But I simply *cannot* abide rudeness from a student.

"Oh no, you don't," I yell. "Are you willing to give up on higher education without a fight? Doesn't education mean anything to you?"

I point to the kids standing with their parents. "What about these future students?"

"Oh lady, please," says Officer Doug. "There are other colleges."

"That's what they always say," I reply. "But this college is *here*. This library is *here*. These are *your* possessions! You need to safeguard them!"

I point at Serenade. "Officer—some of your relatives have jobs here, and some of your brothers and sisters went here."

I point at Alex. "*He* went here."

Someone grabs me. It's the woman cop. She's gotten out of the printer cables and has made it to the top of the barricade without my even noticing.

"Come along ma'am," she says.

"You can't make me," I reply.

I don't know what I'm doing, but I grab her around the waist and arms and try to wrestle her onto the big table.

Suddenly the police dogs start howling. They lie down on the curb and will not move.

And the men climbing over the barricades start screaming.

Marilyn climbs over the desks onto the big conference table to give it added stability.

"O wow ow!!" says a cop. One puts his hand to his face.

"I'm bleeding," shouts another policeman.

Another man trips over a rocky abutment. He crashes to the ground and groans.

"I broke my leg," he shouts.

Serenade keeps filming. The local TV team keeps filming.

All of the police are screaming from injuries we cannot see. They are falling down, getting up, and falling down again.

Raskolnikov climbs down in front of the barricade with Mr. Adonai, and they jump up and down on the porch as only a crazy Russian and a crazy Israeli can.

"Ha ha ha!" they shout.

Then Mr. Adonai looks around. "Dean!" he yells. (At last he gets it right!) "Look behind you!"

I turn on the precarious table and look back behind the barricade.

On top of the registrar roof and all along the top of the fence surrounding the college as far as I can see are people. They are wearing black pants and black shirts and deep hoods, which they have pulled over their heads so that their faces are in shadow. They are throwing dolls at the police. The dolls are large, almost the size of a baby, and they are throwing them with all their might at the sheriff's men.

The policewoman I was fighting has grabbed my arms. But she looks back when I do.

"It's the puppet turners!" she whispers.

Then she faints in my arms.

I hold her and watch the police retreat from the onslaught of dolls.

When a doll hits the ground it disappears sometimes. Other dolls seem to take life and grab the cops by noses and arms. Then they too vanish.

The cops finally unwedge the man with the broken leg, and the woman cop who fought me regains consciousness, pats me on the shoulder, and climbs down.

Officer Doug examines the wounded.

The woman officer moves her arm. The other guy's broken leg turns out to be a sprain.

"I sure thought I broke it," says the victim. "But now, somehow, it feels better."

"What do we do now?" asks one officer timidly. "We can't shoot them. They haven't attacked us."

"Well, someone did," says Alex. "I think you better use your tazers!"

"I can't see any attackers," says Officer Doug very quietly, "Can you?"

There is a silence.

"Heck," says another, "this is really embarrassing."

They get up and go to their cars.

"Wait, where are you going?" says Alex.

"We got to regroup," Officer Doug says. "And then we got to figure out what to tell headquarters."

They pile into their cars.

The dogs get in the cars as well, their ears laid back, and they are whimpering softly.

Alex shakes his fist at us from his car. "You haven't heard the last of this," he shouts. "No one defeats the Evictinators. I'll be back with a SWAT team if I have to. I'll—"

"Try reading *Les Misérables*," I shout to him. "It's never too late to become a more educated person."

His car runs over the curb and drives away.

As soon as everyone has left, the people on the roof and on the fences pull their hoods off. I don't recognize any of them, except for Bernhard. He is at the head.

He waves to me. On his shoulder, Mr. Adonai's monkey waves too.

"We will protect our folk," he says. "We will never abandon you, since you have not abandoned us."

"Who are those people?" Marilyn says to me.

"I think," I say slowly, "those are the Dankers."

"Well," said Serenade, "they sure have been a lot of help!"

The reporter with the short skirt shakes her head.

"What just happened?" she says. "I—I—." She and her cameraman get into the van and drive away.

And as we look on, the Dankers or the puppet turners or whoever they are, climb down the fences and the roofs and walk, in twos and threes, towards the botanical gardens, in the direction of Whispering Pines House and the lake.

It turns into a beautiful day. A gorgeous day of high summer like we get in this part of the country after the snow and the freezing rains come in and go out. We all sit on the porch and finish our donuts and coffee. Except for Serenade who runs off to the library to upload the video footage.

Eventually, we all just stretch out on the lawn and let the sun warm our faces. Moments like these are why I chose the life of the university.

It was a beautiful life.

Raskolnikov has recovered from his euphoria. "They will return," he says. "We must prepare to fight on." He stops.

"Dean," he says, "you were brilliant."

I look at the people sitting on the grass. I don't want anything to happen to Mr. Adonai, and Marilyn, and Serenade, and even Raskolnikov. Because, you see, they are now my friends.

"I think you all need to reopen the library now. You've protested, but now you need to show your good faith. People may need to use the facilities today. It's important that knowledge be available to everyone, no matter what else is going on. "

Serenade comes back. "You guys!" she says, "we've already had hundreds of hits on the video! I've just created a PayPal, Save The Geister College Library page. We're fund-raising!"

I turn to Raskolnikov.

"Make an appointment with the city council," I say.

"*I am not going to give up,*" says Raskolnikov, "*after this incredible victory.*"

"No," I say. "But you need to take the struggle to a different level." I stand up.

"I have to leave. I have a new research project."

And I think to myself, *I will be Hugo's beggar. It doesn't matter. What matters is the work.*

Mr. Adonai says, "But Dean, how will you live?"

"I still have a little money left," I say. "I can maybe rent a room in town for a bit. But I need to borrow something from the library."

"You can stay with me for a week or so," says Marilyn.

"Thank you," I say. "Thank you all for your friendship and your help."

They nod. We hug and kiss, like family. Mr. Adonai and Raskolnikov start disassembling the barricade in front of the library driveway while Marilyn heads back to the library.

I walk into the registrar's office and gather up my Danker notes and my Victor Hugo legal pads, my running shorts and a couple of things, and I put them in a rolling suitcase. I take off my cap and gown and smooth the wrinkles out of my dress. I lay my regalia on the counter. I walk out the door. This time I don't lock it. The student and faculty records are open for them to gather or for someone else to manage.

I walk away from the desks and chairs piled up in the driveway and to the library.

Marilyn is doing phone interviews with a local paper, and Serenade is sorting the mail and checking the PayPal page when she isn't running back and forth from the smoker's patio.

The library is filled with the smell of fresh pine.

"Here's some stuff Raskolnikov said you might want to borrow," says Serenade. It's a box that says, *Old Narrow Interior Documents, Uncategorized.*

"Thanks," I say. I get Marilyn's key from her. I can walk to her house from here.

People start coming into the library. Five people. Twelve. And then more.

"Wait," Serenade shouts. She runs after me. "I forgot; you have mail!"

And there's the legal sized envelope from Benjamin.

"Nice dress, Beatrice!" says Serenade over her shoulder as she walks back to the library.

I open Benjamin's package.

"Here are the signed papers," he has written on a note. "But please won't you give us another chance? I managed to get the cabin in the mountains.

"Please come."

19. Henry:
My Wondrous Adventure

i. Pits

I get off the bus at the Narrow Interior depot. Patrick's letter says:

> Say hello to John Russell, the contractor at the building site. Be nice. But don't <u>do</u> anything decisive. Await instructions. You have a house and a housekeeper, Grusha.

I put Patrick's letter, an enclosed map of downtown, and his directions to "my new house" in my pocket. I start walking.

There are a lot of fences. Everything, including the depot parking lot, has a split rail fence around it. Small bells hang at intervals from chains on the top rails.

Henreeeeeee, they tinkle in the breeze.

I go up the hill past the boarded up college. I find the construction site. The gate is open. I walk in.

There is nothing here. Except for a big hole in the ground. And tall piles of dirt all around the perimeter.

A guy in jeans lopes over. "Mr. Holbein?"

We shake hands.

"How do you like our pit?" John Russell asks.

"It's big," I say.

"Yeah!" says the contractor enthusiastically. "Since, as you know, we don't have permission to build yet." He pauses, and I nod.

"I'm keeping the guys on payroll and having them dig this really huge pit!" he says. "It keeps their spirits up, and this way the team is ready to just leap into construction the minute those permits are squared away."

"Isn't that kind of expensive?" I ask.

"No," says the contractor. "They aren't union."

He points, and I see a bunch of guys in hard hats drinking out of paper coffee cups.

The sky darkens, and my stomach rumbles. "Speaking of coffee, do you happen to have any hamburgers, or any donuts?" I say.

"No," says the contractor, "I only drink herb tea, and I'm on my annual summer cleanse."

I look around. "Where's the meetinghouse?"

"Over there behind the tallest pile of dirt."

I can't see anything, so I look down into the pit. There's very dark water down there at the bottom. The water moves and suddenly—

Mr. Death's white face grins up at me as he climbs out of the pit. Wearing a yellow construction hat. His unblinking blue eyes burn through mine.

"*What do you want now?*" I mutter.

"We want that darned lawsuit resolved," says the contractor, "so we can build your mom's beautiful hotel. A glass structure will encase the meetinghouse, like that atrium for the Egyptian temple at that big city museum. With a lovely gift shop inside!"

Mr. Death climbs back down. Shaking with laugher.

✳ ✳ ✳

I walk down the hill and pass by two old buildings that have a banner in front of them:

NOW OPEN! Seelye Cultural Center of Narrow Interior.

Two identical twin guys are standing outside talking.

"Nice restoration," I say.

"Thanks!" says the smaller one. Come to think of it, they are both small.

The slightly less small man says, "This building on the left was an old five and ten cent store, and it's now an archive of photographs of this entire area."

The other guy pipes up, "And this building was the upscale department store that has been retrofitted as a—"

"—cultural space," they both say at the same time.

I look through the windows. The "cultural space" has highly polished wooden floors and a balcony. It's completely empty.

"We're trying to build community spirit," says the tiny man.

"Is there much interest in culture?" I ask.

"Not really," says the less small man.

"Do you know of a coffee shop around here?"

They both shake their heads. "The food in town is terrible."

I walk "home."

It starts raining.

A station wagon passes me, pulls over, and stops. A woman with bright red hair leans out the window. "That you at last, Mister Holbein?"

Grusha.

"You walk in wrong direction." Grusha laughs and points. She has a mellow laugh: not too high and not too low.

"You turn left here. And I suggest some quickness, partner."

It stops raining. I walk faster and Grusha drives alongside me.

"There are peoples waiting for you at house," she says.

"What peoples?"

"Political," says Grusha. "And men with TV camera."

We turn left at a stand of trees.

She accelerates down the street.

A van with CONFIDENCE VALLEY CABLE NEWS painted on it is parked in front of a yellow house with a cluster of people on the driveway.

Grusha pulls up the driveway and into the garage; the people-cluster retreats to the front porch.

"He's all wet!" says someone.

I stand and smile moistly on the front porch while the news camera crew position the reflectors. I meet a reporter in a short skirt and Councilwoman Suzanne Haring, who represents the downtown district. The neighborhood welcome wagon lady shows up and gives me a basket of detergent and a traditional Narrow Interior iron bell to hang on my fence. On camera. Councilwoman Haring says she is mighty excited about the hotel project that will bring jobs and tourists into town.

The reporter interrupts. "Now I'll bet our folks at home are wondering, 'How do the Holbeins live in Narrow Interior?'"

Grusha bursts out the front door.

"You got to see the vintage furniture we got!"

The camera crew, the reporter, and Councilwoman Haring troop in to go look at it.

Patrick has had the place furnished. He loves American retro.

A burnt orange sofa sprawls over the avocado shag carpet next to four enormous turquoise easy chairs. Above the empty fireplace, prints of clowns and Japanese tidal waves alternate along the mantelpiece.

The tidal waves crash and rise. Crash and rise.

Henry ain't this a funny joint? say the clowns.

I don't know what my taste in furniture is exactly. But this isn't it.

The shooting is over. Grusha starts serving coffee and coffeecake.

I reach for a piece of cake. The councilwoman grabs it.

"Mmm," she says.

Someone turns the TV on, and I see people at a horseshoe table.

"—Not convinced by the Holbein proposal," says the one man to a microphone held up under his pointed chin. "And—"

"Bigger is NOT necessarily better, is it?" adds a reporter in a very short blue skirt.

I look at the reporter who is here now.

"We shot this segment earlier today," she says. "Getting both sides of the debate!"

"What do you think?" says the TV reporter, turning to an indistinct person who looms over her—a spectral shadow.

The picture goes out.

Grusha smacks the TV with a potholder.

A voice emanates intermittently from the squiggly screen. "As members . . . Historic Preservation Commission . . . charged . . . public trust."

"Cable not installed yet," Grusha says.

" . . . our town . . . significant . . . historic . . . sites, and . . . must—"

Grusha turns the TV off.

"Don't worry, Henry!" says Councilwoman Haring. She is sitting on the orange sofa with the empty coffeecake plate on her lap.

The doorbell rings. It's Sean.

"Surprise!" he says. He tries to hug me but I duck around him.

"I'm here to help!" he says, putting his arms down.

"Great," I say. "Meet the press."

The reporter says, "Ooh a monk! Great human interest."

I walk out the door as the camera crew gears up for another shoot.

"Love that skirt!" says Sean.

There is an extremely tall girl cutting roses on her side of the fence that runs along the driveway. She's wearing these old-fashioned high waist capris and a red shirt knotted around her waist. She's got a kind of old-style hairdo with the ends turning up. She looks like Natalie Wood, if Natalie

Wood had been six feet tall.

The bells tinkle all along the rails.

She hands me a rose.

"Thank you," I say.

"Welcome to the neighborhood," she says.

On the other side of "my property" a man and a boy watch the TV people come out and grab more equipment. I walk over.

The man is Gideon, and the boy is his son, Gomer.

They inform me that they live with a lady who is a hoarder.

"You should see the garage," says Gomer. "*She's* the one who should be on TV."

"Would you like to come in?" I say to the guys.

Gomer says yes, but Gideon says no. "We have a big day at the doctor's tomorrow."

"They say I'm going to die," Gomer says. "I have cancer."

"Jesus—Gomer," says his father.

I look around. Mr. Death is standing with the tall girl, smelling the roses.

"Are you scared?" I ask.

"Sometimes," says Gomer.

"Me too," I say. I don't know what to do, so I just give Gomer the rose that the neighbor girl gave me. He takes the stem carefully, not pricking himself on any thorns.

"Is that why you ran out of your own house?" Gomer asks.

"Could be," I reply.

I walk back in. Gideon and Gomer wave to me from their side of their property.

Mr. Death stands on the street.

The TV crew leaves.

Inside, Councilwoman Haring and Sean are reassuring each other that the hotel project will go forward.

"Grusha," I say, "I'm fucking starving."

"Boss, all you got to do is upspeak," says Grusha.

I go into my new bedroom, do my bunraku arm exercises and hope that Grusha's cooking is better than her English.

ii. The Decider

I wake up the next morning to the sound of a vacuum cleaner.

I get up, put on a Ralph Lauren shirt and a good pair of khakis.

I go in to the kitchen and drink some of the coffee that's sitting on the counter.

I open the refrigerator. There's nothing in it except for a bottle of tonic and a dried up lime. I close the door.

Grusha has her hand on her hip, and she's yelling at Sean over the vacuum. "City call five times," she yells. "You such big shot cousin, you answer goddamn phone yourself. What do you think? I personal assistant?"

The vacuum goes off for a moment, and I can hear Grusha's armful of bracelets and Sean saying, "Chill, chill."

The kitchen smells of cigarettes and some chemical perfume.

"Also," shouts Grusha, "*No smoking!*" She grabs Sean's cigarette and puts it in the sink. "Monks can't smoke."

"Sure they can," shouts Sean, lighting up another one. "You just have to be Zen about it."

The vacuum goes back on.

They notice me.

"What you say, boss, about smoke?" yells Grusha. She tosses her head. She's not as old as I thought. The hip in her black pants is smooth and curved.

The vacuum's roar has become a kind of groan and something smells like burning rubber.

I crouch on the floor. Turn the vacuum off. Pull something out of the vacuum hose.

The bell from the welcome wagon lady. I put it on the counter.

"Smoke outside," I tell Sean.

"Whatever," says Sean. His cigarette hangs out the side of his mouth, like he is an old time movie actor. "We have to go anyway."

Grusha turns the vacuum back on.

"We need to appear before the historical commission in twenty minutes," Sean shouts as he walks out the door.

There's not enough time to walk downtown, so Sean drives Grusha's station wagon.

Grusha is not happy. "Be careful with car!" she yells from the porch.

"No worries, Groosh," says Cousin Sean. "I'm a fabulous driver."

Sean peels out of the driveway.

We lurch back and forth in our seatbelts as he tears around the corners on the country roads.

"I think I should do the talking," Sean says. "I can really help you here, because, . . . cuz, . . . you aren't so good at thinking on your feet."

"I want you to just wait for me in whatever nice bar it is that you hang out in."

He turns on the radio and lights another cigarette. "But Patrick said—"

"I know," I say, although I have no idea what Patrick said.

There's a pause in the conversation as we hit a pothole and my head bangs against the ceiling of the car.

My stomach stays up when I come down because it wants to puke out the contents of last night's supper. Cheezits and sardines.

"That's all we got," Grusha said. "I had to concentrate on coffeecake."

"Besides," she informed me as she slammed a plastic plate on my twin bed, "I housekeeper, not nouveau cuisine chef."

I put my index finger underneath my ribs and push.

"Sean," I shout over a cover of *Rock Me Like a Hurricane*, "this will be just some pro-forma thing where they'll just talk at me and give me a bunch of warnings," I say. Then I belch.

"But shouldn't we prepare what you're going to say?"

"I bet I won't need to say much."

"You think?" Sean sounds doubtful. He turns on to Main Street. My head slams against the side window.

"And anyway," I say, "what *could* I do that's official over there?"

"That actually makes sense," says Sean, pulling over to the curb in front of city hall.

We screech to a halt as the guitar solo ends.

"And why would you want to do anything to mess up this sweet deal?" Sean says as he turns off the car. "You've got that totally awesome rent-free house, and so what if the furniture is a little bit gay, and Grusha's a bit of a bitch? All you got to do is obey orders, you know?"

"Exactly," I say. "Just like Goebbels."

"Who?"

"What I mean is—that's really well put, Sean," I say.

I get out of the car, and he tells me to meet him at the Maple Leaf.

I go into the castle-shaped city hall.

The security guards at the desk direct me to the third floor.

There is an elevator, but I take the stairs. Big marble steps. Grand.

I wait for a long time outside in a vestibule with an uncomfortable wooden bench.

I go into that same room that I saw on the TV yesterday.

The board members are there, and the pointy-chinned bald man is there in charge. He gets right to the point.

"Mr. Holbein, we are not going to let you build," the bald guy says.

"That's perfectly fine," I say.

The bald guy is holding his breath. He exhales sharply. "No, I mean it."

I look him in the eyes. I read in a book that if you do that, people think you aren't afraid of them.

I say, "Me too!"

I turn to address the others. "Actually, I am appearing at my mother's request to inform you that the company has recently decided that—upon reflection—Narrow Interior does not—how shall I put it?—fit our profile."

I bow slightly to the assembly, which shows that I'm very high-toned and went to a private high school where we took things like fencing.

"Please send the appropriate paperwork to Felice, Hughes, and Whatchem, so we may rescind the building permit request."

"What about the lawsuit?" says a woman with clanking pearl jewelry.

"Cancelled," I say.

"Just like that?" says somebody else.

I shrug.

The committee members stare at me.

"Bye!" I say. I bow again to the assembly and walk to the door. Then I stand and just *look* at it.

A minute passes. The lady with the jewelry coughs until the pointy chin guy gets up and opens the door for me.

I beam at him. "Gosh—thanks so much!"

I egress.

I walk back down the marble stairs and out the door of the city hall. I go up the hill to the bankrupt college and take a look around the library and the grounds. Then I walk over to the construction site with the hole. The men are transporting the dirt in old-fashioned wheelbarrows to the already enormous piles.

I wave John Russell over.

"Stop the work right now," I say to the contractor. "Pay everyone for six months and send them home."

"But—we have to build," John Russell complains.

"Nope," I say. "The world has enough Holbein Hotels."

I start to walk away.

"What about the pit, Mr. Holbein?" he calls.

"Someone will get back to you on that detail," I say.

I go over and watch by the fence as Russell disbands the workers

Then I remember—I really want to eat something! I march down to the Maple Leaf Bar. There must be something to eat there.

✳ ✳ ✳

I walk into the Maple Leaf, order three hamburgers with fries and onion rings and a large beer, and I inform Sean that the deal fell through and that he can stay at the house as long as he wants to, but that I am going to head out to someplace else.

"What the hell happened?" he says.

I tap my hands on the bar. "Boy, am I hungry!"

"What will you tell Aunt . . . I mean your mom?"

"I have no idea, Sean," I say. "Think she'll be mad?"

"Jesus, Henry." He shakes his head.

Two young women walk in.

"Hey," I say. "Those women act like they recognize you!"

"What women?" he says. And he's off to talk to them.

I start to eat my three hamburgers. They are skinny and the French fries are cold. I stop eating and look up.

An elderly man stares at me from across the bar. On either side of him is a girl who reminds me of Patti, only Goth, and a tall-looking guy in a white medical coat.

"I think that's him," says the girl. The old man nods.

"Not much to look at, is he?"

I look back down at my food and think about where I'd like to go next. South or West. Both places my family doesn't like. I think about how I'll change my name and become an entirely new person.

I'll have to get a job, though. I chew on a soggy onion ring, spit it out on the plate, and wonder what kind of job I'd be good at. I've never had a job. Also, I'm not sure what to do with the Monkey King. He's coming by UPS later in the week. I don't know as I want him with me. Perhaps Sean would like him.

Or I can give him to my young neighbor, Gomer. If he doesn't die, that is.

I pay the bill.

Sean has made friends with the women.

"Yes," I can hear him saying, "I was consulting with the Holbein project. But—," he makes a sign to the bartender for more beers, "just now I'm considering other offers."

I need to call Patti. She's my only friend, I realize.

Sean leaves with the two women.

"Later," he says.

"Yeah," I say.

I walk out the back door.

"Just a minute," says this woman in a long dress and a little white cap on her head. She's standing in the alley near the garbage cans.

"I'm sorry, miss, I don't have time to talk to you right now," I explain. "My cousin and housekeeper are expecting me at home."

She grabs my arm. I try to pull away.

But the woman in the cap is stronger than she looks, and she pushes me away from the door and against the wall next to the cans. Two more women in these long dresses and caps climb out of a dumpster. They are huge. They grab me, and one of them puts a bag over my head.

"Are you terrorists?" I ask. My voice sounds funny inside the bag. I can breathe fine, and the bag is not completely sealed up, so I can sort of see my feet and their feet scrabbling down the pavement until they put me in a car.

"Peace," says one. "Be thee silent."

Cheap carpeting. Big American engine.

We drive.

iii. Letter from Molly Winston to Bernhard Hofmann (Partial)

Geister College Archives

June 20th 16—
Dearest Bernhard, beloved in Christ,

I am making copies of my letters to you, so that I may re-read them, imagining you in Muenster. And once we are together at last here in Confidence, we can merge our writings as well as ourselves. Thus I have double the pleasure, as well as the labor, although I must mind the paper and ink, as they are dear here.

Today I walk through the pine saplings I planted here last spring—brought from the pine nuts by my mother Teruko across multiple seas when she became reborn as Christine, and now they are brought by me to this place. The pines will spring forth from the power of their double origin—the Japans and England—and are watered here by the words and wisdoms of so many: the Muenster survivors, the followers of good Menno, the Swiss brethren, the Calvinists, the children of the first people driven from Spain, and others from even farther away. Other good folk have come and grafted themselves onto our family: a new tree of knowledge, indeed a world tree that grounds the good and gives shade and shelter to any who would seek it.

We build bravely here now that summer is upon us, and I share the glad tidings that the meetinghouse is finally being erected, along with the theater that will serve in the cellar and lead us to the dunking. Joanne and Francesca and Ruth and John and Joachim hope to raise the roof tomorrow. Soon we can begin the Spiele in earnest and the Sabbath as it is meant to be celebrated: with the meeting of bodies—manikin and man—and the meeting of elements—water and earth—indoors rather than outside, as we have had to do. For no house is adequate to hold our numbers.

Francesca worries that errant Puritan neighbors have seen our last Sabbath, and she urges us to cease until the meetinghouse is built. We must, she says, perform in secret.

So I sat with her near the lake and told her of the day my family strolled together in the Leadenhall Market. You had just left Oxford, and it was on that day that I knew I would go to the New World. It was the day I acquired Johnny, who climbs about me now as I write.

It was the day we named ourselves the Dankers.

We had purchased meats and vegetables, and my father had given Henry and me pocket money for sweets. He had the means, thanks to his work as a doctor of medicine.

"Danke, danke!" we cried.

"Who are those strange ones?" a passer-by with fine buckled shoes and a cloak said to his wife, who was similarly adorned. "They keep saying 'dank dank.' Are they wet like an old moldy wall near the water?"

My mother looked abashed. Little Henry, my brother, just turned twelve, laughed at that.

"That's us!" he said. "We are the dankers. People who say thank you and get wet!"

"What a terrible name!" my mother said, looking around. "The sound is so nasal!"

"I like it," I said, putting my hands on Henry's small shoulders. "I hear that the detractors of the Friends have taken to calling them the Quakers, because they quake before the Lord."

Several people around us stopped talking and looked at us, but I kept on boldly, as is my wont. "Why should we not have an equally ridiculous name? To embrace the ridiculous, the laughable even, is this not our Lord's Way? To find the great in the small? The heroic in the seemingly foolish? Is that not what we do with our poppets?"

It was then that my father took me aside and walked me towards a cheese-monger. "Hush," he said. "Not so loud."

That is when I decided. "I will go where there are no secrets," I said to him quietly. With that I laid out my silver, purchased some cheddar, and drew all three of my family to a table. I took their hands, holding little Henry on my lap, although he was too big for that. "Where we practice our faith openly, and where any who wish to join us, may."

My father pursed his lips. "Oh my daughter," he said, "what you say has a dangerous merit. Jesus's ministry was no secret, it is true. But remember, he was not us. And he suffered human death to accomplish his great aim."

"But look at the Puritans and what has happened to them from years of secrecy," I said, and here I did lower my voice, for they are

130

angry—these radical ones—and they seek to do murder here. Even the King himself is not safe, although, to be frank, the crown is corrupt as well. "Look at how the secret eats itself within."

We stood up and perambulated the market, not purchasing any longer for we were hard at our disputation, every one of us a philosopher. My father and my mother remonstrated with me, begging me to remain in England with our dear fellowship, but I told them no.

My brother Henry held my mother's hand and looked at me with his wide blue eyes.

"I will to the New World," I declared again.

It was then that the organ grinder passed among us. He walked by, noting the plainness of our garb, but his monkey leapt onto my basket and climbed up my shoulder.

"My apologies young lady, sir, madam, and the young gentleman," said the organ grinder. "Take this creature for a penny, if you will. He will not perform and is endless trouble."

My father shook his head, but my mother was still thinking of our conversation. "I fear for you, my daughter," she said as the monkey chattered.

And I swear to you, Bernhard, a strange thing happened.

"Fear not, dear lady," said the monkey to my mother, "I shall guard you and your kin throughout the generations."

My mother looked at me. I looked at my father. My brother Henry reached into his pocket and pulled out his name-day money. "Here," he said, giving the organ grinder the silver.

"Thank you, young master," said the monkey. "I shall be with you always and with the inner light."

The organ grinder bit the coin, smiled, and walked away.

That is how Johnny came to be with me in this country.

iv. Swim

Someone has tied my hands.

"Put on his seatbelt," says one woman. We drive for a short time. We stop. But we don't get out of the car.

It's hard to know how much time is passing when your head is in a bag, but it seems like a lot of minutes and even hours go by.

"Art thou certain he is the right one?" asks someone at one point.

"He was on the television," says the other.

"It was said he is the Holbein," says the third.

I think of the rich guy—what's his name—Lindbergh, whose kid got murdered because the ransom didn't work or the kidnappers screwed up. I figure I'd better get the ball rolling on the finances.

"Do you want money?" I say.

Silence.

✳ ✳ ✳

It gets hot in the car. I start shifting in my seat.

"I'm sorry," I say. "I have to pee."

One of them zips open my fly, pulls out my penis. She says, "Purge."

I can't.

✳ ✳ ✳

It gets hotter in the car, and the women make me try to pee three more times. The fourth time, my bladder is so full, the urine basically pours out on its own. At the bottom of my vision I see paper cups in a stack.

Then it gets dark, and I don't see anything.

After the penis pulling, I feel no inclination to talk to my captors.

A car door opens.

They make me get out and walk. We are outside. And then we aren't.

There is a smell of rotting wood. Musty.

I sneeze.

Steps down.

It feels cold all of a sudden. I can't hear cars or birds or anything. But I do hear . . . water.

They take off the bag.

I hear a scratch, smell sulphur, see a match glow. Three times.

Three candles are lit. Each woman holds one.

The women in their shapeless dresses surround me. Close in. They are all taller than me. And much bigger. I can feel the flames near me as the water that I can't see slaps against itself.

"*Du*—you—are in the *untergrund*," the tallest one says.

I think this is the one who first accosted me outside the bar. She wears glasses.

We stand there for a long time.

One woman disappears and comes back with a box. She places the box in my tied-together hands.

The woman with the glasses turns me while the other two go away with their candles.

Against a wall, the women put their candles down and, in the flickering light, are making shadow-shapes with their hands, arms, and even their bodies.

I see a procession of figures. Four shadows. Now six as the leader joins them.

The procession becomes a story.

"Gaze upon the shadows, Holbein," says the leader.

The shadows become silhouettes, and the silhouettes become people. I see women carrying candles like the ones I just saw. A long stick held aloft. A big cup follows. And a person with a crown lying on a pallet; the others carry him. The king raises his hand toward another, who kneels before him.

The women return with their candles. They encircle me.

I can hear the water. Is it coming closer? I am afraid to say anything. So I don't.

The candles burn on the floor in front of each woman.

My legs begin to shake. I have been standing a long time.

"He says nothing!" says one.

"He is ignorant," says the second. She has long braids hanging down from her cap.

"Speak!" says the third. "What do you see?"

I squeeze my eyes shut.

I don't see anything.

But I smell mold, rotting wood, and failure.

And I hear Oma saying, "He fails the test because he will not speak."

"Thou must know what you look upon!" says the first woman. "*Du bist* the descendent."

"He knows *nothing*; look at him!" says the third.

My legs fold, and I land on the ground. I am not I anymore. I am... nothing.

The leader pulls me to my feet.

"Now what?" she says to the others.

The one who has been quiet speaks.

"Let him stand the test of the immersion," she says.

A moment passes.

A heavy door clanks open, and the water rushes in.

I realize now that they are just going to drown me.

"No," I say.

The water comes in fast.

The women stand in a circle. One of them unties my hands. And they push me in the direction of the tunnel, another enormous hole.

The middle woman says, "You must watch for the opening. There is a light, an electric light."

I am still holding the box. How can I swim with a box?

"You don't understand," I say. I want to tell them that the slimy cold water will open my eyes, and that the water will make my eyeballs pop out. Then Mr. Death will take them.

"You swim down the tunnel and come up the other side."

The water is at my hip joint. I shit my pants. As my shit flows away from me, I realize, *That's why Mr. Death has those human looking eyes. He takes them from his victims.*

I retch, but there's nothing to puke up.

The water is at our waists. The skirts of the long dresses float around the women like bloated corpses.

The woman with the braids blows out her candle. The quiet woman blows out hers.

There is one candle left, and the women are nodding and murmuring together.

"This too was tradition, Holbein," they say in a sing-song voice. "Repeated immersion, inherited from the others—not the Japaners—the first people who came to Europe: the dispossessed, the eternal wanderers."

The water is up to our chests and rising fast.

"*Please,*" I whisper.

They chant as the water comes up to my shoulders now, up to my chin.

> *After the fall of the Kingdom of Muenster*
> *Those exiled from Jerusalem offered us shelter,*
> *And with protection they showed us how to make the* spiel.
> *Preserve through dissembling the history of the real—*

The water rushes up. Then it enters my mouth, making my silence complete.

v. Woman 4 and Woman 5

I should drown. But I don't.

I am lying on the ground on the shore of the lake of the college.

The security lights are on around the perimeter. I can see the library and the piles of dirt. On the ground are the box and something else.

I get up. Walk, bend over.

A big moon is out, and I can see the cover of an old book.

A book that says: *Der Märtyrerspiegel.*

As I look at the title, its letters shift and reform to read: *The Martyrs' Mirror.*

The book is not wet. Neither is the box. Someone brought them out and put them here.

I sit down on the shore again. I open the box.

A child-size wooden hand is inside. The book flutters open.

There is a fourth woman waiting in the moonlight. She is not dressed like the first three. She looks . . . like someone in a Thanksgiving costume.

"Hello," she says.

She comes to me and picks up the book and the box, lays them at my feet.

"Who are you?" I ask.

"Molly Winston, called the seer of the inner light, daughter of Franz and Christine Holbein, betrothed and beloved of Bernhard Hofmann, descended of beloved Menno."

"Are we related?" I ask.

"Yes," she says, "by the might-have-been."

"So—" I say, "are you real or not?"

"Touch me," she says.

I figure that not much else can go wrong for me tonight, so I take her hand.

I feel warmth and a pulse, but the pulse is very fast.

"You are the first man to come for me," she says. "Bernhard...he never came, although we waited for him and built the fences, and we forged the bells and constructed the meeting house. But he was delayed, so we had to begin the *spiel* as best we could."

"What is *spiel*?" I say. I pull my hand away but she grasps it.

"Do not let go," she says. "The feel of you is good."

"*Spiel*?" I remind her.

She smiles, takes my hand between both of hers.

Her hands are hot.

"I forget you do not speak German. *Spiel* means 'play.' But it is no profane mummery; the *spiel* is a ritual, wherein we become the things we show, but we do not display ourselves."

"The women said something like that," I say. "The women who abducted me."

Molly laughs at that. She begins to count my fingers.

"Why are you so hot?" I ask.

"The fire," she says. She is counting and recounting, as though this were a game, taking each finger between hers and counting under her breath: one, two, three.

She kisses each one, her mouth warm on the digits.

"You are Jonah," she says.

"No," I say, "I'm not Jonah. My name is—"

She holds my fingers to her forehead and closes her eyes. "You have undergone the immersion so now you are Jonah, who persists through water."

She opens her eyes. "A new man with a new name. So tell me, friend, what is it that ails you?"

"I'm in big trouble with the women who took me, Molly," I say. "I failed some test."

"That's nothing," she laughs. She lets go of my hands. "We faithful fail tests all the time. What is needed now is persistence. And play."

I try to understand what the maybe-not-real-Molly is talking about. But it is late, and I've been kidnapped and almost drowned, and so, in spite of myself, I yawn. I'm tired, and I'm not one for puzzles, even with a mysterious spirit-lady from the past or heaven or my imagination.

"Go home, Jonah," she says. She pats my head as though I were a small boy, picks up the box and the book again, and places them in my hands. Pats my shoulder too.

"Find the attempt you are supposed to make."

"What about these?" I show her the two items.

She laughs at the book. "This will not help you. I am of it, but not in it."

"What about the hand?" I ask.

There is silence. I look at her, and there are crystalline tears falling from her eyes. Hard like diamonds.

I reach up and touch one. It sticks to my finger. I put it in my shirt pocket.

"The limb is all that is left of the original," she says.

Then she begins to burn.

Her skin peels off in black layers. The smell though, that's what's hardest. The smell of burning flesh.

Molly is still talking, though her skull is showing, and even the bones are blackening in the red-blue flames that surround her.

"Do what you can," she says. "Assemble what has been dispersed."

I faint or collapse or something.

The fifth woman of the night comes along. It's the professor from the bankrupt college. She helps me up.

I try to explain what has happened. But I can't.

She leaves with a snarling, bear-like man. He's got a gun but talks like a librarian.

I pick up the book and the box with the wooden hand in it, and I walk back to the house my mother bought for me, but where I do not really live. Wearing the clothes she had someone choose for me, but which I did not select.

I walk and look at the super-big moon.

As I walk I remember Oma telling the story that I did not like.

The shadow play that I just saw was about that dumb guy—the knight called Parzival. And Parzival fails the test because he didn't ask the questions. There were a bunch of questions. Of course, I have forgotten them.

vi. Clothes Make the Man

I get up the next morning, go out to the kitchen in my boxers, and drink some coffee. Outside the sliding doors to the backyard, Grusha is hanging clothes on a clothesline.

"Everything in move get washed," she announces. "And hung in air. Better for soul. Also bedbugs. They travel easily."

I see my pink shirt hanging on the line. And the pants.

"These smell like shit, boss," she says. "Had to wash twice."

I go back into "my" room. It's true. All my clothes are gone.

I go into another room. I see a woman's cosmetic bag. And a fuchsia electric guitar.

I go into a third room. It smells of smoke and feet. A single mattress on the floor. A grease-stained pair of jeans and a torn t-shirt lie in a crumpled heap next to the bed. I pick up the t-shirt; I'M WITH STUPID, it reads in big red letters. These must be Sean's car-fixing clothes.

I put them on. They are a bit big on me, but they make me feel thinner. I find some paint-spattered tennis shoes by the front door. They fit.

I go outside.

The woman from next door is there again, standing at the fence that divides our property. Today is she is dressed like a nineteenth century newspaper boy, complete with knickers, suspenders, and a cap tilted at what I think they call a rakish angle.

She smiles this time.

I walk over, hitching up my pants.

"Hey," she says, "are you the electrician? They've been talking about how the place needs rewiring."

"Handyman," I say.

My new neighbor looks me up and down.

"Where are your tools?" she says.

I think for a minute. "These people are so rich, they have their own tools they want me to use."

She snorts at that. "I'll bet."

"Still," she says, "doesn't it look more official if you have one of those belts?"

"Yeah," I say, leaning on the fence, "but those belts make me look fat."

The woman puts her hand on the fence and laughs. She has a low laugh.

"So, what brings you out here this morning, miss . . . "

"Serenade," she says. She lifts her basket; once again it's filled with roses. She is wearing large yellow gloves. On her side of the fence are white roses, and next to that are pale pink ones, then red, then orange. They go on all the way to the mailbox. And around the front of the property.

"Your roses are amazing!" I say. "But don't they require a lot of work, like food and pruning?" I remember Mr. Gilbert telling Oma about them.

"True," she says, "but I just love them. And once you get them going, they give so much back to you." She sighs and looks at the basket. "That's it for now. I have to go to work."

"Where is work?" I ask.

"The college library." Serenade stops. "I mean the city library, historic downtown branch, is what they're calling it now." She looks at me and smiles again.

She has a plump upper lip above a square jaw. Her face looks like a lady schoolteacher mixed with a lumberjack. It's not a beautiful face, exactly, but it's for sure a sexy one. She's taller than me. But then, most of the women around here are.

"What's *your* name?" she says.

"Jonah Gilbert," I say. I put my hand out. She takes her hand out of the glove and shakes.

Smooth skin. Strong grip.

"But my friends call me Joe," I say.

❋ ❋ ❋

I walk downtown as Joe.

Joe meets the old hippies sitting on the bank steps, has a few laughs, and then Joe goes into the bank.

I use the ATM for Henry Holbein, but Joe Gilbert goes inside the bank in his loose pants. "How would I find out about what mortgage money one owes," Joe asks a man at a desk.

"No worries, sonny," says the man. "They'll find *you*. They mail you a bill every month, and if you don't pay it, they show up and throw you out. What, you never owned property?"

"No," I-as-Joe say. "I'm just asking. I'm . . . trying to plan my future."

The man chuckles. "Well good luck to you, son."

Two desks down there's a woman with two kids saying, "I really need you to reconsider my loan request." Another woman sitting behind the desk wearing a big string of fake pearls is shaking her head, and she's looking over the woman's head at the security guard.

I walk out with my $200 and I-as-Joe wonder how long $200 lasts in today's economy.

I walk past the fences, and the air smells like roses.

Outside the Seelye Cultural Center, a truck stops in front of the building, lowers its ramp, and a bunch of people are getting green lumpy-looking sacks and bringing them to the front door.

At the door, a young guy with a goatee is talking to three people as they each hold a sack.

"Be careful with those," says the guy. "We need to bring them into the gallery and unpack them, get them into those earthen pots, and arrange them according to the plan."

One of the workers—a woman—says, "Man this is hard. Those things may be made of cloth but they still prick you all the same."

I would just pass them by. But Joe has other ideas.

"Hi," Joe says.

The woman raises an eyebrow.

"Pardon me for asking," I say. "But aren't those the cloth cacti by the artist Pedro de Caballo-Kinsky?"

"Yeah," she says. "How do you know that?" The guy with the goatee is directing, but he is also listening, I can tell.

Pedro, whose real name is Peter Rivers, spent a week with my mom at our apartment one summer. He dressed like a guy flamenco dancer, wore loud boots, and insisted on having a fresh Magnolia to wear in his lapel every day. He also insisted that two Spanish-speaking girls stand in flouncy dresses and snap castanets whenever he entered or left the room. He was a raw foodie and a general pain in the ass. But what Joe says is this: "I worked on setting up one of his exhibits in Fulcherton." I name a gallery farther south.

"Hey Mitch," she says to the goatee-guy who's in charge, "this guy says he's worked on one of Caballo-Kinsky's exhibits."

"Just as a day laborer," I say. "He's a very important exponent of postmodern, postcolonial consciousness, at least that's what they tell me."

We chat for a few minutes, and I explain about working for the Holbeins. The story gets truer with every telling. Joe throws in going to the bank and looking at his somewhat meager finances.

"God, I wish you could help us here with this exhibit," says the woman. Her t-shirt says, DON'T MESS WITH SUE. "The artist isn't coming until right before the show opens, and we don't understand the blueprint for the installation."

We briefly admire each other's witty t-shirts, and then she goes over and talks to Mitch. Mitch is working with two other workers. Very young, shy looking.

Mitch shakes his head.

"Oh come on," Sue says. "Have you ever seen a more honest face?"

"Dude! Where the fuck have you been?" Sean is barreling down on us, all orange toga and flip-flops.

Sue says, "Sean, this guy says he works for you!"

Sean looks at me, opens his mouth and—

I look at him. Joe lifts his two hands like a conductor at the beginning of a symphony.

"Oh, yeah," says Sean. He adjusts his sari and looks at my outfit. "Uh— what's your name again?"

"Joe," I say.

"Of course," says Sean. "Joe, he's our . . . "

"Handyman," I say.

"Right," says Sean. "He's a great guy." Sean smiles and puts his arm around me. "He's like family!"

"Interesting that you couldn't even remember his name," says Mitch. He crosses his arms. Cocks his head.

"Late night, again, Sean?" I say.

"Oh yeah, cuz, I mean bro. Crazy late."

We hug each other and then beam at the crew.

"How's that hotel project going, anyhow?" asks Mitch. "I hear there's been some trouble over at the construction site." He pauses. "And at the historic preservation commission."

Sean glances at me.

"Remember the chemistry set fire?" I say quietly.

"What did he say?" says Sue.

"Joe says the Holbeins have a lot of chemistry." Sean pulls his toga up over his shoulder. "I wouldn't worry about yesterday," says Sean. "Whatever shit went down will work itself out."

He looks at his watch. "Maple Leaf opening time," he says. "See you guys at Happy Hour!" He looks at me. "Bye, uh, Joe."

I breathe out.

"For gosh sake," says Sue, "if he's working for those Holbein people, he must be reliable. And Sean knows him!"

"Take these pots inside," says Mitch to the three helpers.

They carry the pots into the building.

Mitch crooks a finger at me. I walk over to him.

"Truth is," says Mitch quietly, "I could use some help today, maybe tomorrow, and maybe the next day. But this has to be off the books, man. I can't hire you legally. I'll pay you cash on a daily basis, or rather Myles and Giles Fairweather will. They're the center directors. You'll have to be discreet. We're kind of on a shoestring here."

"It's hard to make ends meet with a gallery," I say. "I had a friend who worked for a guy who owned one."

"OK," he says. "Come on." He turns back to me. "Just don't piss me off. I've got something of a temper."

vii. As You Like It

The next two weeks are Joe-Heaven. I get up, put on Sean's car-fixing clothes, walk into town, and help out at the Seelye Center.

Then I walk home and say hi to Serenade while she tends her roses at the fence. I explain to her that the Holbeins have me living right there in the little house so I can be available and on call 24/7.

"That family clearly never heard of unions," she sniffs over her pruning shears, "or treating the help like actual *people*."

Every day Serenade has on another incredible vintage outfit. Sometimes she's got a forties style "gal Friday" suit on, and sometimes she's wearing a Four Seasons-like men's suit, and sometimes she's just wearing a white bathing suit like Elizabeth Taylor wore. I look forward to bathing suit days.

I notice, though, that she is rarely inside her house. And, that there's a tent pitched in her backyard.

"You ever seen Jean Cocteau's *Beauty and the Beast*?" she asks me one time.

I tell her yes.

"I love her bedroom, because you can't tell whether you're indoors or outdoors—I could totally live in a place like that."

On the weekends, I shut my bedroom door and practice with the Monkey King.

"So how about taking that chick out?" he says, putting his hands on his hips.

"I think she has a boyfriend," I tell him.

"How do you know, daddy-o?" he says.

"She acts like someone who's attached."

"Well, I ain't ever *seen* the cat," says Son Gokū. "Besides, he can't be much in the sex department." Monkey thrusts his hips back and forth. "Why else is she hanging out on the driveway with those flowers all the time?"

I clap the two wooden sticks together and put Monkey King back in his suitcase.

The next day I help Mitch cut the two by fours for a big table he's making to put Pedro's soft "welding tools" on.

"They aren't part of the exhibit, really," says Mitch, "but he wants them included."

I arrange the cacti in the pots along the hallway. Then I help Sue re-paint the gallery walls white.

"Thin coats, Joe," she yells at me. "Otherwise we'll have to strip the wall and re-plaster it."

"Why?" I say.

"Bumps. The paint forms lumps, and after a few gallery shows we have to start all over again and re-plaster the whole damned thing."

"Mr. Holbein," say a couple of sharp alert voices, "such a pleasure to have you stop by and see us."

I stiffen but Joe starts climbing down the ladder immediately.

Patrick walks into the entrance hall with Myles and Giles Fairweather.

Joe tells me to bend over, so I do. "Argh," I groan.

"Jesus, Joe," says Sue, "what's the matter?"

"I feel sick," I say.

The men's room is right past Patrick. I'm not much of a darter, but I do my best to rush past him.

Patrick sees a worker in loose pants and a cheap t-shirt. He doesn't even bother to look at my face.

"One of Pedro's less provocative installations." Patrick runs his hand over a cactus pot. "Still, it's an appropriate curiosity for the local popu-lace."

I pull open the bathroom door and run into one of the stalls.

From time to time, I tiptoe out, listen, then crack open the door to the men's room. Patrick keeps on being there, holding forth about Pedro to Myles and Giles. I wash my hands periodically.

Someone comes in, and I run back into the stall.

"Joe," hisses Mitch.

I come out.

"Don't go out there!" says Mitch. He puts his back against the door, rolls his eyes, and sighs.

"What if Holbein recognizes you, and sees you're moonlighting for us?"

"Gosh, I hadn't thought of that!" I say.

"And what the hell will he think if he learns we're hiring people ille-gally?"

"Good point," I say.

Mitch takes another look out the men's room door. Then he walks over to a supply closet, opens the door, takes out the BATHROOM BEING SERVICED pylon, puts it outside, and shuts the door again.

"Just between you and me," he says, "he's a bit of an asshole, isn't he?"

"Oh yeah," I say. We guffaw.

I wash my hands again, but Mitch takes drops of water from the tap on his index finger and puts them all over the mirror. The water drops slide down. He takes out his mobile phone and takes pictures with us reflected in the spotty bathroom mirror.

"You're an artist, too!" I say.

"Photography and installation." He steps back from the sink and shows me a slide show of the pictures he has just taken: several of me semi-hiding in a stall, one of him picking his nose while the drips slide down the mirror, one of both of us looking in the spotted mirror.

"These are cool," I say.

He smiles briefly, puts the phone away. "Problem is I have to eat and pay the rent. So I work here, and then I do stuff on my own time."

"What stuff?" I say.

Mitch wipes down the mirror. "Fences, he says. The fences of Narrow Interior."

"Show me," I say.

"It's kind of hard to explain."

"Make me see it," I say. "Help me see."

Mitch looks at me for a second. Then he goes over to the supply closet and takes out a bunch of paper towel and toilet paper rolls. He starts lining them up and down on the bathroom floor.

"See. I want the installation to ask questions about how we are continually separated from each other, but that the barriers we erect are both meaningless and influential. How we can't get anywhere *with* the fences, but we also have to acknowledge that the fences exist."

"Will you have bells?" I say.

"The bells are seen as welcoming but they are also a warning." He takes a bicycle bell out of his pocket and puts it on top of one of the towel rolls.

"The fence would have all different kinds of bells and buzzers running up and down it, with motion detectors set to trigger and there will be recordings on little iPods or whatever that are buried in plastic bags all along the way. Saying, 'Don't bother me' or, 'Stay away' or, 'Who goes there?' or even, 'Come on in!' and, 'Howdy Neighbor.'"

Mitch adjusts the lines of the fence-model. "The devices will be geo-cached so people can find them with their GPS devices."

"Could people add to the fences too?" I say. "They could decorate them with materials they have lying around the house. So they deconstruct as they construct, and the fences will become a living monument to who we have been and why we are the way we are."

"Good idea," Mitch says.

I take my sneakers off, and I put each one on top of a toilet paper roll that goes at an angle to the main fence.

Mitch is moving around the rolls of paper, taking pictures with his camera phone.

"Where would you put the first fence?" I say.

"Around the old Danker meeting house," he says. "And the fence would run all the way to the center of town here, and there would be geo-caches that would connect with the Seelye Center and with the photo archive of the history of the town."

"Do you know much about the history?" I ask.

"No," he says. "But people could make their own archives and add pictures and imaginings in the geo-caches, so it wouldn't be an artist just saying, 'This is such and such history'; it would be art that asks, 'What do *you* think?' and, 'What do you remember?'"

"Narrow Interior could become the town of endless fences," I say. "People adding to them all the time, some running along side the fences that already exist and some new ones. Awesome. Why don't you make it?"

Mitch looks at me. His eyebrows lift. "I need a grant and institutional support, and no one has heard of me. The Seelye has already made all these commitments to important artists, and they are saying relevant things about borders and post-imperialism, like you said yourself."

"But the Narrow Interior fences are really cool," I say. "They are the first things I noticed when I got here."

"We've always had them." He nods. "As long as I can remember."

Mitch finishes photographing and starts picking up the rolls.

"Do you know anything about a book called *The Martyr's Mirror*?" I ask as I hand him the toilet paper rolls, and he puts them back in the closet.

"No," says Mitch. "I'm not a big reader." He hands me my shoes.

"Do you know anything about a small wooden hand?" I show him approximately how big with my hands.

"Funny you should ask," he says. "The museum has a bunch of—I guess you'd call them doll parts—downstairs. We keep finding them buried around town."

"I bet they aren't dolls," I say.

Mitch looks out the door, raises his finger. Goes out. Comes back. Patrick is gone.

I work some more and walk home.

Serenade is back by the fence with her yellow gloves and a basket full of roses. Now she's wearing a red polka-dot sundress. Her long black hair hangs down in a single thick braid. Sitting next to her are two huge bags of fertilizer. She picks one up with one hand, rips it open with another, and puts it down.

She's really strong!

"You like to spend a lot of time outside," I observe, after telling her I like her dress.

She says, "I—don't—like—indoors." She points at something.

I glance at the tent in the backyard.

"Is your name Serenade because you like to sing?" I ask, because I don't want to ask about the tent.

She nods.

"Will you sing a song for me?" I ask.

She stops pruning and smiles at me.

"No one ever asks me that," she says. "They always think I'm going to be like super untalented or something."

She opens her mouth and takes a breath, but then looks back at the house.

"I think Harold is calling me," she says.

"I can't hear him," I say.

"He calls silently," she says. She looks at the house again.

"He needs me to stand next to him as he writes his dissertation." She pauses. "Harold wants a lot of things: he wants to get a post-doc at Cambridge or London and then become a professor."

"What do *you* want?" I ask.

"I want to sing—in front of people," Serenade admits. "I sang in the choir at the local Presbyterian church, which has an outdoor chapel that we use in the summer and that worked great for me—" she swallowed.

"But the board said I was too tall, and they made me sit down at the back row, and no one could see or hear me!—I complained, and then they said I was strange looking and intimidated the children. They said I made people uncomfortable because I don't look like a normal woman."

I say, "I think you look just fine."

Serenade sets the basket down and puts her gloved hands in mine. Her hands are bigger, but that's ok. Her brown eyes grow large too. "Thanks."

"Tell me what kind of songs you'd like to sing," I say.

"I actually wanted to sing opera," she says, "and I studied German and Italian with a lady from the big city who came here for some peace and quiet." She squinted for a moment. "But my problem is—the venues."

I nod. I keep holding her large hands.

"I like folksongs and kid songs too. There's something past-ish and hidden-y about them. You know, like 'Ring Around the Rosies' which is about the Bubonic Plague. Old songs do that—they indicate another time and an event or a feeling—something that mattered to people. The song keeps it even though the memory gets lost."

I keep nodding. Holding.

She thinks. "I know! There's a kid's song I know that's German—my grandma taught me:

"*Klatshe Klatsche in die Hand*

Fuer den Puppensang und Tanz"

She has a high voice—surprisingly high for someone so tall.

"*Klatsch fuer Frankreich und Japan—*"

I watch Serenade sing. Her lips blossom with the words she's intoning, and I notice that she has the best eyebrows I have ever seen on anyone. Sharp, black, elegant. She has a big nose, but it suits her. Everything about her suits her.

Then Grusha comes out and waves to me from the porch. I let go of Serenade's hands and run up the driveway and pull Grusha into the house before she can say my name out loud.

viii. Busted

"Boss," says Grusha, "Mr. Patrick looks for you. He calls here like fifty times. He comes here twice. He says you got to come meet him at inn downtown, or else."

"No problem," I say.

I walk into "my" bedroom. My clean clothes are hanging in the closet. I put my pink Ralph Lauren shirt in a shopping bag, along with my khaki pants and Patti's shoes.

I come out.

"I give you a ride on my way to rehearsal," says Grusha. She's holding a guitar case. "He says he want you at Oak Bar at Narrow Interior Inn by six, and it's five thirty now."

"Ok," I say. "But if we run into anyone, you need to call me Joe until I get inside the hotel."

"Why?" she asks. We open the front door.

"I am pretending to be a handyman so people will like me for myself and not for my money."

"So that's why tall neighbor girl keeps on talking about handyman when I see her," says Grusha.

We go outside, get in the car, and she revs the engine. "Peoples are pissed off when they find out."

I say, "Won't they be happy I'm rich when they thought I was poor?"

We back out of the driveway. Serenade yells, "See you later, Joe!"

Grusha arches her eyebrow really high, sort of like a silent movie actress.

"You think she'll be glad you lied to her?" Grusha observes. "I only name one example." Holding the wheel with her right hand, she snaps a black bra strap underneath her black t-shirt for emphasis. Her dark green painted nails drum on the wheel as she drives.

We arrive downtown.

"Pull into the parking lot behind the hotel," I say.

The four hippy veterans have left their position on the steps outside the bank and are now stationed behind the hotel.

Grusha drops me. I walk over to the guys. "Here to see the big boss," I explain.

"Glad I'm unemployed," says one of them. I give them the thumbs up, and go inside. I visit the men's room on the other side of the bar.

I change clothes and shoes. I wash my face. I smooth my hair. I walk into the oak-paneled bar with my shopping bag.

The TV is on. CNN. Muted, with the closed-captions running.

Patrick is sitting at a table with a martini in his usual Brooks Brothers suit. His back is to the television, so he can't see that our mother is on the screen. She is hustling out of the limo and into our apartment. She looks the way she always looks these days—harried and upset.

Mathilde Holbein firmly denies the IRS tax evasion charges. And in other news . . . The Dow Jones fell another 100 points . . .

I slide into the booth.

"Henry! Thank God you're all right!" he says.

I tackle the issue head on.

"Patrick," I say, "you know by now that I told the Historic Buildings Preservation Commission that we are abandoning the hotel project," I say. "I said we would drop the lawsuit."

Patrick looks in my direction. But he doesn't see me any more than he saw Joe.

"I'm glad you're in one piece. Mother was worried."

He takes out his cell phone. "He's fine. More later. No, don't talk to any reporters about the—" He looks at me, hangs up, and begins checking messages.

"The project isn't—" I start.

Patrick interrupts. "Don't worry—I'll fix it," he says. "I'll speak with the commission and with the contractor. The hotel project will proceed."

"It should *not* proceed!" I say. "It's a stupid idea."

Patrick continues tapping on his phone.

I lean across the vast wooden table and grab his arm. "Patrick, listen to me. Don't build that hotel. This is a compelling town with a complex history."

Patrick puts his finger up.

I try another tack. "Tell me," I say, "how is architecture going? Building anything exciting lately?"

"I'm too busy running the business," he says.

I keep holding his arm. "Remember the eco-garden house you said you were going to make: the one where you couldn't tell exactly which was outside and which was inside, that moved between exterior and interior with the help of retracting doors and roofs?"

"What the hell are you talking about?" Patrick pulls his arm away and starts fiddling with his breast pocket handkerchief.

"When we watched Cocteau's *Beauty and the Beast* that vacation before you started architecture school," I say. "You said you wanted to build a house like the Beast's. You called it a postmodern garden house."

He frowns. "I don't remember. Sounds like a pipe dream."

I am pretty tolerant, but Joe has no patience for denial. "What's wrong, Patrick?" I ask. "You're sad all the time just like Mom. Why? Your husband isn't dead. Your—"

Patrick leaps to his feet. "Don't talk to me about husbands!"

Then I get it.

"But Patrick," I say, "there's no problem now in being gay . . . Everyone accepts it, and it's totally fine, and I'm ok with it. In fact the girl I like, she's kind of—"

Patrick throws down a credit card. "Now that I've fixed your mess, and verified that you haven't killed yourself or something, I have to go back to the city and deal with the real world," he says. "Just stay away from the business. Go back to your fucking puppets." He marches out the door.

I sit for a while at the table.

Mom is in trouble. Patrick is in trouble.

Patrick comes back in. "I forgot my card," he says.

That's when Myles and Giles Fairweather, the Seelye Center directors, come in.

"Mr. Holbein!" they cry as they set eyes on Patrick.

I leap to my feet, run over to the bar, clamber over it, and dash into the kitchen.

The kitchen staff is busy getting the dinner orders ready for the nice home-style restaurant that's in the inn. I see an apron, put it on, and I say to the sous-chef, "Please, my big brother is out there and—"

"He's drunk," the assistant chef finishes.

"Yeah," I say, "and he wants to beat me up because my mom has always liked me best."

"Bro," he says, "I feel your pain. Take the apron but don't cook anything. Run out the back way over there."

I wish I had time to get my shopping bag with my Joe-clothes. I mess up my hair and put on a hair net.

The vets are still in the parking lot.

"Joe?" they say. "Are you a cook now?"

Jimmy pulls into the parking lot with the limo as Patrick walks out. "He was just here," he is saying on the phone.

Serenade rounds the corner with a tall blonde guy. It must be Harold. She sees me just when Patrick does.

"Joe?" she says.

"Henry?" says Patrick.

So I do what anyone would do in my position.

I climb on top of the nearest car and wave my apron around over my head.

"Aieeeee," I yell, jumping up and down. "Time to fricassee! I am the monkey king, lord of sautéing! Come and watch me prep! I'm a super-crazy chef!"

I climb on top of another car. The car alarms start chirping, so I have to yell louder. "See me make banana cake and then throw it in the lake!" I jump to another car. And another. Then I stand and pound my chest.

"Come on, you schnooks, ain't you ever seen a monkey cook?!"

"Jesus Christ," says Patrick. "He's finally flipped his lid!"

"Is that our neighbor?" says Harold in a hushed sort of voice.

"No," says Serenade, "that's the handyman."

I leap off the cars, still holding my apron. There are two old garbage cans with metal lids. I whoop, holler, and pick them up and bang them together like cymbals. "Give me a hand as I play my pots and pans!"

Then I run down the alley.

Straight into Mitch and Sue and the other art gallery workers, heading out of the Maple Leaf's back door.

"Henry!!!" shouts Patrick as he runs down the alley. Jimmy drives the limo, and after them come the vets, Serenade, Harold, and Myles and Giles Fairweather.

"Mr. Henry, don't do anything crazy!" shouts Jimmy belatedly.

Myles and Giles are trying to inquire politely about what the trouble is.

"That's my fucking younger brother," yells Patrick.

Sue and the workers gasp.

Mitch looks at Patrick and at the limousine. Then he looks at me.

"Is this true?" he asks.

I nod.

Sue shakes her head, and the workers shuffle their feet.

"You *lied* to me so I would I hire you, and in so doing risk my own job?" says Mitch.

"What the hell is going on here?" says Patrick to Myles and Giles.

"Wait, what?" says Serenade.

"I—I," I stutter. "I was trying, that is, I *am* trying to become someone different."

Mitch says, "You're an asshole, just like your brother."

"Now just a minute!" says Patrick, but no one listens.

Mitch punches me. I punch him back.

I have never hit anyone before, and I'm not very good at it, but Mitch hits me again, and so I have to try again.

Eventually I get better, or perhaps I should say that Joe does. Joe punches Mitch in the face. It hurts like hell, but then Mitch's nose starts bleeding, and that's really cool, and he pushes Joe and Joe grabs him and we, I mean, they, fall down, and roll around on the ground.

The person who I thought I was and who I've been performing for twenty-plus years wants to merge with the person I've been pretending to be for the past few weeks.

We will become a third thing. "I" can sense it.

Although who or what is "I" really?

(It's an interesting question.)

Meanwhile, one part of me witnesses while the other part acts.

"Hey, who's beating up my cousin?" Sean runs out of the Maple Leaf.

"You!" yells Patrick. "This is all *your* fucking fault!"

In between punches from and at Mitch, I can see that Patrick and Sean are at it.

There are four of us fighting now in the alley.

"Stop fighting this instant," says Serenade, but we ignore her.

"I . . . trusted . . . you," says Mitch, between jabs to my ribs.

"You . . . let . . . him . . . get . . . complete . . . ly . . . out . . . of control," says Patrick.

"You're an asshole."

"No, you're an asshole."

This is fun.

I get up and so does Mitch, and we punch each other around the corner onto Main Street. Patrick and Sean follow, and so does everyone else.

Cars stop.

The vets follow at a distance, urging us on.

Serenade screams to stop. Harold is trying to get her to walk away, but she won't, so he starts talking about late capitalism and the fascist state. The

Fairweathers have gone home.

Two cop cars come.

We all stop what we are doing. Sean is laughing. Mitch is swearing.

Then Patrick starts telling everyone who he is.

"Mr. *Holbein*?" says the officer in charge. The cops look at each other.

"What a summer!" says the second guy.

"Yeah," says a third. "First, the professor and now, *this*."

They look at each other some more.

It's clear that they don't want to arrest Patrick or me.

But in my new incarnation, I insist that we ought to be arrested. I spit on one officer, and then while Patrick is explaining that I am "disturbed," I punch my brother in the stomach as hard as I can.

"Why?" Patrick grunts as he clutches his ribs.

I keep right on punching. He punches back.

He's bigger. But I am angrier. "This one is for Oma," I say with what I think is maybe a jab.

"And this one is for making Cousin Sean your servant." Uppercut.

I am tired, and Patrick has just punched me in the eye, but I go on anyway. I punch him in the nose.

Something cracks.

"That's it," say the cops.

"Jesus," says Mitch. "And they say *I'm* the one with the bad temper!"

They put us in two different cars.

Serenade stands on the street as we pull away. She is clutching a huge purse to her chest. I notice she is wearing a tight black dress and very high heels. She looks gorgeous.

Patrick looks out the window and notices Harold and Serenade.

"Sven!" he says. "Sven, is that *you*?"

ix. An Absolute Beginner

I apologize to Mitch in the holding tank while Patrick arranges with Mom's lawyers to get us all bailed out.

"Rich people do fucked up things," I tell him as we sit side by side on the metal bench. "I wanted to be a regular person—for just a while."

"That's classist bullshit," says Mitch. "*No one* is a 'regular person.'"

"I know that now," I say.

Patrick is escorted back into a different cell, where I can hear Sean "ohming." Patrick shakes his head and mutters, "Sven, what have you done?"

"What is happening with the hotel?" says Mitch.

"It's a no-go," I say. "Mom is being indicted for tax fraud."

"So now what?" says Mitch.

I take a deep breath and tell him about the abduction.

Mitch nods. "Sounds like the Narrow Interior Mennonites," he says. "It's a break-away sect. My mom was from that community, but she said they were too weird, even for her, so she became a professional sex therapist and started the Caligari Institute here in town."

"I think they want me to put on a show," I say. "Will you help me? Then we'll build your fence."

"Tell me why the hell I should help you," says Mitch. He stands up.

So do I. "I will be a different man," I tell him. "I promise you."

Then he squints. "Did you get taller since you moved here?"

I hold out my arms. The sleeves of my pink shirt no longer reach my wrists. My shoes feel tight.

"I must be bloated," I say. "But Mitchell, I will be—I *am*—changed."

Mitch looks at me. He has very dark brown eyes, a little like Serenade's. He lifts his chin and smiles. "Fuck with me again," he punches my shoulder, "and I'll kill you."

✳ ✳ ✳

We are released at midnight, thanks to the Holbein special relationship with the city. Patrick walks straight to the limo, gets in. Drives off.

Sean waves as he heads back to the Maple Leaf.

Mitch and I walk to the Seelye Center. I explain to him what I know about the Danker puppets.

The center looks different at night. Outside, there are tables and chairs that I haven't noticed, and pine trees that I don't remember being there, and a fountain and some sculptures that I don't remember seeing before. The retrofitted steel and glass entrance makes the pink, illuminated pillars inside the center look at once old and new.

During the day the place feels empty, but now that it *is* empty, it looks full.

Mitch disables the alarm and gets out his keys.

We walk in, and I look up at the high ceiling in the atrium. It, too, is pink.

The lights shimmer and start to shift to green.

"The lighting automatically alters," says Mitch. "It's a bit disco, but I like it."

"It's pretty," I say as the pink-green illumination becomes aqua blue, like water.

We swim through the space, gliding over polished wood floors towards the back of the gallery, and Mitch unlocks an almost invisible door in the smooth white wall.

"Are you afraid of enclosed spaces?" says Mitch.

"Not anymore," I tell him.

We walk through narrow white hallways to a tiny metal elevator. We ride down to more white hallways and more doors. Mitch unlocks each one till we enter a low ceilinged white room lined with cabinets.

He pulls out a drawer.

I see a tangle of arms and legs made of wood. The limbs are blackened and scorched looking.

"Spare body parts. Don't let them freak you out," says Mitch.

"They don't." I put my hands in the drawer and rummage through the remains. They click and clatter. There are no bodies, and just a few heads. No faces on the heads that remain. They have been cut off jaggedly with knives or axes.

The air-conditioning whispers, *we stand in for those who were burned and drowned and buried. We replicate, we symbolize.*

"Do you hear something?" Mitch says.

"Always," I reply.

He looks at me.

I look back. Mitch's dark brown hair has red flecks in it. I inhale his smell of metal and lime.

"Folks keep finding appendages," Mitch says, "all over town."

"Dispersed," I say. "To maximize the chance of their being discovered."

Mitch strokes a burned hand. "It's sad," he says. "These were artfully made."

"We shall revive them," I say. I pick up one head that has a neck with a second head attached at the other end. I show it to Mitch.

Etched all up and down the long neck are words: *Defaced we save face. We protect the truth till its time of revealing.*

"Perhaps the faces aren't as important as we think they are," Mitch says.

"True," I say, "but I wonder if we shouldn't use photographs of our own family and friends as models for the new faces. That way they will look, just a little, like somebody specific."

"That's a weird idea," says Mitch. "What made you think of it?"

"Your fence did, and something else too," I say. "The past has to be connected to the present, to who we are now, and to people we know."

"What's your other idea?" he says.

"Serenade's roses," I say. "The beautiful is only the beautiful when we care for it, when it lives for us."

"I think someone has a crush," Mitch says.

I close the drawer.

"Are you aware that she's a bit different?" says Mitch.

"It doesn't matter. I've had so little experience with sex that I wouldn't know where and how to start with anyone anyway."

"Sounds like you need to visit my mom's sexual healing center," says Mitch.

He is still holding the puppet hand.

"But first," he says, as he places the hand very lightly on my cheek, "you can start with me."

I almost say, *I'm not gay*, but the fact is Joe doesn't know who or what he is, and Henry doesn't know either. But Jonah—the man birthed through drowning by the oversized Mennonite women—he *wants* to know. And inside Jonah there are other selves yet, trembling to express themselves. And put together, we all want to, and *do*, learn quite quickly in this white subterranean room that fills quite suddenly with writhing, living limbs.

✳ ✳ ✳

The next morning I go to the municipal library at the bankrupt college and ask for assistance with local history. The librarian makes a phone call, and then gives me a home address. I walk over, ring the doorbell. Dean Beatrice Bell—that professor—answers. I tell her I need help researching the Dankers, and I convince her to move in with us for a month.

"All right, young man," Dean Bell says. "We'll need a preliminary discussion with all the other researchers if you want to engage in a meaningful historical assessment and reconstruction."

I nod.

She looks at me over her glasses. "You look different."

"So do you," I reply.

I walk her and her rolling suitcase over to the house, and Grusha settles the dean in Sean's room.

"You never here anyway," my housekeeper says to my cousin. She plops his bedding on the retro orange sofa.

Sean grumbles an assent, an unlit cigarette hanging out of his mouth.

She turns to me.

"And by the way, I quit," Grusha walks into her bedroom and slams the door.

After I move Dean Bell in, I go for my session with Mitch's mother at the Caligari Institute for Hypno-Therapy and Sexual Healing.

She's a tiny doll-like blonde who wears a witch hat and black stilettos.

"We like to start our clients off with sexual role-play involving puppets," she explains. "Then we move on to hypno-therapy."

"I can play with puppets," I tell her. I remove her hat. "But I'd rather learn on a real person."

❋ ❋ ❋

Afterwards I walk back downtown to talk to the vets.

It turns out they are all poets. There are six of them.

"You need to organize," I say, "form a collective and take part in something bigger than yourselves."

"The sixties are dead, man," they say.

"All the more reason to create a community."

They roll their eyes at me. "Listen to the hotel man," they scoff.

"Do you want to reach people, or don't you?" I say. That's something both Patrick and my mother have said to me on more than one occasion.

And they listen to *that*.

"You—" I say to the guy who's name is Barry. "Come with me across the street."

We go talk to Myles and Giles at the Seelye Cultural Center.

Mitch is already there. He waves to me and gives me a thumbs up, which means, I guess, that he hasn't been fired because of the fight/jail thing and/or that he doesn't regret last night.

"We are thinking about an event at the center that will bring in the community and will also celebrate the history of Narrow Interior," he is saying as we arrive.

Myles and Giles put their hands together, their faces folded up small.

"At this point," says the less tiny one, who I think is Myles—clenching and unclenching his hands, "money is so tight that we're just trying to stay open."

"We really prefer offerings like film festivals," says Giles.

"Is that the best use of this space?" I ask. "People can stay home now and look at a screen."

"There's nothing like the heat of the real," says Barry.

"Yeah," I say, "like Barry says. What's your last name?"

"Murakami," he says.

"Are you by any chance Japanese?"

"Well, part."

"So, Myles and Giles," Mitch continues, "we're thinking the Seelye Center should sponsor an interactive event about the town's Danker origins, which will—"

"Not that cult!" says Myles. He looks at Giles who shakes his head emphatically.

"The Seelye Center's mission is to create a new narrative about Narrow Interior!"

"But there's *nothing new* to narrate about Narrow Interior," Mitch and I say at the same time. Mitch nods at me, and I continue.

"Except that you have a rock band who lives here, and some rich people from the big cities who come here, and you seem to have more than the average number of poets."

Barry says, "Shouldn't the past be confronted?"

"If you don't remember, you repeat, Freud said," Mitch points out.

Myles and Giles are still shaking their heads and squeezing their hands together.

"We don't . . . "

I take out my checkbook. "I would like to make a sizeable donation to the Seelye Center," I say.

Myles and Giles beam at me.

* * *

That evening we order in some pizza and have an organizational meeting at my house. Sean, Barry and his five poet friends, Mitch, Sue, and the two student assistants from the Seelye Center help themselves to sodas and beer.

Dean Bell arrives, bringing a former student named Allison, and Allison brings an old man named Mr. Olsen and his helper, Mr. Calvino.

"I remember you from the bar!" I say, shaking their hands.

"Thank God you put the kibosh on that idiotic hotel project, young man," says Mr. Olsen.

"I just hope this isn't going to be stupid," Allison says. She goes to the door when the bell rings. She brings in the pizza delivery boy. He grins enormously as he holds out two large boxes.

"Allison tells me you are engaged in creating a performance," says the pizza guy. "May I share that I am very fond of amateur theatricals?"

Mr. Olsen turns to the dean. "Is that really what we are doing?"

The dean responds by putting him on a subcommittee along with herself, Allison, and me to work up a rough draft of a script. Then the poets will make it lyrical.

Grusha would have been in charge of musical accompaniment. But she's in her room packing.

"Do you play an instrument?" I ask the pizza boy.

"Ali," he says, shaking my hand. "I have been known to attempt the harmonica."

I sigh. So, no music.

We must all learn how to handle the puppets.

I go into my bedroom, pull the Monkey King out of his suitcase, and bring him out to the group.

"Now we're cooking!" says Monkey, rubbing his paws together as he surveys the crowd of people in the living room.

"Damn!" says Sean. "It's amazing how you do that without moving your lips or even your arms!"

Grusha comes out of her room to get some pizza. She jabs Sean in the ribs. "Don't be stupider than you are already are, *malchik*," she says. "This is magic like in *Petrushka*."

I give Monkey to Barry. He takes him but immediately cries, "this stupid monkey is heavy!"

Monkey clenches his fists. "You're cruisin' for a bruisin', Clyde!" he shouts. "You better cut the gas or I'll—"

Mr. Olsen hobbles over and raps Monkey sharply on the head with his A.T. Cross pen. "*Cool* it right now with my friend Barry," says Mr. Olsen, "or you'll agitate the gravel." He pauses. "You dig?"

Monkey rolls his eyes towards Mr. Olsen, puts his paws together. "My apologies, big daddy," he says. "Didn't mean to frost you." He bows to the old man.

At lasssst, says the huge octopus tattoo rippling on Allison's chest. *Ssssomeone to keep hisss majesssssty in check.*

We all stand there till Barry breaks the silence.

"Mr. Olsen," he says wonderingly, "were you ever a beatnik?"

"Briefly," is the reply.

Mr. Olsen speaks in crisp tones about an ill-starred friendship with Jack Kerouac while I go get a dining chair for him to sit on. I bend, lift the chair, straighten up, and hit my head on the chandelier hanging over the table.

"Watch yourself there, big guy," says Sean.

x. The Best of All Possible Worlds, Almost

Over the next few weeks it gets hot, and Serenade's roses bloom so abundantly that they cover the top of the fence with rich, vibrant colors. The air is filled with their fragrance.

I buy a barbeque at the Narrow Interior Swap and Save Mart of the Inner Light and teach myself how to grill. Now I can have hamburgers any time I want them.

During the morning I visit the Caligari Institute, then I meet the dean at the library. At the end of the day, Jack LaLanne comes on the local TV station, and Sean and I do jumping jacks in the living room.

"Well now, Henry, just look at you!" Mr. LaLanne says.

I nod and start on my pushups. "I'm t . . . rying . . . Mr. La . . . Lanne," I huff and puff. "I'm trying as hard as I can."

The organizational meeting becomes a rehearsal, and the rehearsals happen every night except for Friday. No one likes to work on Friday nights in this town.

Everything's going great.

Except for two things.

Grusha has quit, but won't move out. She spends time in her bedroom, makes periodic trips to the kitchen, gets something to eat, and goes back in. At night she takes her car and her guitar case someplace, comes back late, goes to bed.

The house quickly becomes a mess. I add house management to my schedule. After each rehearsal, I run the vacuum cleaner and wash the dishes, check the laundry and take out the garbage.

"Did something happen?" I ask her as I clean out the vacuum cleaner brush's bristles. It's crazy how fast they get dirty.

"Boss, if you can't figure it out, then I am not gonna tell you," she says. Then she goes back into her room.

In other words, she's not talking to me.

The other problem is that Serenade isn't talking to me either.

Every morning when I look out the window and I see Serenade working on her roses, I walk out the door. The minute she sees me coming down the driveway, she rips off her gardening gloves, throws them down, marches back into the house, and slams the screen door so hard it bounces. Then I see her sneaking out the back of the house into the tent pitched in the backyard. Although, the hedges are growing so high I'm imagining that part rather than seeing it.

The first time this happened, I picked up her bright yellow gardening gloves from the rosebush. When I came back the next day, there was a new pair—bright pink sitting on the grass—that she threw down as I came running out. The next day the gloves were lime green. She has an infinite supply of them. Or else is ready to purchase them infinitely.

So I try returning the gloves. I walk over and ring the doorbell.

Harold the boyfriend answers. He has enormous pale blue eyes. He's tall and blonde, and I guess he's pretty handsome.

"Hi Harold," I say. "I'm your neigh—"

He interrupts. "Listen, I don't have time to talk to neighbors—I'm writing."

He's also very thin.

"I found Serenade's gloves." I hand him the three pairs.

"Ok then," he says.

"Could I speak to her?" I say. "Is she in her tent?"

"She's at work," he says. "Look, I'm very busy theorizing about Nietzsche and the will to power."

I experience the will to punch him in both of those blue eyes with my own personal power. But Dr. Caligari says that this sort of anger is not appropriate to express directly.

"Please tell her I said hi," I say as he's shutting the door.

✳ ✳ ✳

Sometimes when I am between my appointment with Dr. Caligari and my appointment with the dean, I walk around downtown N.I. Today, I run into Allison and we have a cigarette and talk. I light mine but don't inhale because frankly cigarettes are disgusting. Still, I want to be sociable.

"What should I do about Serenade?" I say to her.

"Nothing," she exhales. "You work on your puppet play thingie and you just proceed."

"I've spent my whole life waiting for things to happen, and quote-unquote proceeding," I say to her.

"Sometimes waiting is really cool," she says. She looks across the street, and I follow her gaze. Ali has come out of the Bollweevil Café and Literary Pizzeria and is sweeping the sidewalk.

"How's that waiting thingie working out for you?" I say. She looks at me as her octopus tattoo hisses a warning. She leans her head down and confers briefly with her chest.

"We kind of like it when you're an asshole," she says, looking up. "It's a lot more interesting—well it's a BIT more interesting—than the bland man-without-qualities thingie you were doing when you first moved here."

"Thanks," I say.

The tattoo whispers something, and Allison stands up.

"Mr. Olsen is expecting me for tea."

"Can I come?" I say.

She rolls her eyes. "Jesus, man, you really have no life do you?"

"That's my entire point," I say. "And the only way to start one is to—in the words of Dr Caligari—'connect with others in social situations,' which means going to have tea with that interesting old gentleman."

She shrugs her shoulders. "Ok, I guess."

We walk up the street. I have to say that I never get tired of downtown N.I. Myles and Giles are directing new young people to put up posters for the Danker re-enactment outside the gallery. There are punked-out high school kids skateboarding and swearing, although the minute they see Allison, they skate away FAST. The poets are declaiming to each other on the steps of what used to be the bank, and young moms with strollers are looking in the stores, sashaying in very high heels and short shorts, which is a surprising look in such a small town.

It's a great place.

Ali is still sweeping the sidewalk in front of the Bollweevil when we walk over. Allison stops to talk with him. She just stares and stares at him. Waiting. They finish talking, and he pats her on the back. She says goodbye and gets ready, in the slowest way possible, to walk on. I decide that waiting just may not work at all in some cases.

"Hey Allison," says this guy who looks like a Botticelli angel. Flowing golden hair. Aquiline nose. Perfect peaches and cream complexion.

"I'm not fucking talking to you," she says.

"Oh come on," he says as he tosses long, waving locks

"Fuck, no," is the answer.

This immediately makes me interested because I have not one, but two, people not speaking to me.

"Hi there," I say.

The angel boy lifts his chin in an aristocratic sort of way. Clearly, he went to private school too.

"Ah," he says. "The hotel man." His voice is also perfect. Surprisingly masculine for such a pretty face. Resonant, like he's about to announce the arrival of John the Baptist or a bunch of saints.

"I have to go," Allison says to me.

"*Former* hotel man," I say to the beautiful boy Allison isn't talking to. I introduce myself.

"Carter Bergman," he says, shaking my hand. "I'm a former as well."

"Goddamn it," Allison says. "Henry—are you coming with me or not?"

"Who is he?"

"He's the fucking drug dealer," says Allison. Allison's octopus thrusts out a tentacle: *You're bbbbbad.* The octopus shoots all its tentacles at the angel-boy who bats them away with languid fingers til Allison loses patience.

"I'm out," says Allison. "*Asshole,*" she finishes.

"*Former* drug dealer," Carter Bergman says to me, as she goes, Ali looking at her in wonderment as he continues to sweep (that sidewalk is dustless at this point).

"But no one ever wants to believe you. No one ever wants to hear your side of the story."

I nod noncommittally.

"Let's get a cup of coffee," he says, "and I'll tell you how it is."

xi. The (Former) Drug Dealer Tries to Tell His Story

We walk into the Bollweevil Café and Literary Pizzeria.

FIND YOUR FAVORITE AUTHOR HERE! it says in dripping yellow paint on the glass of the front door.

I realize I've never actually been INSIDE this establishment. And, looking around, I understand why no one has ever taken me here.

It's a junkyard. Dark red velvet on one wall. Graffiti on another. And on a back wall with windows, three sagging bookshelves with a mess of books—some piled on top of each other, some half-open, some double stacked, but none standing straight in the shelf like they're supposed to. There are busts of authors—I presume—in niches in the corners of the ceiling, which is festooned with hanging Tiffany lamps, chandeliers, Calder-style mobiles, Chinese lanterns, wooden fans, and Christmas lights.

On the wall with the red velvet are Charles Dickens mugs and Jane Austen teacups, commemorative plates of bookstores, authors, and famous literary quotes hanging on any space not taken up by the other stuff I just mentioned, and on every table as well as on every other available space there is some kind of objet d'art or action figure. On a coffee table near the sofa, I spy Edgar Allen Poe, and, whimsically—because he wasn't an author—Jesus. Next to him sits a chubby orange Buddha—also not an author, strictly speaking. Over them looms a fancy porcelain statue of Moses holding the Ten Commandments.

Lladro, I think. My mom has a collection of those.

"I'll take a latte, hotel man," says the (former?) drug dealer.

I go up to the counter and order two lattes and a slice from Ali who's working the register while the server is on break. I sit, and Carter starts right in.

"So in June I go to the Narrow Interior post office to pick up the package of weed that Sergei told Andrew was coming in the mail, and I get my paper slip out of the P.O. box."

"Wait," I say. "You ship marijuana by MAIL?"

The ex-drug dealer nods. He flips his long hair behind his ears. "And I go to the counter, and I'm always a little nervous at the P.O. because if things are going to go wrong, they are going to go wrong *here.*

"I'm in a hurry because I want to go home and eat lunch and think about the anniversary of my dad's heart attack, which happened on that very day, and drop some acid, which is what I do every year. And of course organize the delivery to the party of the local rock star who remains, you will not be surprised to know, a pretty big customer."

I shift a bit in my seat.

"How does this connect with Allison?" I ask.

"It will—anyway, the man right in front of me in line at the P.O. is really old, and he is talking nervously to the old crumpled up woman who is with him. I think at first Dutch, but I spent a summer in Amsterdam, doing acid and fucking prostitutes, and don't recognize any words.

"That means they must be German. But they are funny-looking Germans if you stop and look at them, which I am doing because this is the post office and everything takes a fucking long time. They aren't wearing Lacoste t-shirts and shorts and socks with their Birkenstocks or sandals, which even the old people do. They stand sort of huddled up with their arms crossed. When they open their mouths, their teeth have metal in them."

"Excuse me," says a tiny voice to someone.

"Andrew, for the record, positively hates Germans. He always quotes his grandfather who insisted, and I quote, 'You can't trust the Germans, because any German is a Nazi, the son of a Nazi, or the grandkid of a Nazi no matter what they tell you about being a member of the Green party.'"

"Who's Andrew?" I say.

"Andrew is my friend and business partner. He came out with me from Denver when I moved here to attend Geister College. Andrew always complained when we sold to German exchange students because, to quote him, 'Germans always act like they run the place.'"

"Excuse me Herr Holbein!" says the tiny voice again. I look around.

"What the hell *is* that?" I say to Carter.

"There," Carter points a professionally manicured digit.

I look down at the table. In front of my napkin stand two plastic salt and pepper shakers. They are shaped to look like tiny versions of the busts in the niches. But these have holes at the top of their heads for the spice. White and black. The white one is the one addressing me, because he hops forward and makes a little bow.

Carter sighs. "The tableware here always does that—just ignore them."

But I can't.

"Pleased to meet you, Henry Holbein," says the white plastic head.

"Wolf and I hear you're putting on a play." The other shaker hops forward.

"AND WE DEMAND to take part."

The pizza and lattes come, and the drug dealer is momentarily distracted by his drink.

I put my elbows on the table and move my face closer to the salt and pepper shakers. The white one has long hair tied back with a ribbon, a little like Thomas Jefferson, and the black shaker has short hair cropped close around his high forehead. He has expressive eyes and a determined chin.

"We would like very much to be involved with your production," continues the first one—who seems to be younger and looks sort of dreamy if you squint at him.

"But I must have top billing," says the pepper shaker head, who has a gruffer voice. "You see I'm a world famous author, and—"

"Wolfie, please," says the salt shaker in an injured tone. "No one *cares* about how famous you are. I wrote the words to Beethoven's 'Ode to Joy,' and you don't see me carrying on about it do you?"

"You just did," yells the pepper shaker who is tipping back and forth with rage. "You ALWAYS sneak in something about what you wrote when *I'm* the one who's really famous."

"Who are you two gents supposed to be exactly?" interrupts Carter. "I'm trying to tell a story here."

The pepper shaker leaps off the table and smacks the former drug dealer on his perfect nose, which—now that I look at it—is so perfect that I figure it has got to be a nose job.

I catch the pepper shaker in my hand on the rebound and put it—or rather him—back down.

"Easy does it, mister," I say.

I can't say I've ever heard a pepper shaker growl before.

"I apologize for Wolf, sir—may I call you Henry?" says the salt shaker. "It frustrates Wolf that we are not so well known in this century. But I assure you—we are quite crucial to the development of continental romanticism, and we continue to exert a considerable, if unseen, influence on American literature."

The salt shaker pauses to catch its breath.

"Please," I say. "You have the advantage of us. You know us, but we do not—yet—know you."

The salt shaker nods.

"Gentlemen—" he says. "Allow me to introduce my distinguished colleague, holder of the pepper, Wolfgang von Goethe, author of *The Sorrows of Young Werther*, *Faust*, and—"

"And don't forget all those fucking poems I wrote," interrupts Wolfgang von Goethe.

"Please be patient with him," says the salt shaker, shaking his head. "He has an enormous ego."

Despite himself, Carter is interested. He puts his latte cup down and leans in.

"And you?" he says to the salt shaker. "Who might you be?"

The salt shaker inclines his whole self in an even deeper bow—a gesture whose graciousness is slightly counteracted by the tiny plop of salt that falls out on the table from his head. "I am Friedrich Schiller, playwright, historian, and philosopher, who made Mary Stuart, Joan of Arc, and William Tell household words."

"Awesome," says Carter. "The author of *On Naïve and Sentimental Poetry*."

I look at Carter. He shrugs his shoulders.

"What? A person who has an alternative business model can't be well educated?"

"Blah blah blah," interjects Wolf Goethe. "What about our parts in the play Herr Holbein? And our DRESSING ROOMS?"

Friedrich Schiller looks up at me. Tiny etched eyebrows arch imploringly.

"Can you please put us in your play? Wolf is really suffering from insufficient artistic visibility."

"I'd be happy to involve you," I reply, bowing back over my pizza plate at the two important miniature German authors. "But you're a bit small to be puppets—"

"What about shadow puppets?" says Schiller. "Can't you magnify us somehow through a projection on a screen?"

"Speaking of shadow puppets," says Carter. "That was what was in my package from the post office!"

"Reduced to the status of marionettes," mutters Goethe. "We'll never hear the end of it from that goddamned Kleist."

"How curious that there are shadow puppets in our quaint village!" says Friedrich Schiller to Carter. "Do please tell us your story."

xii. The (Former) Drug Dealer Tries to Tell His Story, Continued

"As a matter of fact it WAS highly interesting," says Carter, hailing the server for another latte, even though this is a place where you're supposed to go to the counter and order.

"Because, as it turned out, these Germans that I saw at the post office were East Germans—and they were smuggling shadow puppets that made fun of the government into the country."

"Just a minute," says Wolf, "there's no East Germany anymore so no one cares about *that* government."

"You don't get it, boys . . . " says Carter the former drug dealer. "These puppets were making fun of the *current* German government. And the feds tried to intercept the package because—such puppetry might give people in the US ideas."

"How do you know that for sure?" I ask him.

He shrugs. "I'm in graduate school for public policy now. We learn how the behind the scenes stuff works. Also—I retain certain connections."

Goethe nods enthusiastically. "Yes, we attorneys also learned such things—about how government surveillance functions."

"That's the theater for you," Friedrich Schiller observes. "The stage is always a place where progressive political comment happens—the regime doesn't matter."

"That's not always true," says Carter. "The theater can also be a repressive space where the hegemony can reinscribe its—"

I go up to the counter and get another slice of pizza and pick up Carter's new latte while the three of them argue about the theater and enlightenment of the people. Some books by Bertolt Brecht and Caryl Churchill tumble off the shelf and land on our table, which makes the salt and pepper men squawk a bit.

While I'm up, a girl comes in. She's a teenager, not a skater, and she's carrying a square suitcase. She sits over by the books, opens the case, and takes out an accordion.

"Entertainment?" I say to the server.

"She always comes in after school," she says. "Just talk over it. She's not very good."

I'm paying for my second slice and the coffee when someone else comes in—a man.

Ali follows him in.

"Sir," he says to the man, "I can tell you that they aren't hiring here."

"I'll do anything, Marie," the man says to the server. "See, I was work-ing construction on that big hotel, and then the project went bust—"

I go back to my table and sit down. Quickly.

"How are you doing, Steve?" says the server.

"I'm trying to learn how to be hungry," he answers.

I slide down in my seat a little.

The kid with the accordion starts to sing:

And I roam and I roam and I roam and I search
For the narrow house that ain't no church
For the brown eyes that ne'er crossed the sea
That stranded keep longing for you and for me

Carter says, "So, about the puppet play—" But I'm listening to the singer:

I heard the words from a forgotten past
Of dollies, and dunking, and a love that lasts
Of brown eyes that sank in the cold North Sea
Still waiting and looking for you and me
In the house that ain't no church.

The girl has a pretty, if not always on-key, voice. She sings as a guy with a chef's hat tosses the pizza dough, decorates the pies, and slides them in and out of the oven—the door creaking open and shut. The girl sings as Ali comes in and out of the shop with a mop and clanking bucket, and the construction guy keeps saying he really needs work. And she sings with passion and intensity, as Carter gives a long, not very interesting descrip-tion of the party he ended up at after he delivered the marijuana, and how he dropped acid there and saw a puppet show.

I miss some of what the girl sings. But I catch the final verse :

Tell the builders of stone, leave the dankers alone
I heard the wind a calling
Let them perform the play, keep the pastors away
The birds sang all night long
And I cry to the trees, water rushing at me
Tell me where be the dollies I'm seeking

But the place we sought's been forgotten
For the house is lost and fallen.

The song ends, and the girl sits quietly with her accordion. The construction worker—or rather the guy who used to be a construction worker—gets his pizza box (I guess he got it for free) and leaves.

"So—" says Carter, leaning back in his chair. "Isn't that a wild tale?"

I look down at the salt and pepper literati.

"This town is filled with songs and ghosts and fragmented memories and sadness for what has been lost."

"You don't know the half of it, young man," says Goethe. "There's more to us than the Dankers, I can tell you. You hover on the edge of a larger mystery."

"What do you mean?" I say. I'm super hungry now and am thinking about just going ahead and ordering a whole pizza. "And who is 'us'?"

"The thankful ones," both Schiller and Goethe say at the same time.

I stand up and go order the meat lovers pizza—what a pizza would be if it was also a hamburger. I pay and sit back down.

"I don't understand what you're talking about," I say.

"Let me get someone who can explain," says Schiller. He calls out, "Count Georg!"

Schiller confides, "He's a former student of mine—his last name is Hardenberg, but he calls himself Novalis. He wrote a wondrous novel once about a man named *Heinrich*."

I tremble a little hearing the German version of my name.

A book flies off the back shelf and lands on the table. The author on the back cover smiles brightly.

"Freddy—what is it? I was drinking coffee with Wordsworth and—"

"The thankful ones . . . " prompts Schiller.

"Ah!" says Count Georg as he surveys the company. "We comprise believers who began even before those that called themselves the Dankers. They are a branch of us, but not the tree. The tree grew already in the Holy Land."

Carter peers at the objects on the table.

"I take it you are referring to the Crusades?" he asks somewhat sarcastically.

"Earlier, actually," says Goethe. "But we were there too—with the Knights Templar outside of Akko."

"The point is," interjects the Count, "we have been a part of German-ness all along and before German-ness even was—in the Holy Land, and then with the peasants in the Peasants' War, and with the Anabaptists, who claimed our name, but we continued everywhere we went, through the failed revolutions to the Great War, even to the White City of Tel Aviv, even to—"

"Bullshit!" Carter interrupts. He pounds the table so hard that the latte, the pizza, the book, and the shakers bounce.

Schiller says gently, "*Mein Freund*—we were also with your family in the place that cannot be spoken."

"Who?" I say. "What?"

"Anna?" Count Georg calls out. "Come help us."

Anne Frank's famous photograph—which has been transferred onto an elegant white commemorative plate—soars off of its hook on the wall, where it is hanging next to porcelain memorabilia with the photographs of Hannah Arendt, Marge Piercy, and an old-fashioned looking lady with a large nose, who, Schiller whispers to us, is the eighteenth century author, Rahel Varnhagen.

The gold-edged plate hurtles towards the ceiling and then circles down-ward like a small flying saucer and sticks a perfect landing on the table.

I notice that Anne Frank is wearing a necklace like my mother's.

"Greetings, friends!" says the Anne Frank plate.

She notices Carter.

Her plate rears up on its edge, twirls upward, and strokes his face.

"*Landsman,*" says Anne to Carter, "Never fear—we were with your *Leute* even at the end."

Carter puts his hand to his face and says, "Fuck." He says it over and over while the tears fall from his eyes, but harden—glistening like dia-monds on his peaches and cream cheek.

It gets quiet. I look around. All the people in the Bollweevil Café are frozen into position. The server has her knife poised over a fresh pizza pie, and the man making the pies has thrown the dough in the air, where it hangs suspended a few inches from the ceiling. He looks up at it.

I hear something: whispering at the back of the room, where the book-shelf is.

I try to get up out of my chair. I can.

I walk past the sofa where the girl with the accordion bends motionless over the instrument she was in the process of putting into its case. I follow the sound.

A group of books huddle on the table near the bookshelf.

"This *always* happens," an Elie Wiesel's *Night Trilogy* boxed set explains to *The Poetry and Prose of Tadeusz Borowski* and *Paul Celan: Selections*. "It will pass in twelve minutes."

"Things *should* come to a halt," says *SparkNotes to Primo Levi's "The Periodic Table."* *The Complete MAUS Summary and Study Guide* adds, "Time freezes because we have not overcome this history."

"Why can I move?" I ask.

"Because somehow you are linked," says the essay collection by Jacques Derrida.

That's when the Moses statue waves me over to his smaller circle, consisting of himself, the Jesus action figure, and the little orange Buddha.

"T-t-take a look," says Moses. He extends the tiny porcelain tablets to me.

I take the tablets, and as I look, the Hebrew letters morph into the English words:

Once upon   *there was a boy*
a time   *named Henry.*

I hear the room begin to come back alive. I hand the tablets back to the Moses statue.

He nods as he takes them, stuttering slightly:

"K-k-keep search-ing for—your truth."

"Mo is right," Jesus adds. "Dare to live your story, Jonah—dare to understand what your story means." They both turn to the Buddha.

"Yeah, and while you're at it, try to let go of things that don't matter!" the orange statue says, chuckling.

The pizza chef catches the dough, and the phone starts ringing.

"Henry!" Anne Frank calls. "Come back to the table."

I sit down again.

"Are you Jewish?" I say to Carter.

He wipes his eyes with a napkin. "Not practicing."

"I wonder sometimes if my mother's family may have been Jewish originally," I volunteer.

"If she is, then you *are*," says the Anne Frank plate, twirling a little. "Your roots matter—just like I am German, even though I wrote in Dutch."

Schiller hops over and up onto Anna's plate. Her arms reach out of the picture and embrace the salt shaker.

"Oh Fred," says Anna.

"I'm her favorite author," he volunteers shyly.

Goethe growls.

I remember at last why I sat down with the drug dealer in the first place.

"Carter—" I say. "Why is Allison so mad at you?"

"Oh that—" says Carter, shrugging his shoulders. "I had gone to the party to make the delivery, and I kind of had a misunderstanding with Allison's friend—the really cute, slender one . . . "

Schiller cocks his head, which means he tilts his whole self toward Goethe.

"Wolf, this sounds like your kind of story."

"Oh, shut up," says the pepper shaker. He march-hops to the end of the table and looks out the window.

"What happened?" I say. Carter shrugs again. It occurs to me that he is a big shrugger. "I thought she was just a bit drunk. It turns out she was very drunk."

"Did you have sex with her?"

"I tried."

"And what does she say?"

"That I tried too hard."

"What did you do afterwards?"

"What did you expect me to do? It was totally a misunderstanding."

I stand up and look over at the sofa. The girl with the accordion is gone.

"Would you like to come with me?" I ask Schiller and Goethe. They both shout "*Jawohl*" and jump into my hands. I put Schiller in my left pants pocket and Goethe in my right, so they will have equal billing and won't bicker too much.

"That was an illuminating story," I say to Carter.

"Seriously," says Carter. "Why can't people just get *over* things?"

I walk over to the counter and put some change in the tip jar. I start to ask about the salt and pepper shakers, but the server speaks up first.

"Just take them," she says. "They make a heck of a racket. Customers can handle most of what goes on in here—but those two are always over the top."

I walk to the door.

"So, maybe you and I can hang out sometime," Carter says to me in his resonant voice.

I shake my head. "I don't think so, man."

He shrugs. Takes out his phone.

"Come back soon, boys!" cry Anne Frank and Count Georg together. "We'll want to hear about the play!"

I wave to them.

"Andrew?" says the perhaps former drug dealer, moving perfect golden hair away from the ear pressed to the cell phone. "Andrew—where the hell are you?"

xiii. *Genji* or *Gawain*

That night, I run the vacuum cleaner, wash the dishes, check the laundry, and take out the trash. I set Schiller and Goethe on the kitchen counter where they admire the house and argue about whether mid-century modern is sentimental or naïve, aesthetically speaking.

After Sean goes to the bar and Grusha goes to bed, I sit in the backyard with Monkey King on my lap. I hear Serenade come out of her house and crawl into her tent.

"That octopus tattoo," Monkey King says to me one night, "do you think she digs me?"

"Don't know," I tell him. "Why don't you just ask her?"

"Jesus Christ," says Monkey, "haven't they taught you anything at that sex place? You can't just blurt the words out. You gotta be gallant and smooth with the chicks."

He jabs me. "And even more so with the cats!" He chuckles and lies back against my chest.

"You have to rock and roll like Prince Genji who had all those girls and whose every gesture's like a work of art."

"But Gokū-san, you can't act smooth when the girls in question aren't even talking to you . . . "

"Yeah . . . " he answers in a sleepy voice. "Then you gotta resort to being one of those tin-plate cubes in King Arthur." He stretches and curls up against me.

"They're squares, but they generally get the job done."

"Like who?" I say.

"I don't dig that stuff much," says Son Gokū. "But what about what's his name, Parzival's pal, who fights the jolly green giant?"

"You mean Gawain and the Green Knight?"

"Yeah, him."

I squint as the stars come out, trying to remember that story.

"What happens?"

"He makes with, like, the big 'I'm sorry' to the whole court!"

"But he doesn't get the girl, does he?"

"Henry, sometimes, you are so dumb I don't even know what to do with you. Just say you're sorry to the chickie."

"What if she doesn't accept the apology?"

"Then, you move on."

"I don't know if I can do that."

"Then you're still just a boy who's hiding."

When Monkey says that, I do something I never do.

I hold my puppet monkey to my chest.

And I cry.

Then, for some reason, I remember my dad. I stand up, carrying Monkey in my arms, and I walk down the driveway. We go up the quiet street, and I look at the woods that border it all the way to downtown. I remember walking with my dad outside my grandmother's house when I was very young. "The night sky," he said, "always makes me feel small and big at the same time, and I feel that whatever happens will be all right. There was a poet who said that once—that you could feel the power that rolls through things when you're outside."

Monkey and I look at the stars for a while, and then we walk back down the street and up our driveway. I look over at Harold's backyard, and I see the huddled shape of Serenade inside her tent, her shadow illuminated by a light inside.

I walk back to the porch and sit down on the rocking chair.

"The kind of gallantry you're talking about is a tall order, Gokū-san," I say.

"Don't I know it," he whispers. He pats my shoulder and immediately falls asleep.

✳ ✳ ✳

Another week goes by.

The Friday night before the Danker show at the Seelye Center, we don't rehearse. I look out the living room windows. The lights are on in Harold and Serenade's house.

I put on my pink Ralph Lauren shirt that I wore when I first came to Narrow Interior. I put on my chef's apron, and I fire up the grill and make myself a hamburger. Then I make two more: one for Serenade and one for Harold. I put them on multigrain buns with mayo and onions and the really good round pickles, placing the burgers on the blue willow china plates I inherited from Oma. I will take them over.

As a peace offering. An "I get it and I will be friends with both of you and I wish you all the best" offering. But I will talk too. I will say something like, "I'd like to apologize for my behavior towards both of you. Serenade,

I was very wrong to misrepresent myself as a handyman when I was really your eccentric rich neighbor all along, and Harold, I admit, I had designs on your girlfriend, and I was out of line. I hope you can forgive me."

It's what a gentleman would do, I figure. Gawain and Parzival would be pleased. Genji—I'm less certain of, but I'm no samurai. I take off my apron, pick up the plate, and walk down the driveway.

A shadow appears just in the corner of my vision.

I look around. Mr. Death hasn't appeared in a long time, but right now I feel him, just like a shadow on the edge of the seeable. "Stop that lurking!" I say to him. "Show yourself."

He does. But he starts morphing; he begins changing outfits like a monster from a horror film trying to find a final terrifying shape: the Sherlock Holmes get up, the cowboy, the Wall Street, the construction worker look. And then lederhosen, and after that a uniform that looks suspiciously like an SS outfit.

"Cut that out!" I say. "You know the German branch of my family resisted Hitler and then fled the country!"

Now Death cavorts like Fred Astaire, in white tie and tails. On his skull, a gleaming black top hat. Sometimes, I think he just likes to fuck with me.

"I'm busy right now," I tell him. "Go away or else help me!"

Mr. Death nods. He crooks a skeletal finger at me. I follow him up to Serenade and Harold's front door.

Death raises his/her hand in warning.

Death cups his hand to where his ear might be if he had one.

I press my ear against the front door and listen.

xiv. The Sorrows of Serenade

Serenade's voice is loud. Harold is harder to hear, but his voice gets louder as the conversation gets uglier.

"You promised," says Serenade. "You vowed you'd take me to the University of London. I have family from there. My ancestors came from London to Narrow Interior. I want to get in touch with my roots."

"I can't, baby," says Harold. "The post-doc is for one person and the money is tight and it's only a little more than a year."

"It's two years!" shouts Serenade.

I realize the hamburgers are getting cold, and they are excellent burgers so I figure I had better just eat them while I listen.

"Well, eighteen months *in tota*—" There's a rustling sound as someone tries to touch someone, but they get up and walk away

"And you'll save and come visit on vacations and we'll Skype and we'll chat, and I'll make it home at least one or two times, and it will be ok, and then I'll be poised for an actual tenure-track job—"

"No, it won't be ok," says Serenade. "You said you'd take me. You *promised* you'd take me."

"Well, I can't," says Harold. "And I can't say no to the Circumstantial Fellowship —it's a chance of a lifetime—it will never come again—it's the chance to really research and prove that Nietzsche and the will to power concept is connected to the various British empiricisms and not German idealism as has been traditionally believed and the work has got to come first if I'm going to have a chance at a real job in this challenging market, and I'll have to schmooze a lot of people and turn on the charm."

"You're ashamed of me!" says Serenade. "That's the real reason—you're ashamed of me because I never finished college and I want to be a singer, and I'm just a local girl who works in the library."

The pickles in the third burger slip out of the bun and onto the ground. The pickle is one of my favorite parts, and without the taste of the pickle the hamburger really loses something. It's starting to get dark, and I can't see where it fell.

"No no," says Harold. "Although—it wouldn't kill you to get a bachelor's degree. And perhaps wear clothes that are slightly less outrageous and perhaps learn to eat with your mouth closed. Be more fem or maybe more androgynous but stop changing your mind all the time. It's hard to explain this gender-queer thing to people."

"I think they're pretty fucking fashion-forward in London," says Serenade. "And as for gender, what about Carnaby Street, Bowie, Punk, Boy George, and Grace Jones FOR FUCKING EXAMPLES."

"Grace Jones is Jamaican—and would it *kill* you to eat with your mouth closed?"

"So you DO want to change me."

I finish chewing and get ready to knock on the door. *Hello there!* I will say, *I happened to make an extra hamburger, and I was wondering if one of you—*

"Well there are a few things that could stand some changing, LIKE THE INDOOR THING."

Silence.

"I'm indoors now," she says so softly I can barely hear.

"Yeah, but you're already perspiring. I can see it on your lip and on your skin."

"That's make up, you idiot," she says.

"Come on—" he says, "be honest—it's getting to you. The walls are closing in—I can see it."

"I could learn," she says.

"I know honey. And the eighteen months will give you time . . . you know?"

"No, you don't," she says. "You've never accepted me for who I really am—warts and all. And what about how I was going to try and get my singing going in London?"

"Oh Serenade, honestly," he says. There's a long pause.

"What?" she says.

"Honey, it's just not that good of a voice."

I drop the plate and the third hamburger. The plate hits a sprinkler.

"What the hell was that?" says Harold.

There is a backlit shadow at the side window next to the door. I don't crouch down or slip away. I'm ready to be seen.

Harold peers out the side windows. He doesn't notice me.

"That ridiculous neighbor gives me the creeps," he says as he moves away from the door. "Do you know he looks out the window all the time and watches our house?"

"Well that must mean that you're watching HIM," is the response.

Now there is murmuring that I can't make out. I hear stuff scraping and objects being moved around. The back door opens and closes.

I start feeling around for the remaining hamburger and the plate.

That's when Serenade says, "I'm leaving."

My foot connects with something. I pick up the plate and the hamburger that has fallen on the ground next to it, and, despite it being a little bit dirty, I shove hamburger number three into my mouth. I feel incredibly hungry.

The front door opens as I swallow the last of burger three.

Serenade walks past me with her tent bag and another bag. Harold follows her.

"It's over," she says.

"Hooray!" I say, but neither of them hears me.

Harold says "Don't leave, baby" sorts of things as Serenade gets into her car and drives away. Then he walks back into the house and shuts the front door.

I have succeeded in becoming completely invisible, just when visibility started to seem like a *good* thing.

I run into my house.

Grusha has come home and is practicing guitar in the kitchen with a skinny woman on another guitar. The dean stands there with them shaking the Schiller salt shaker and moving her head.

"Serenade's gone," I tell Grusha.

"Go after her," she says.

"Yeah," says the other guitarist. "She probably hasn't even left town yet."

The phone rings.

Serenade! I think. I go to answer.

"Who is *that*?" I ask Grusha, pointing at the skinny guitarist.

"It's Cassandra," says Grusha. "She and I like to jam."

"Hello?" I say.

"HENRY-IT'S-PATRICK-DON'T-HANGUP!" shouts Patrick.

"What do you want?"

"It's Mom," he says. "She's being indicted. She's under house arrest!"

"Did she ask you to call me?"

"No," says Patrick. "I don't know what to do for her and I'm afraid she'll do something—desperate."

I am silent.

"I need you to come right away. I have a situation here," he says.

"Well, I've got a situation *here*," I say. "I'll have to get back to you."
I hang up.

❋ ❋ ❋

I don't know who to call about Serenade. So I do three things I've never done before.

I borrow Grusha's car, and then I drive it to the Maple Leaf. And then I actually ask my cousin Sean for some advice about women.

Sean is sitting at a table with Mitch's mother.

I tell them about Serenade.

"Jesus," says Sean. He looks at Dr. Caligari and then takes a gulp of beer.

"What does she fear most?" asks my sex therapist.

"Being inside," I say.

"Well, where's the most OUTSIDE place you can think of around here."

"I have no fucking idea," I say. "I'm not an out-of-doors person!"

"Cuz, that's not really true anymore," says Sean. "What about all that walking you do?"

They think—too slowly in my estimation.

"I am afraid she's left town," I say.

"Did she take all her things?" says Dr. Caligari.

"No . . . " I say. "She had her tent and a totebag or something."

Dr. Caligari lets out a deep breath. "Well, then she can't have left town—she left all her clothes there and she'll want to get them!"

I think about Serenade's many different outfits and hairstyles.

"You're right," I say to the doctor. "She must be planning to come back and get all that."

"Groovy," says Sean. "So that means she's gone off some place to cool off."

"And pitch her tent, I guess," I say.

"Well," says Dr. Caligari, "then that's where she is."

"So . . . where can you camp around here that's open and not get like arrested or molested." Sean smiles at himself for this rhyming set of *bons mots*.

We all look at each other.

Geister College campus. Near the lake.

"Ok," I say. I turn to go.

"Wait," says Sean. "She maybe needs some space. I mean, don't let her leave town, but . . . "

My cousin pauses. "Don't go talk to her with whatever declaration you have to make and think she's just going to love you." He looks at Dr. Caligari, who presses her tiny hand on top of his meaty one.

"What I mean is, I have learned that you can't force things. You can only—"

Sean takes a breath. "Be present, offer yourself to that person—all of you, in any way they can use it, even if it's not a way you want or like. If you love the person, you want to serve them in a truly unselfish way."

"Right?" he says to Doctor Caligari.

She smiles at him. I turn to go.

"Wait!" says Sean. "Let me drive you." He stands up.

"No," I say. "I need to do this myself."

"But Henry, you haven't let me help you yet," he says.

"Come on, Henry," says Dr. Caligari. "Let Sean drive."

✸ ✸ ✸

We drive up the hill, and I tell my cousin to wait in the car.

I go through the fence and around the hole that is or was the site for the Holbein hotel.

And there I am by the lake where I almost drowned and where I saw Molly and where I thought I had transformed myself. But in the end, you are always just who you are. Just as Monkey has to be Monkey and Tripitaka has to be Tripitaka and Gawain has to be Gawain. And Parzival has to go back and ask the questions to Amfortas, but he needs that whole huge book to figure out how to do it because he's what you call a super-slow learner. Because you are locked into your incarnation or your fate or what God or destiny or I don't know what has got you locked into.

The moon is out, and Serenade is sitting outside her tent, near the water.

I walk over and ask if I can talk to her.

"Have at it," she says.

"I am sorry for many things," I say, "but I am most sorry for lying to you about who I was. I hope you can forgive me." I crouch on the ground when I say this. I look into her eyes. They are pissed off looking brown eyes.

"Go on," she says.

"I'm sorry I lied to you and then kept up with the lie—"

"Which you would have just kept up," she interrupts.

"Yes," I say, although it's extremely annoying when you're trying to apologize and the other person feels they have to correct and amend what you're saying, as you are trying to say it.

"Which I would have kept up indefinitely."

"That was a complete bullshit thing to do," she says.

I bow my head in assent to this assessment.

"Why should I trust you now?"

"Honestly?" I say. "No reason other than the fact that I genuinely like you." I decide against "love" which is not tactically advisable under the given circumstances.

Then I say, "Because I am genuinely trying to change."

Serenade leans forward, til her face is rather scarily IN MY FACE, and says, "Are you normally this much of a liar?"

"Yes I am," I say, looking back at her. "I became a liar because of my family, but that's no reason to take it out on anybody else."

She's quiet for a moment, thankfully. She sits back.

"Please forgive me," I say.

"I'll think about it," she says. "I'll *consider* it, if you come swimming. I like this lake, and it's fun to swim in your underwear, and I think you'll look ridiculous and that will please me, rather."

We strip down to our underwear and start walking into the water, which is fucking cold because it's a lake and lakes are cold.

Truth to tell—I will not remember much of that swim.

Only that I do it. Eyes closed most of the time. Trying to remind myself that at least I'm not in a tunnel after having pissed in a cup in front of three enormous women and almost drowning.

I open my eyes only when Serenade calls to me to get out before we both freeze to death.

I get out and lie on the bank next to her.

Serenade's underwear is almost, but not quite, transparent. She's got buff muscled arms, and small but pretty breasts—at least that's what the bra shows. Her waist curves in, and her legs go on and on to surprisingly small feet.

"Do you ever wish you were dead?" she asks.

"Sometimes," I say.

I can't think of anything else to say.

We lie side by side. I listen to her breathing for a long time.

Finally she rolls over onto her stomach.

"Do you think I'm pretty?" she says.

"I do," I say.

"Harold always thought I looked too masculine."

"I think you look fine."

She snorts.

"I cross-dressed as a man for a while," she says. "But I got tired of it. It wasn't the entire truth either."

"So you play with identity," I say. "You're fluid."

She snorts again. "Well, you'd be the one to know about *that*."

Then we just get quiet. We lie there for another long time. There are birds singing in the trees, and frogs croaking, and crickets chirping. I guess this is what they call a pastoral moment.

Finally, I stand up and offer Serenade my hand. She waves it away.

"I don't know what I'll do without Harold," she sighs. "And my dream of London."

I want to say things like, "Are you crazy sleeping outside in public by yourself at night?" and, "How do you plan on getting your clothes back when Harold retains possession of the house?" and, "You'll have to take your career into your own hands if you want to be successful and not rely on some pipedream, young lady."

I realize for the first time that my mother and I may not be as different as I thought we were.

"Well, I'm here if you need me," I say. "You can even pitch your tent in my backyard if you want."

"No thanks," she says. "I'm still mad at you."

"I don't blame you," I say. Then I put my clothes back on over my semi-dry underpants.

"See you," I volunteer.

She says, "Try to stay out of trouble!"

"You know me," I say. "Good as gold."

In the moonlight, I can see that she is giving me the finger.

I walk back to Grusha's station wagon, but when I get there the driver's door is open.

Sean is sitting in the driver's seat, one leg hanging out.

I lean in.

Sean is soaking wet. Unlit cigarette in his mouth. Eyes closed.

"Sean!" I say.

My cousin opens his eyes. "Sean," he mumbles. "I used to be called that."

He staggers out of the car, and at first I just get out of the way. Sean throws his cigarette on the ground. Then he takes the entire pack out of some hidden sari pocket and dumps the death sticks out.

I take his arm to steady him. He must be drunker than I thought.

"Let's just go home."

"I think I prefer to walk," he says, squinting.

"Since when?" I say.

A cell phone rings. Sean looks through his robes, pulls out a square device.

"Where'd you get that?" I say.

He ignores me. Listens.

"I'll do my part," he says curtly into the black square. "I just gotta— NO—DON'T FUCKING SHOW UP. Dude, I mean, Sensei, I mean— whatever—I'm ON THIS."

I get in the station wagon as my cousin hangs up, wrings out his wet monk's robe, and strides away from the car.

I drive back home. Then I go inside and sleep.

I dream that the bed keeps shrinking, and that my feet dangle over the edge.

xv. The Play's the Thing

On the Saturday morning of the performance, I phone Mr. Marlin, the family accountant.

"My Narrow Interior account didn't get its monthly deposit," I tell him.

"I'll take care of it," he says. "But you should know—things aren't going so well with your mother's appeal."

I hang up, and Sean stumbles into the house.

"Where have you been?" I say. "You need to stop buying everyone drinks at the Maple Leaf."

He looks at me. "I've been thinking," he says.

I raise my index finger. I don't have time for a bullshit explanation. "Have you ever considered seeking employment?" I continue.

"Joe," he says, "there are no jobs anywhere."

"Then help out around here," I say. "Wash the car. Do something about those weeds."

Amazingly, he nods and goes right out and does both jobs.

I remember a story my Oma told me that ended with the hero saying, *We must cultivate our garden.*

It's too early for hamburgers, so I fry up some pancakes and eggs and bacon in the new frying pan I bought at the Narrow Interior Thrift Shop.

Grusha and the dean watch the news on TV while Sean comes back in and washes the frying pan. Then he sets the table.

A lot of bad stuff is happening in the world. I walk in and turn the TV off.

"Hey!" I holler. "Who wants a hearty breakfast?"

✳ ✳ ✳

At eleven thirty on the Saturday end-of-summer weekend, Sean, the dean, and I drive over to the Seelye Cultural Center. The show is supposed to begin at twelve noon. All six poets are present already. Allison comes in with the pizza guy Ali, and Mr. Olsen arrives soon after on his new Segway along with Mr. Calvino. We put on our black sweatpants and our black t-shirts. And over that, black hoodies. We all have black masquerade half-masks to put over our faces.

In my pockets I have the German author salt and pepper shakers. I have told them they can be my prompters, in case I forget something.

"*Wunderbar!*" says Fred Schiller (we are now on a first name basis). "It's like being a director!—All powerful but behind the scenes."

"*I'm* the director, then," says Wolf (I told him Wolfgang was too hard to say). "You're just the assistant."

Mr. Olsen interrupts, "I feel like a goddamn idiot in this outfit." Since he has refused under any circumstances to wear sweat pants in public, he is sporting a black Brooks Brothers suit, a black shirt and tie, and a black Fedora.

"You look like a Mafia boss," Mr. Calvino says. "And I mean that in a good way." Mr. Olsen harrumphs at that until Allison soothes his feelings.

"I think you look sophisticated," she tells him. The old man thinks, then nods.

Mitch, Sue, and the museum workers have brought the new puppets and a bunch of props. The chairs are set up while Myles and Giles stand near the front door to greet visitors.

Twelve o'clock arrives.

Then twelve fifteen, and then twelve thirty.

No one comes.

Myles and Giles smile their tight smiles. "This has happened with several of our events, so I wouldn't feel too badly. We can proceed anyway and see who comes in, or we can—"

The space at the Seelye Center has lost the magic of the other night. Now it feels truly empty.

"No," I say. "We can't just do this for ourselves. We've done that already. The show needs to go out to others."

I walk outside. I need to think what to do.

"Dude," says one of the skater kids who are cruising up and down Main Street.

"You're not a—mime—are you?" The others groan in exaggerated horror.

"Or a clown or a folk-guitarist playing like BOB DYLAN?"

"Van Morrison's worse," says another.

"Wait!" says a fifth guy or maybe it's the first one. "Aren't you that hotel trust fund loser who like went crazy downtown and went to jail and like your eccentric rich family like bailed you out?"

"That's me!" I say (NOT TELLING ANY LIES). "And if you wait right here, we'll show you something even more eccentric!"

I go back into the Seelye Center.

"We're going to take this show outside," I announce. Myles and Giles are already folding up the chairs. The poets get our props, and all of us take the puppets, and we walk out of the building and march towards the old bank.

"Lookie here," say the skater boys, "it's Narrow Interior Occupy!"

"Shut the hell up," says Allison, "or I'll set you on fire for real this time!"

"Yessss sssstupid boyssssss," says a voice emanating from her chest.

The skater boys get silent. But now they're curious, so they glide alongside of us.

I carry the Monkey King, even though he isn't in the play. He refused to be left behind, and I couldn't refuse my old friend's request.

Serenade is standing outside the bank.

Wearing black.

"I'm here to do the play," she says.

"How do you know it?"

"You're not the only one who knows how to spy on the neighbors," she says.

I shake my head at her genius.

"Great—we'll need to make a couple of changes to the script you heard," I say to Serenade. We walk up the steps.

"My voice isn't loud enough to carry outside," I tell her. "So I'd like you to do some of the narration and your own puppet voice."

End-of-summer Saturday shoppers are getting out of cars, and tourists are here for a final run at discounted maple syrup, postcards, and Cassandra t-shirts.

She stops walking.

"Wait," Serenade says. I wait.

More people get out of cars and walk up the street. There's talking and complaining and kids saying they are hungry and already bored.

"I'm afraid," Serenade says.

"But this is your dream," I tell her.

"That's why," she says.

I look down at my sneakers. Women can be frustrating people to deal with.

Thankfully, Monkey King raises his arm and puts it on her shoulder.

"Don't you worry, dolly, I'll take care of you," Monkey says.

"I don't understand it," she says. "I wanted to—make the show—happen and I wanted—to be a part of it. But now I—" she pauses and shakes her head.

"I don't want anyone *seeing* me." She looks up at me with her brown eyes.

I realize that I am finally taller than her.

"No one will see you," I say. "That's the beauty of *bunraku*." I squeeze her arm with my own hand, let go of it, and then I gently pull her hood back up and move her mask down over her face.

"You can be visible and invisible at the same time! People look at you, but really they don't see you, because all they see is the puppet."

Serenade shudders. "Really?" she says. Very low.

"I promise," I say.

I embrace her. I hold her in my arms and kiss her very lightly on the lips. They are salty from her tears and a bit sweet from pink lip-gloss. But all in all, it's a pretty satisfying experience.

A smile trembles up under the black half mask.

I go to the top of the steps of the bank building, and we arrange ourselves on different levels sort of like a Christmas pageant.

I hold the Monkey King to my chest and clack the sticks. I know this part of the play by heart.

But before I can say anything, an enormous voice emanates from Serenade:

"ONCE THERE WAS A WOMAN WHO DRESSED AS A MAN," she chants.

People walk by.

Monkey King lies inert in my hands.

I close my eyes for a moment. I think of Oma and Mr. Gilbert and the others: the puppet troupe from years ago.

"LISTEN," I shout.

The skaters start shouting too. "Listen, you stupid people! Pay attention!"

I nod to Serenade who takes up the recitation:

Listen! In 17th Century old Japan
a beautiful woman dressed like a man
travelled with her father across the sea
to meet the pope in Italy.

Teruko, which means shining child, becomes Christine
She and her husband—folks you've never seen
Lost in history without renown
Are the parents of Molly who founded our town—

A lot of people don't look, but a few do.

I give Serenade the signal, and she raises her arms like a conductor. We all shout:

This is our hidden history
How Narrow Interior came to be—
What is close starts far away
The unremembered haunts today.
The fences, the bells, everything you here see
Starts with Christine from Japan and her puppetry

"What's with the hoods?" someone says.

"Mommy, look at those Halloween people!" says a small boy. He and a bunch of kids start pointing as their parents drag them towards the stores.

Serenade looks at me. I tilt my head.

"Let's follow them!" she says.

So we do. The skaters help Mitch and Sue with the props, saying, "Yeah, yeah!"

People are beginning to look at this group of people all dressed in black marching up the street. I raise Monkey King up at the front of the line, and Serenade joins me as we all repeat the lines from the opening:

The hidden history of what's come to be
In a play right now for you to see.

"See! See!" chant the skaters.

There's a Saturday end-of-summer sale going on at the bakery/mill that is now a mall, and everyone is piling in there, so we all pile into the main lobby area after them.

Then I realize something. I look at Serenade.

She looks up at the huge skylighted atrium. And gives me a thumbs up.

A security guard gets ready to stop us, but Sean knows him, goes over, and says quietly, "Brother, we're doing some performance art sponsored by the Seelye Center. Can you help us?"

"Sure," says the guard. "Buy me a beer afterwards?"

So much for saving money, I think but don't say.

Sean, Mr. Calvino, the poets, and Mitch have been lugging the puppets. But they've been holding them backwards, their faces concealed in their arms and chests till now.

We make a quick huddle in the entrance, and Serenade jumps out of it, holding a beautiful lady puppet, like the Japanese lady Oma gave me long ago.

"Look at that big puppet!" says someone.

It's Gomer, finally out of the hospital.

Serenade moves the arms and head of the beautiful lady. I give the Monkey King to Sean, and I work the lady's puppet legs.

The play is actually happening—we are underway. Serenade breaks through our circle and swoops among the surprised shoppers like a composite ninja warrior. I watch her go.

"Woah!" says Sean softly as he struggles to hold on to the Monkey King, who squirms in his grasp. "Excuse me," he whispers to two moms as he steps over their strollers.

Serenade tilts her head and she chants.

"*OH I am a-grieved!*" she chants in a high strange voice that is no longer quite her own.

> *To dwell in a land where I must be masculine to attain value*
> *and where my Christian faith cannot be shared. Oh I am a-feared!*

A lady wearing an enormous crucifix, who is buying potholders at the Potholder Shack, turns at the word "Christian."

The dean nods at Gomer, who steps up to help her carry a samurai puppet past the Cookbooks 'n' Things Shop.

Mr. Calvino nudges Mr. Olsen.

"Oh," says Mr. Olsen, "uh—" He speaks rather than sings like the old guy in *My Fair Lady*:

> *Do not weep, oh my own! We shall journey to the Bishop of Rome!*
> *I, Hasekura, Samurai, will receive his blessing and bring Christianity*
> *back home triumphant to our nation.*

The crowd sighs as the samurai puppet strokes the face of his puppet daughter with an elegant hand. Serenade's puppet inclines her head and makes an elegant gesture with both sets of long tapering wooden fingers.

> *Do not bewail your feminine station—*

The shoppers applaud loudly at that line.
Mr. Olsen as Hasekura keeps chanting:

> *Verily, you are my most beloved child.*
> *Thus, I would never leave you behind.*

Serenade has her puppet bow reverently to Hasekura while she chants:

> *Have thanks, noble father and now on to the ship!*

Serenade points her puppet's arm towards the candle kiosk. I manage to get over to her so I can start moving her legs.

> *But first—*

Mr. Olsen says.

> *A disguise*
> *To conceal yourself from prying eyes!*

"Ooh," say the moms with strollers, "don't you love those?"

> *To protect you as you sail the perilous seas.*

Two poets come and put a pair of pants on Serenade's lady puppet over the bottom of her kimono. Mr. Olsen the samurai explains.

> *The secret of your gentle gender*
> *must be kept until we may safely tender*
> *Our humble greetings to His Holiness*
> *Once we've arrived in the Christian West.*

Serenade makes her puppet shake her head no and then comically shrug her shoulders and nod yes finally.
The parents in the mall laugh.
I give Mr. Olsen the signal, and he starts talking again while the dean moves the samurai's arms.

> *And on the long voyage to give us cheer*
> *The artists of the small—bring my puppet turners here.*

The shoppers from the kite store and the chipmunks store and even the maple syrup tasting room gather in the lobby of the mall. Those of us not performing spread out to form a circle around the puppeteers.
"Look," we all shout, "BEHOLD THE MASTER PUPPET TURN-

ERS!"

Allison, Mitch, Sue, and two of the poets march into the circle, holding Mitch's masterpieces.

Puppets that are miniature bunraku puppeteers. And they hold tiny puppets, and these puppets work.

Allison cries,

> Oh Lord Hasekura, we too are Christians of low degree!
> We too would travel the open seas!

"*Pray let us attend you*," they all say in unison, "*and our musicians too.*"

We pause here for a moment because we were going to use recorded music but can't because we don't have that equipment.

In the pause, the woman with the crucifix shouts, "This is a mockery of Christianity!"

"I blame you for this, Larynx," she hisses at Allison. She glares at Mr. Olsen and strides towards the door. A few members of the audience start murmuring and shuffling as the cash registers start up again.

"Excuse me, *please*, I'm trying to get out," says the imperious lady with the crucifix to someone.

"Be thee silent," says a familiar voice.

Nine Mennonite women enter the mall with Grusha and Cassandra. G and C are playing guitar music that goes pretty well with what we've been doing. I guess Grusha's been spying on the rehearsals too.

Three familiar women walk into the bunraku circle. They are so big that they just push through the crowd, which falls back on either side of them.

I know those women, and there's no way I'm going to try to stop them from doing whatever it is they want to do.

Only Mr. Olsen seems unabashed.

"Excuse us, ladies," he says. "We are in the middle—" They brush by him and go straight to Serenade.

"Proceed with the *spiel*, sister," they tell her.

Serenade smiles at them.

"Hey," says the Maple Leaf bartender—who was looking for some aftershave at the Smells R Us counter—to the salesperson, "isn't that Cassandra?"

Complicated scenes follow: one involving a pretend ship, another involving a storm, and another involving an emergency landfall in France. Then there's the meeting of two lovers—one European and one Japanese—who are Molly Winston's parents. The whole thing culminates with the dean's explanation of what the Danker religion may have consisted of.

Serenade leads us as we all chant:

> *Daughter Molly creates yet another sort of practice,*
> *Merging east and west, Jesus, German legends, Buddha, and the acts*
> *Of good people throughout time and space—*

While we're finishing up, the three Mennonite leaders grab the Monkey King from Sean. The largest woman looks at me and rips the Monkey King's head from his body.

I feel a terrible pain. This was the last thing I have from my grandmother.

The crowd gasps. And I gasp too.

Because there's a second head on the other end of the Monkey King's neck.

The Mennonite woman flips the head around and sticks the monkey head back in the puppet body.

The new head . . . well, it looks a lot like Jesus.

None of us know what to do next.

It's the dean who saves the day.

"Why it's Bernhard Hoffmann!" she proclaims. "Molly's intended!"

The three women hold the puppet while Mitch and I quickly grab the clothes from the Molly's Dad puppet and put them on the former Monkey King now Jesusy-looking puppet.

They hold the puppet up while I quickly chant:

> *But that my friends is another tale*
> *We'll end our play here and wish you well!*

Then I clack the sticks.

Serenade pulls off her hood and mask and shouts: "Walk with us to the old Danker meetinghouse! Come learn how to operate the puppets, and learn more about our town's Danker history!"

The rest of us take off our hoods and masks and bow.

Applause is followed by a hubbub as we line up to march up to the meetinghouse.

The three Mennonite women and Serenade go to the head of the line, followed by the dean. The rest of us mesh in with the audience.

"What the heck kind of story is this?" asks a woman next to me.

"It's kind of like *Shōgun*," says someone else. "They have to go get a doctor to help the old guy in the fancy robe. The puppet with the sword."

"Isn't the son really a girl?" ask two teenagers.

Someone else asks, "Is this show free?"

"Sure!" I say. "It's sponsored by the Seelye Center!"

We start walking. People chatter and make comments.

I walk by myself in line until John Russell, the hotel contractor, catches up to me.

"Say, Mr. Holbein," he says, "are you in charge of this thing?"

"No," I say, "Serenade is."

"She's amazing," he says. "Really a local hero. A visionary."

"Isn't she?"

"Henry," Serenade calls, but then she gets distracted talking to people and shaking hands.

John and I walk up the hill with the crowd.

"Are a lot of people out of work because of the hotel cancellation?"

"I won't lie to you," says John. "It's hurt quite a few folks."

Just then a little girl jumps out of line and hugs me. I hug her back.

"The tall lady said to do that," she says.

The bells on the fences are ringing.

Henreeeeee

Somehow Mennonite women hand the puppet who was the Monkey King down the line, and he ends up in my arms. Now, I guess he's Bernhard Hoffmann, Molly's fiancé.

"What's going on?" yells something in my pocket.

John Russell holds the Monkey King while I fish Fred and Wolf out of my pockets.

"Look!" they say.

All along the fences and on top of all the buildings are the shimmering forms of people. Some look like the Dankers and are holding puppets, but, behind them, still others stand wearing strange hats, turbans, and veils. Still others glimmer behind them—so many. They are waving at us.

"This is something," says John.

"You see them too?" I say to him.

"Of course," he says. He shudders. "I'm just glad that skeleton friend of yours isn't with us this time."

I smile. Then I turn my attention to my bunraku figure.

"Who are you really?" I ask my puppet, although I think I know the answer.

My puppet smiles back at me.

"I am all of them," my grandmother's bunraku figure replies in a voice at once new and familiar.

"Including you."

"Good to know," interjects John Russell. "I'm a universalist myself."

"This is quite a successful production we put on," Wolf Goethe tells Fred Schiller.

❋ ❋ ❋

Back at home, I fire up the grill and start making hamburgers with the help of the salt and pepper shakers. I'm cooking for the performers and their partners and friends, and people who've just turned up after the dunking in the lake. We're all wet, and we are sitting on towels or outside on the patio.

The TV is blaring.

Grusha calls me inside because we are on the news.

"Performance art comes to Narrow Interior through the puppetry of Serenade Hoffmann and a troop of local residents, including a local scholar, a gutsy senior citizen, a group of Vietnam vets turned poets, a college dropout, and one very brave little boy," says the Confidence Valley anchorwoman.

"Here's Samantha with this heartwarming story."

We see our local TV reporter standing in one of her very short skirts with Myles and Giles Fairweather in the Seelye Center.

"Tell us, Myles and Giles, how this performance came to be."

"The Seelye Cultural Center believes strongly," says Myles, "in bringing art *to* people in meaningful and user-friendly ways."

Samantha nods and wrinkles her forehead.

"This was why we decided against a traditional performance in an actual building," says Giles. "And why we felt it was crucial to begin addressing the local history."

I serve Grusha and the dean their hamburgers as the segment cuts away to the professor standing with the Narrow Interior Mennonites outside the Danker meetinghouse. She is wearing her cap and gown, and she is grinning with excitement. She is flanked by a woman and a bearish looking man, both wearing LIBRARIANS RULE t-shirts.

"It was a fortuitous discovery at the municipal college library, but actually—" The professor gestures toward the nine enormous Mennonite women. "These women are the real experts," she says. "They still practice the Danker ways."

Samantha turns to them with shining eyes. "What happened to the Dankers?" she asks.

"Mother Molly was martyred," say my three ladies.

Samantha turns back to the professor. "Can you translate that, professor?"

"We believe that most of the town may have been murdered," says the dean. "See, the bells rang whenever anyone walked down the Main Street, and there were probably lookouts stationed to warn the populace of strangers. The lookouts failed, and Molly Winston and her community were overpowered by a larger force of Puritans and consequently burned and then drowned. That was the common treatment of the radical Anabaptists, of which the Dankers were probably an offshoot."

"Yikes!" says Samantha. "Quite a gruesome story here in the quiet town of Narrow Interior! Back to you in the studio!"

"But grim thoughts were not on the minds of the participants on this sunny Saturday of end-of-summer weekend," says the anchor. "Take a look at this footage of a remarkable community performance with a surprise appearance by rock star Cassandra! More at eleven!"

Next, I offer a burger to Councilwoman Haring. She is sitting on the living room floor with Dr. Caligari and the Fairweathers as Mitch explains to them his idea for the Narrow Interior Fences art installation. They look up at the TV for some great takes of Serenade singing, and later there are some good shots of Mr. Olsen on his Segway and of the puppets, with Mitch explaining to Cassandra and her kids how they were constructed using puppet remains that had been buried under fences all through downtown. There's even a short interview with Gomer, who explains why puppets are really just like action figures and how puppetry will contribute to his recovery.

There are shots of the dunking as well: the Mennonite women leading whoever wanted to, to walk into the water of Geister Lake and get wet. We players all went in, holding the puppets above our heads.

In yet another shot, there's Ali, standing next to Allison and holding up a checkbook in one hand and a pizza box in the another and saying something about buying the college, but I have to go back out to grill some vegan hotdogs for the Mennonite women who are all sitting outside with Serenade on the grass.

"Yes, sister," says one to her. "The being large and strong is not an easy matter for a woman, is it?"

My three Mennonite women sit together smiling at Serenade.

"You are the one to explain our ways! You are a descendent of the beloved."

"I don't know about that," says Serenade. "I'm from here. My family is from here."

The women listen as Serenade talks, but I have to go back to work.

I concentrate on my barbecuing job. I grill the hot dogs and the burgers, turning and re-turning them carefully, waiting patiently, so the meat cooks evenly and I may serve my guests the best I have to offer.

Although I'm pretty intent on my job, out of the corner of my eye, I see Ali and Allison talking. He takes her hand and kisses it.

I serve my friends their food.

xvi. On the Road

I dream that night of the three Danker women and the shadow play in the cellar of the meetinghouse.

"What of Parzival?" says the woman with the sword. "You have neglected to ask his question."

When I wake up it is almost light. The early morning has a chill to it, and that sharp, dry smell that signals it's almost fall.

❋ ❋ ❋

So I go now to put the question.

I do not take the train, because no train goes there, and I do not take the bus, because there is no one to pick me up at the parking lot in front of the carpet cleaners, where the bus drops you off. I cannot have Jimmy drive me there. And since I don't have a car of my own and don't like to drive and have certainly asked the people I know in Narrow Interior for enough favors, I start walking from Narrow Interior to Oma's house.

The dean says that people in the nineteenth century thought nothing of walking ten miles a day or even twenty. Victor Hugo did it, so I guess I can too. I figure it will take ten days max. Less, if I don't rest much. I think of the German Romantics who loved the mountains, and my father who loved to sleep outdoors in tents, but my mother would never let him because she was crazy for hotels and always wanted to stay in one, and so he travelled alone when he went mountaineering. Which is why he died and she didn't.

That's how Patrick told it to me once when we lay in our bunk beds in the blue bedroom at Oma's house by the sound.

Although, that story may not be strictly true. In a way my mother died when my father did. Then she died more inch-by-inch as the years went by and as the hotel empire grew. Holbein Hotels lived, but they thrived as they took life from her. Perhaps. This account may not be strictly true either.

What is true is that I don't know much about my father. I am puzzled by why he would want to spend so much time in Switzerland. What was he looking for on those rugged mountain peaks?

"The origin," Patrick told me that night. "He kept saying he was looking for the origin."

Even though I don't understand my father, I still want to behave like I think my father's son would. So I go on my own solitary expedition. I pack a small backpack with legal papers, a toothbrush, and a towel and a hoodie and one change of underwear and two pairs of socks, and I put Patti's walking shoes to the test and set out.

Back in a week or so, I write on a note addressed EVERYONE on the envelope. I leave it on the kitchen table with a Narrow Interior bell—the one I got as a welcome gift—on top.

P.S. Monkey King wants to visit Allison's octopus tattoo. So please take him over. Be sure to switch his head before you do.

The air is almost-autumn crisp, and I feel fresh and strong when I set out along the empty driveway. Sean must still be out partying in Grusha's station wagon, despite her continual protestations.

At first the journey is fun. I walk on the country roads around Narrow Interior.

I remember a song my dad used to sing to me:

> *I love to go a-wandering along the mountain path . . .*
> *And when I go I love to sing my knapsack on my back.*

Then I walk along highways, and sometimes I walk past strip malls. I avoid the big cities, and I go to the bathroom at 7-11's, and I buy food to eat there. I sleep on a towel on some grass at the rest stops, but when I get near the cities, I can't do that, so I use my credit card and get rooms at cheap motels.

But I can't sleep in those motels. There are overcrowded rooms filled with parents and kids and grandparents trying to go on a family vacation, but they don't have enough money for everyone to have a room, and so they are all stuffed in, and there is complaining and showering and the constant flushing of toilets.

I go outside one night at a motel near one of the smaller cities, and there is a man crying on the balcony right next to mine.

"I will never get another job," he says. "I'm finished."

The woman saying, "No, don't say 'finished.' It sounds like dying."

Him saying, "I'd be better off."

Her saying, "Don't ever say that."

Him, "Even if it's true?"

Her, "It only *seems* true."

I wait for them to continue. I feel like I understand them, although I know that's wrong and stupid and incredibly arrogant of me. You can't ever know how someone else feels. But I won't leave those people on the balcony. I have to stand outside till they decide to do something or say something, which is going to give me a message about what I should do next.

"I wish," says the man, "I wish I had something to believe in."

I walk down the stairs of the motel. I have left my cell phone at home, because I don't want to receive calls, and I don't want anyone to hassle me. But now I wish I had it, so I go to the broken down payphone near the ice machine and I call Serenade.

"I am calling," I say in the voicemail, "I am calling because I miss you, and I am also calling because I am your friend whether or not anything can happen between us, but I'm also calling because I want to be close to you sexually, however we decide to go about doing that. I am calling to say that I have learned some things at the Caligari Institute for Hypno-Therapy and Sexual Healing that might surprise you—in a good way. But I am calling mostly because I care about you and want the connection between us. I *need* the connection. I'm sorry if I didn't say that before or if I said it so poorly it wasn't comprehensible. But it's really true. It is also true that for me you are the beautiful itself. Beauty incarnate. So that's why I'm calling."

The space on the voice mail runs out before I can finish. My heart is full, as the Germans like to say, or rather, as my Oma used to say: My heart is full.

Jack LaLanne says if you exercise regularly you can do what you have to do physically when you have to do it, so I guess all that exercising has paid off at last, because I walk a lot and I walk pretty fast for about three days.

I walk like Little Red Riding Hood, although my grandmother has already been eaten. I walk like the brave little tailor although I am not brave. I walk like Jean Valjean and Wilhelm Tell, and Shane, and Sherlock Holmes, although Sherlock took hansom cabs mostly. I drink a lot of water-fountain water, and I eat a lot of hot dogs. I just don't feel like a hamburger.

On the fourth day a truck pulls up, and the guy reaches over and opens the passenger door.

"I saw you at the motel," says the man behind the wheel. "How about a lift?"

"Thank you," I say. "But no. My mother is in trouble," I explain to him. "I must come to her as a pilgrim, in the guise of a beggar."

The trucker looks at me and thinks. "Kind of like in *The Odyssey*?" he says.

I say yes.

"But aren't we beyond that sort of story?" says the trucker. "Don't we need to tell a less violent, more generous tale?"

"You got a point," I say. I get in, and I ride with him for a while. We don't talk much. I sleep.

I wake up, and he asks if I know any good stories.

I tell him the story of Parzival.

"So *he's* the grail guy!" says the driver. "He's a bit of a nut, isn't he?"

He turns off the highway, and I get out. I am close to my destination.

"I hope things work out with your mom," he says. "Look at it this way—at least you still have her. My mom killed herself a couple of years back."

He drives off in the early morning.

I am back in the country now. I'm walking on roads with traffic lights and then stop lights and then nothing. There are still a few places left like this here in the U.S., although they are disappearing. I turn the corner of one road, and I turn several more corners. Then suddenly, I can smell the sea. It smells like fish and seaweed and birds and it smells like being a boy.

I walk the graveled country road, and wild swans honk at me from the reeds in a nearby pond, although I guess it isn't a pond if it's so near the salt water. I wonder if the swans are bewitched brothers, waiting for a sibling to knit sweaters for them out of beach palms and transform them back into men.

Then I am standing in front of Oma's house.

It's a blustery day filled with unexpected wind, and I feel cold, although I have my hoodie on.

Oma's house is a wreck.

The shingles are hanging off the sides, and the red paint on the front door is peeling. On either side of the front door are two flowerpots with the remains of some dead plants. The windows are dust-covered, and the garage door is not properly closed.

The outside area is a mess too. There was grass in front of the house when I visited. Now it is dry and dead, with choked weeds and beach grass sprouting and strangling itself.

But the worst is the split rail fence. The beams have fallen down. There are no flowers there anymore.

That was to be expected. No one came to care for the house after Oma lost herself and became like Snow White lying in suspended animation from within her glass coffin. I knew that nurses' aides came and went, but they were not roofers or gardeners or handymen. Mrs. Gilbert died, and I don't know what happened to Mr. Gilbert. The lady who ran the gardening store retired and moved to someplace hot and moist. Bonnie? I don't know what happened to her either.

They are gone. Just like the flowers.

I stand in front of the ruined house.

I never went to see Oma after she got sick. That was cowardly. My mother stopped me from visiting of course. But I could have, and should have, disobeyed.

I don't think she even had a funeral.

I walk up to the front door. There are two bags of groceries sitting there with a yellow slip that says HOLBEIN WEEKLY DELIVERY on one of them.

I look in one flowerpot and then in the other. I put my hand in the dirt and pull out my orange plastic gun. I reach in again and something pricks me. I close my hands around the sharpness. I pull out my sheriff's badge.

I do not ring the doorbell; I put my badge in my pocket and lay the gun on the top step. I pick up the grocery bags and walk around the back of the house, past the garage, and down some concrete steps. In front of the sliding doors, a rusted lawn chair that had been lemon yellow but is now just the color of earth flaps its ribboned strips. A painted white metal table sits next to that along with a couple more chipped white chairs.

The black curtains have been drawn over the slider. I push them aside and lean on the sliding door. It's not locked, but it groans open slowly. I fold back the curtains all the way.

And there is my mother in the room with the red paneling. She's set up a bridge table, and she's sitting on a folding chair.

The giant Buddha statue is gone, as is the screen I hid behind. Now it's just a room, devoid of magic.

My mother sits at the bridge table in her bathrobe with stacks of newspapers in front of her. She is cutting them up with a pair of scissors. She is wearing my father's old black glasses. I guess she doesn't want to bother having an optician come in.

And she still has on her necklace with the hand pointing down.

I can see the house arrest anklet blinking a red light on her left leg.

"Just leave the groceries here," she says. "The gratuity's been handled already, so you can—"

I sit down in the chair across from her. She starts a bit when she sees

me.
    "What do you want?" she says.
    I tell her, "To ask you a question."

xvii. The Fisher Queen

"Henry, I don't want to answer any more questions," my mother says.

"This is a simple one," I tell her.

Then I ask the question that I have needed to ask for a long time, but like Parzival I did not know to ask. And then could not ask. And then refused to ask, because I felt so angry that I had to ask it at all.

"Why does Parzival have to pity the Fisher King?" I asked my grandmother once, petting the dog and feeding him a bit of the leftover coffee cake from Oma's breakfast. "He's a *king* after all. He has everything."

"Because he's sick," Oma said. "And because pity is important."

"So, what does Parzival say to the Fisher King?" I asked Oma.

"'*Was fehlt Dir*,'" she said to me, "is how you say it in German. '*Was fehlt*' means also 'what is lacking.'"

I stand before my mother in the red paneled room where the bad things happened.

"What's the matter, Mom?" I say.

This is no fairytale, and my mother, predictably, does not answer.

"Mom," I say again, "What can I do?"

I cannot see my mother's eyes behind her glasses, but I can see her chewing on the inside of her lip and fingering the necklace.

"There is nothing to be done," she says. "I am finished."

Right at that moment I want to hit my mother as hard as I can for sounding like that family man in the cheap motel.

I don't though.

Instead, I say this: "I'm sorry you feel so discouraged, but I don't think you're in such bad shape." Then I move all the junk on the bridge table to the outside table.

"Come," I say. "It's nice out."

Amazingly, she actually walks outside.

I get her situated at the metal table, and she takes off my dad's glasses and puts on a pair of sunglasses.

Then I open my backpack and put in front of her on the table the paperwork that the lawyers have sent me and the spreadsheet from Mr. Marlin, together with a letter from Patrick.

"You have to pay what you owe, and you will be under house arrest for three years," I say, "but the government is kinder now because of Martha

Stewart."

My mother takes her sunglasses off. She has pale brown eyes, and they are very beautiful.

"My reputation," she says, "my friends. No one will talk to me. My opera subscription . . . they claim they lost the email . . . I've lost the family box. And I've lost the box seats to the ball game. Football and baseball. The grand jury. The invitations to the museum openings. It's all gone."

"But you still have plenty of money," I say. The spreadsheets are highlighted, showing pretty big numbers.

"Many of the hotels are empty," she says.

"Then sell the empty ones," I say. "And for God's sake, don't build another one of those glass monstrosities in Narrow Interior."

Now she looks at me.

"Henry," she says, "did you really tell the Historic Preservation people you were abandoning the project?"

"Yes."

She shakes her head. We sit.

"Although," I say, "abandoning the project may have been a bit hasty."

But my mother is thinking about something else.

"Abandoning," she says. "Well, I'm an expert on that—"

Despite myself, a hope springs up in me. *She's going to apologize to me. It's going to happen.*

"I never went to see your grandmother after her stroke. But she left me her house anyway!"

"Sometimes," Dr. Caligari says, "people just can't take responsibility. Because they fear it would kill them."

My mother pushes aside the newspapers and scissors. I notice that she has a bottle of glue on the table as well as big pieces of blank sketch paper lying nearby.

In front of her are individual letters she has cut out from a headline and arranged in the following order:

T-O-X-I-C

E-V-A-S-I-O-N-S

"And you loved her so much," she says.

"But I have always loved you most," I say. It was a lie until now, but when I say it, it feels true, and perhaps it *is* true and I just never noticed because I was so busy missing my elusive, falling-off-a-mountain father whom I never really knew. And feeling bad about my grandmother. And being angry with Patrick.

And, of course, I was very busy hiding.

I would like to touch my mother, but she does not like to be touched. So I look at her and nod encouragingly instead.

"And that religion of hers," says my mother, "or whatever it was. When Patrick told me about the Danker meetinghouse in Narrow Interior, I thought, 'good,' let's root out these tainted histories, these crazy cults. I thought I was sending you there to do away with it, to cement its destruction, not bring the whole nonsense back!"

"Mom," I say, "it's ok."

My mother looks down at the cut up photographs. "It's why I've always been an atheist." She points at the papers. "All of it—the problems today— they all come back to religion!"

"Your problems don't."

"We'll never agree on this," she says. "This ritualistic madness, my mother lighting candles in the closet because *her* mother did. She almost set the house on fire, and so Jane and I said, 'Forget it!'"

She sighs.

"But Mom," I say. "You still wear the necklace."

"My mother gave it to me."

I put my hand on my mother's necklace. She cringes a bit, but then allows it.

"Mom," I say. "Do you know what the hand means?"

She shrugs. "Mother said it was a protection sign."

I think but don't say the word: *hamsa*.

She holds her necklace and keeps on talking. I let her.

"And your father—I thought he wanted nothing to do with your grandmother's cult—and then—things—changed. Then, after all *that*—you react against us, and there's Sean and his nutty—"

"What are you making, Mom?" I interrupt, pointing at the letters in front of her.

"A collage," is the answer.

"I didn't know you liked to make art," I say. Then I tell her about Serenade's singing and about Mitch and the rolls of toilet paper and how we hid in the bathroom from Patrick.

My mother chews the inside of her lip before answering.

"Sounds insane," she says. But her voice conveys that she's amused.

As I sift through the clippings on the table, I come across a photograph of my mother in her Hermes suit. The photographer wanted to capture her entire outfit, so it is a color photo that included my mother's Birkin bag and her high-heeled shoes.

I pick up the cut out and make it walk jumpily across the table.

"It's not fair," I say in a shrieky high voice.

My mother studies the paper scraps and chews her lip.

"It's not fair that I have to take care of all these hotels," my paper doll mother declares. "I'm just a girl from Oklahoma." The doll starts stamping on the headlines that say, "TAX FRAUD: QUEEN OF HOLBEIN HOTELS BROUGHT DOWN."

"Washington State, not Oklahoma," says my real mother. She is looking at my cutout version of her stamping on the headlines.

"OH, whatever SHALL I DO?" my cut out mother shouts. "I don't want to be a magnate. I just want to swim in the OCEAN!"

"I can't swim," says my regular sized mother. She picks up the scissors.

"I didn't know that," I say in my regular voice. "Why didn't you learn?"

"This singing girl—is she your girlfriend?" she says.

"Well . . . she's a girl . . . a kind of girl . . . that I really like."

In the meantime, my paper doll mother continues to prance and jump on top of the headlines.

"How I just LOOOVE the SEEEEA!" she screams.

"No," my mother says. "It's the desert. The desert is what I've always longed for. The heat of it. It's pure, dry light."

Then she opens up the scissor blades.

"YOU SHALL NOT BE FREE," she booms at her paper doll self. "YOU MUST SAVE THE HOLBEIN LEGACY."

"Shan't do it!" says my paper-doll mom.

My mother extends the scissors and snips the head off of her photographed self.

"YOU MUST DIE FOR YOUR TRANSGRESSIONS AGAINST THE SOCIAL ORDER!" she hollers.

I pick up my paper doll mother's head and make it and the headless body continue prancing on top of the headlines. "You can't kill me so easy," I say in my shrieky paper doll mother voice. "So THERE."

I grab some tape and stick the head back on top of the suited body. Then I put my paper doll down and pick up a handful of clippings.

"Come on, people," I say in my regular voice. "There's got to be more to life than this!"

My mother picks up her own handful of clippings. "Here's to the dissolution of the empire," she says in her own voice.

She looks at me. I look at her. Together we rip apart the headlines and the pictures of the lawyers, the jury, and the judge. We throw them in the air like confetti.

"DOWN WITH GREED!" we shout as the broken limbs and phrases rain down on the outdoor table.

A skeletal hand reaches out from behind me and grasps the figure of my paper doll mother.

"Why, hello there!" my real mother says to Mr. Death.

He is wearing an attractive if somewhat old-fashioned flannel shirt, elegant Bermuda shorts with cuffs, and old-style lace-up hiking boots. But over all of that he wears my father's trench coat. On his head he wears one of those green felt hats that look like he's about to yodel or play the accordion. He is carrying several lengths of rope in a coil, as well as a large green knapsack.

He looks like my father must have on his last mountain climbing trip.

My mother smiles at him brightly.

"Won't you sit down?" she says. "I don't receive many visitors, but I feel as though—" she pauses and raises her hand to her forehead.

"This is Mr.—" I begin, but my mother cuts me off.

"I feel as though we know each other well already. Don't we?"

Mr. Death nods, bows, and takes a seat on one of the rusting metal chairs. He smiles back at my mother. Of course, as a skeleton he's always smiling, but his grin is particularly wide, it seems to me.

My mother glows at the attention.

"You know," she says confidingly as she leans over to speak with him, "I've had all sorts of problems with the law because of these hotels I've been managing."

Mr. Death leans over the table and takes my mother's hand.

"Watch out, Mom!" I say.

"Oh, Henry, don't be such a prude," she rejoinders. Mr. Death ignores me. He trains his human-looking blue eyes on my mother and only on her. He holds her hand, but apparently has no immediate plan to kill her, which is comforting, I suppose.

"Anyway, as I was saying, such *trouble* with these hotels, and I think that perhaps I *will* retire, as my son Henry here suggests. Do you know

Henry? Well of course you do, it's why you came here isn't it? But now you must stay and visit with me. Where was I? Oh yes, I think I may take up making art as a hobby. Do you like collages? Yes? Well, I agree that they are a crucial moment in avant-garde art and—"

Mr. Death's jaws open and close as he says something to my mother that I cannot hear.

"Ha-ha!" she says, "it's true. Patrick *does* take things awfully seriously." She lowers her voice. "Yes, I know he's gay. No, I don't worry anymore about Henry. I have my own problems. Besides, he just told me he has a girlfriend, so that's promising, don't you think?"

As is undoubtedly clear by now, I am not a big fan of Mr. Death. Still, my mother is delighted to see him, and I figure she has a right to spend time with whomever she pleases.

So I leave the papers on the table as she talks to Mr. Death. He sits attentively, inclining his head towards hers, resplendent in my dead father's mountaineering clothes.

But before I do that, I think of something. "Mom—did you pay them severance packages?"

My mother shakes her head. "Who?"

"The workers at the hotels you've had to close!" I say.

My mother smiles at Mr. Death, but he looks up at me and shrugs his bony shoulders.

"See if you can convince her," I tell him. "It's not too late to do the right thing."

I walk inside through the ruined house to the kitchen and phone Patrick.

"Get some people out here to take care of her," I tell him.

"I will," he says. I'm about to hang up when he says, "Henry, I need to talk to you about something."

"About Sven?" I look out the kitchen window and watch my mother chatting merrily with Mr. Death.

"No," says Patrick. "I figure . . . that was such a crazy night, it was my imagination, probably." He pauses. "No. I mean about Sean."

"What about him?" My mother throws back her head and laughs now, as though Mr. Death has just told her a very witty story.

"He's . . . gone."

I breathe in and breathe out. I look out the kitchen window towards the water.

I just say the words. "Is he dead?"

When I ask the question, Mr. Death lifts his skull head and looks up at me through the window.

"He wrecked your housekeeper's car," Patrick says quietly. "He drove it into a pine tree."

"So, he's dead?" I say again.

Mr. Death stands up, pushes his chair in, and says something to my mother.

"I don't know how to begin to answer that question," says Patrick.

"Either he is or he isn't," I say. "Unless he's in a coma. Is he?" I say.

"Not exactly," says Patrick, as Mr. Death walks over to the kitchen window and taps on the glass.

"He walked away from the accident, left the car where it was, and checked himself into a rehab place run by Zen monks in Riverfield. Not the Materialist Pureland people—this is an actual monastery."

Mr. Death motions for me to open the kitchen window.

"So he's alive," I say. I breathe in and out again.

"He's—changed," says Patrick. "I went to see him this morning."

Patrick visiting Sean in a rehab place run by Zen monks. I try and fail to picture it. I give up and open the window.

"What?" I say to Mr. Death. He doesn't answer. Typical.

"How is he different?" I say to Patrick.

"He just *is*," says Patrick.

"What does this mean?" I say to Mr. Death.

"Well," says Patrick. "There was this strange friend of his with him at the rehab place. A weird fellow in a skeleton costume wearing a cowboy hat. Sean said he—the friend—was with him in the car, and the man checked him into this place, because he—Sean—and the cowboy had made some kind of deal."

"What kind of a deal?" I say.

"I don't know. Sean asked the cowboy friend to tell me, and the cowboy wouldn't say," Patrick replies.

"That figures," I say.

Mr. Death waits by the kitchen window while I listen to Patrick explain that Sean insists that his name is now Brother Francis Kuro Matsu, and that Brother Francis plans on staying in the monastery after his recovery.

"Well—that sounds pretty different," I admit.

"Yeah," says Patrick. "He's even planning on taking—what do you call them—"

"Vows," I say.

Patrick says he has to go.

"Oh—and Patrick, I want you in charge of designing and building the Narrow Interior Cultural Retreat and Learning Center project."

"What the hell project is that?" he says

"It's a construction project that is going to be a charitable donation by the Holbein family—not a hotel, but a retreat and learning center. You'll figure out the details. Call John Russell."

"What about the preservation people?"

"Your contact there is Lars Lenard Olsen. He'll work with you on convincing the Historic Buildings Preservation Committee to allow construction of a space that actually does some good."

"So—we're back on track?"

"You bet we are," I say.

"Also—" I say, "I want to commission Mitch Gaynor to do a set of installations involving fences."

"Isn't he the guy who knocked you down?" Patrick asks.

"Yeah," I say. "But he's a very talented artist—these people always have—"

"Temperaments," says Patrick.

We hang up. I smile thinking of the future interactions between Patrick and Mr. Olsen. And Mitch.

Mr. Death taps on the frame of the kitchen window.

"So—you killed Sean AND saved him?" I say to him..

Mr. Death nods.

"What do you want—a medal?"

Mr. Death nods again.

I think for a moment. I reach into my pocket and pull out my sheriff's badge. I lean out the window and hand it to him.

Mr. Death pins the badge on his mountaineering shirt. When he does, the shirt turns into a black cowboy vest and the rest of his clothes change back into his western gear.

"Thanks, partner," says Mr. Death. He tips his hat, and strolls back over to where my mother is sitting. As he walks he pulls out a black square cell phone and starts talking to someone soundlessly.

I shake my head. I'll never understand that varmint.

I call Patti.

"What the HELL is going on out there?" she says.

"It's a long story," I say. I explain a little, promise more, and hang up.

Then I walk outside the front door and stick my orange plastic gun in back of my pants just under the belt. I survey the ruined front yard of my grandmother's house.

I want to know how my father died and what he was looking for in Switzerland. How much did he know about the Dankers? How much did he believe? And I want to know how the Dankers died and who they really were, if it's possible to know that. And how and why they got started in the first place.

This means I need to go to Europe and then maybe even to Japan.

And maybe Israel. My perhaps Jewishness is connected to this story too. Or at least, it's connected to *my* story. The one that I now get to live in plain sight of others.

Maybe Serenade will come and she'll get her adventure abroad.

A lot of maybes.

But first I'll get to work on fixing Oma's fence.

I lift the grey rail and ease it into place. In the dirt where it had lain, a tiny blue flower juts out an inch above the ground.

It's a start.

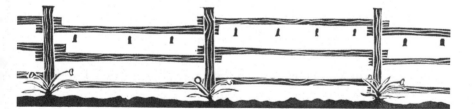

20. Beatrice:
1 letter and 1 diary entry

Autumn

Dear Henry —

I send you greetings from the Café on the Place de la Co-
médie in Montpellier. Montpellier is—as I think I have told
you—a strange city, filled with small feral monkeys that came
here long ago—no one knows how. But the food is delightful,
the people friendly, and it is a fine thing to re-visit the city
after so many years. Retracing my steps to Montpellier has
freed me somehow. Ben is with me. I've made no promises
to him. And yet, I feel—for the first time in years—hopeful,
vibrant, and, dare I say it? young.

A grant from the Ali Foundation for Inter-Religious
Understanding and a reading fellowship from the city have
allowed me to go through the drawers of materials in the
university library at a leisurely pace—giving me ample time
to prepare this material for a new book. Typically French,
the library is in a complete state of chaos, but they do have
in their possession a mass of diary pages composed by the
man who I presume is Molly Winston's father...Franz Holbein—a Swiss-German doctor who trained here in Montpellier. In this same collection are twenty-odd pages of writing
in Japanese, which I imagine belong to his wife, Christine,
née Teruko—whom he mentions and about whom I will
have occasion to say more in a moment.

Franz Holbein's diary entries are written in English, because he was practicing the language for a move to the New World. It seems that he and his wife envisioned emigration but apparently never got to America due to the difficulty of the many wars raging during the early seventeenth century. They travelled perhaps as far as London (our play indicates as much), but I can't tell that from the materials archived here. How this book came to be left behind is a mystery I cannot—at this point—account for.

On the last pages of Franz Holbein's memory book, Christine adds her own entries in French, which she has learned very well. She is, in my estimation, a compelling writer, and I enclose a segment that I have translated from the archive.

It made me think of you, somehow.
Wishing you all the best –
Beatrice

Copy of diary entry by Christine Holbein:

Today we practiced our holy play of poppets—to be performed before we baptize ourselves in the sea Friday night. After our repetition, as we packed our dolls safely away, Franz told me a strange and lovely tale. It concerned a legend his mother Ursula of blessed memory told him of a knight who was destined to save and to heal. The youngest son of a lordly family, he was hidden by his mother, who— desperate to protect him—concealed him in the country.

"As both of us have been concealed," I said to him, "you a secret Anabaptist, and I, a seeming son with a secret purpose, on the open seas."

He laughed at that, and said, "God chose this knight, my mother told me, as I suppose He has chosen us to reveal HIS goodness. Thus, like the young knight of Mother's tale, we can and must fulfill God's will, which can never be thwarted, although in human arrogance we often think it can."

Then he told me of the knight's seeking of the thing they

call the grail.

"What is 'grail'?" I asked, folding our black hoods and placing them in a cabinet.

Franz explained, "What my mother told me was that the grail was no idolatrous cup as is oft believed—to be worshipped and adored. It is rather the philosopher's stone—a thing of earth—such as we. Made of dust but blessed by God." He kissed me and said he wanted to make a play about him—using our poppets we would tell the tale of the knight who sought the wounded fisher king, who possessed this grail.

"Yes," I said. "But we must also have a play that is not so lofty. For folk can learn only in tasty bits." I put my hand on his face. "And beloved, sometimes, the spiritual can also be at once poignant and droll."

With that, I told him the story of the Gautama's incarnation as the monkey king. Monkey was mischievous and curious as all monkeys are, but in the end he was heroic. He sacrificed himself for his people by laying himself across the chasm between two cliffs surrounding a raging waterfall. His people crossed over the raging waters safely, though it broke Monkey's back.

"You see, my love—the stories of virtue may all be connected," I told him, and I took out my favorite of the poppets for example. "Just as this beautiful lady is both the Virgin Mary and the beloved Kanzeon, the deity of mercy. A human, she is also a god, a wife, and a mother."

We sat together for a long time, holding the lady with her one perfect arm and hand (the other has fallen off). Her fingers are spread—two against two—in the priestly blessing of the daughters of David. Wounded yet lovely, her serene face looks back at us, waiting for us to give her life and words.

The End

Acknowledgments

The author thanks the following living, dead, real, and fictional entities: Kobbie Alamo, Jackson Alberts, Kathleen Alcalá, anyone I might have forgotten, Jeff Arnold, Awaji Puppet Theater, Back to the Grind, Eric Barr, Bashō, Larry Behrendt, Lillian Behrendt, Peter Behrendt, Belgian Village Camp, Aimee Bender, Erith Jaffe Berg, Gordon Berger, Linda Besemer, Susan Block, Christopher Bolton, Ann Brantingham, John Brantingham, Brian Brophy, Erika Brummett, Mark Budman, Janet Buttenwieser, California Museum of Photography, the cast of *The Cabinet of Dr. Caligari*, Adalbert von Chamisso, Jane Carroll, Ezra Chatterton, Micah Chatterton, the cast of *The Children of Paradise*, City of Claremont, City of Coupeville, City of Goshen, City of Manhattan, City of Northampton, City of Riverside, City of Southampton, City of Watermill, College of William and Mary, Jean Cocteau, Jo Scott Coe, Justin Scott Coe, Melissa Conway, Coupeville Library, Culver Center, Jill Davidson, Kathryn Lynn Davis, Jacques Derrida, Liselotte Dieckmann, FeLicia Elam, Ziad Elmarsafi, Wolfram von Eschenbach, The Fall, Carol Frischman, Lilian Furst, Bil Gaines, Claire Gebben, Idee German, Wolfgang ("Wolf") von Goethe, Tod Goldberg, Jamie Beck Gordon, Joscelyne Gray, Robert Gross, Andrea Grossman, Barbé Hammer, Leonard Hammer, Friedrich von Hardenburg, Marie Hartung, E.T.A Hoffmann, Homunculus, Andrea Hurst, Inlandia Institute, Sankai Juku, Qonnie Kim, Heinrich von Kleist, Cheryl Knobel, Rich Kremer, Jack LaLanne, Kaye Linden, Daniel Lockhart, Christi Love, Kim Lundstrom, Mandy Manning, Ellen McGrath, The Mission Inn, Charlotte Morganti, Patricia Morton, Robert Murphy, Hilary Henry Neff, Elizabeth Newstat, Nielson Library, Northwest Institute of Literary Arts, Vivian Nyitray, Jeremiah O'Hagen, Elizabeth Peabody, Pitzer College, the Plaza Hotel, The Pogues, Joe Ponepinto, Cati Porter, Ōtagaki Rengetsu, Rivera Library, Rob Roberge, Bruce Holland Rogers, Boris Romanov, CloClo Romanov, Oleg Romanov, Stephanya Romanov, Vladimir "The Boss" Romanov, Sandra Sarr, Friedrich Schiller, Peter Schlemihl, Christoph Schweitzer, Seattle Library, Theda Shapiro, Smith College, Soup Burg, Ana Maria Spagna, Ben and Judith Stoltzfus, Erika Suderburg, Sweeney Gallery, University of California, Riverside, Wayne Ude, Historic Williamsburg, Wu Cheng'en, Z Pizza.

CPSIA information can be obtained
at www.ICGtesting.com
Printed in the USA
FSOW04n0002170615
7919FS